## JAMES WASN'T LEAVING T.J. BEHIND

No matter what.

"I need a lead, Mack," Calvin James stated. "Hal gave me the runaround. French security moved T.J., and we're no longer trying to figure out where he is. The hit team that came after me was stripped clean. I've got no clues, no bread crumbs to follow."

Bolan sighed. Every man who had signed up for Stony Man duty, including himself—especially himself—had understood that it could come to this.

Everyone had gone into the offered deal with his eyes wide open. Every man on Phoenix Force and Able Team had agreed, and now that the mission - had gone south, that the worst-case scenario had finally occurred, Calvin James didn't want to play by the rules anymore.

Bolan frowned. He wasn't much on rules himself.

The Executioner picked up the phone.

*Other titles in this series:*

| | |
|---|---|
| #34 REPRISAL | #67 ECHOES OF WAR |
| #35 MESSAGE TO AMERICA | #68 OUTBREAK |
| #36 STRANGLEHOLD | #69 DAY OF DECISION |
| #37 TRIPLE STRIKE | #70 RAMROD INTERCEPT |
| #38 ENEMY WITHIN | #71 TERMS OF CONTROL |
| #39 BREACH OF TRUST | #72 ROLLING THUNDER |
| #40 BETRAYAL | #73 COLD OBJECTIVE |
| #41 SILENT INVADER | #74 THE CHAMELEON FACTOR |
| #42 EDGE OF NIGHT | #75 SILENT ARSENAL |
| #43 ZERO HOUR | #76 GATHERING STORM |
| #44 THIRST FOR POWER | #77 FULL BLAST |
| #45 STAR VENTURE | #78 MAELSTROM |
| #46 HOSTILE INSTINCT | #79 PROMISE TO DEFEND |
| #47 COMMAND FORCE | #80 DOOMSDAY CONQUEST |
| #48 CONFLICT IMPERATIVE | #81 SKY HAMMER |
| #49 DRAGON FIRE | #82 VANISHING POINT |
| #50 JUDGMENT IN BLOOD | #83 DOOM PROPHECY |
| #51 DOOMSDAY DIRECTIVE | #84 SENSOR SWEEP |
| #52 TACTICAL RESPONSE | #85 HELL DAWN |
| #53 COUNTDOWN TO TERROR | #86 OCEANS OF FIRE |
| #54 VECTOR THREE | #87 EXTREME ARSENAL |
| #55 EXTREME MEASURES | #88 STARFIRE |
| #56 STATE OF AGGRESSION | #89 NEUTRON FORCE |
| #57 SKY KILLERS | #90 RED FROST |
| #58 CONDITION HOSTILE | #91 CHINA CRISIS |
| #59 PRELUDE TO WAR | #92 CAPITAL OFFENSIVE |
| #60 DEFENSIVE ACTION | #93 DEADLY PAYLOAD |
| #61 ROGUE STATE | #94 ACT OF WAR |
| #62 DEEP RAMPAGE | #95 CRITICAL EFFECT |
| #63 FREEDOM WATCH | #96 DARK STAR |
| #64 ROOTS OF TERROR | #97 SPLINTERED SKY |
| #65 THE THIRD PROTOCOL | #98 PRIMARY DIRECTIVE |
| #66 AXIS OF CONFLICT | |

DON PENDLETON'S

# STONY

AMERICA'S ULTRA-COVERT INTELLIGENCE AGENCY

# MAN®

## SHADOW WAR

A GOLD EAGLE BOOK FROM

# WORLDWIDE®

TORONTO • NEW YORK • LONDON
AMSTERDAM • PARIS • SYDNEY • HAMBURG
STOCKHOLM • ATHENS • TOKYO • MILAN
MADRID • WARSAW • BUDAPEST • AUCKLAND

Recycling programs
for this product may
not exist in your area.

First edition February 2009

ISBN-13: 978-0-373-61983-2
ISBN-10:    0-373-61983-9

SHADOW WAR

Special thanks and acknowledgment to
Nathan Meyer for his contribution to this work.

**Printed in U.S.A.**

# SHADOW WAR

# PROLOGUE

Barbara Price opened her eyes.

She awoke clearheaded and alert, knowing exactly where she was and what she needed to do. There was a war being fought in the shadows and like the ringmaster of a circus, she was at its epicenter. Her eyes went to the window of her bedroom. It was dark outside. She looked at the clock on her bedside table and saw she had been asleep for exactly forty-five minutes.

Price sat up and pushed a slender hand through her honey-blond hair. She felt revitalized after her power nap, and with a single cup of Aaron "the Bear" Kurtzman's coffee she knew she'd be ready to roll.

She got up out of the bed, smoothed her clothes and picked up the copy of the *Washington Post* she had placed on her table before stepping into the upstairs hallway of Stony Man Farm's main house. The headline screamed out at her.

Colombian Businessman Busy Senator

Marcos Sincanaros, renowned currency specula-
tor, has been tied to campaign contributions ex-
ceeding five million dollars to Maryland Senator…

Disgusted, Price stopped reading. She had too much
on her mind at the moment to worry about Washington
politics. She frowned. The name "Sincanaros" was familiar, however. She resolved to ask Akira Tokaido, one
of the Farm's computer wizards, to see if Stony Man had
a file on the man.

As Price walked down the hall, she began clicking
through options and mentally categorizing her tasks.
She had men in the field, preparing to step into harm's
way, and it was her responsibility to coordinate all the
disparate parts into a seamless whole.

The Farm's mission controller was headed to the
basement when the cell phone on her belt began to vibrate. She plucked it free and used the red push-talk
button.

"Price, here," she said coolly.

"Barb," Carmen Delahunt began, "the teams are in
jump-off mode."

"Thanks, Carm," Price told the ex-FBI agent. "I'm
almost in the tunnel now."

"See you in a minute," Delahunt said.

Price put her phone away, entered the tunnel that
joined the main house to the Annex and got into the light
electric rail car. The engine began to hum and the vehicle quickly picked up speed as it shot down the under-
ground tunnel. Things were starting to click, to come

together, and Price could feel the tingle she had first felt as a mission controller for long-range operations conducted by the National Security Agency. It had been there that she had made her bones in the intelligence business before being recruited by Hal Brognola to run logistics and support at the more covert Stony Man operation.

Stony Man had operated as a clandestine antiterrorist operation since long before the infamous attacks of September 11 had put all of America's military, intelligence and law-enforcement efforts on the same page. As such, it operated as it always had—under the direct control of the White House and separate from both the Joint Special Operations Command and the Directorate of National Intelligence.

Stony Man had been given carte blanche to operate at peak efficiency, eliminating oversights and legalities in the name of pragmatic results. It also, perhaps most importantly, offered the U.S. government the ability to disavow any knowledge of operations that went badly. It was a brutal truth that if things turned wrong for the Stony Man action teams, Phoenix Force and Able Team, they would be left out in the cold.

It was one of Barbara Price's most sincere prayers that she would never be called upon to make the decision that left compromised operators hanging in the wind.

She pushed aside the morose reflections as the electric car slowed and she exited the vehicle, then entered the Annex building after passing through security. Things were ready to go hot—she could not afford to be distracted now.

As she stepped into the Computer Room, she was

met by Aaron Kurtzman, the wheelchair-bound head of cybernetics at Stony Man Farm. The big man reached out and handed her a steaming mug of coffee. She eyed the ink-colored liquid dubiously.

"Thanks, Aaron. That's just what I've been missing. Something that can put hair on my chest."

"David called for Phoenix Force in Marseilles," he said, grinning. "They're set up to go in the hotel. Carl did the same for Able Team in Louisiana. They're in the air and heading toward the target."

"Good," Price said. She took a drink of the strong coffee and pulled a face. "Once we're sure everything is unfolding, I'll give Hal a call and he can pass the information on to the President."

Kurtzman glided over to his work area, where it looked as if a bomb had exploded. His desk was covered in faxes, paperwork and the exposed wiring of half a dozen devices.

Across the room at his workstation, fingers flying across a laptop while monitoring a sat com link, Akira Tokaido bobbed his head in time to the music coming from a single earbud. The lean, compact hacker was the youngest member of Stony Man's cybernetics team and the heir apparent to Kurtzman himself. The Japanese-American cyberpunk had at times worked virtual magic when Price had needed him to.

Across the room from Tokaido sat his polar opposite. Professor Huntington Wethers had come to the Stony Man operations from his position on the teaching faculty of UC Berkeley. The tall, distinguished black man sported gray hair at his temples and an unflappable manner. He currently worked two laptop screens as a translation program fed him information from monitored radio traffic coming out of France.

Carmen Delahunt walked through the door of Computer Room and made a beeline for Barbara Price. The only female on the Farm's cyberteam, Delahunt served as a pivotal balance between Tokaido's hotshot hacking magic and Wethers's more restrained, academic style.

Delahunt finished her conversation and snapped her cell phone shut as she walked up to Price. She pointed toward the newspaper in the mission controller's hand.

"You see that about Sincanaros?" she asked. "As soon as I saw that name, it rang a bell. I ran a profile—not pretty."

Price smiled. "You read my mind, Carmen," she said. "Once we have Phoenix and Able taken care of, why don't you send me a summary in case anything comes of it."

"Will do." Delahunt nodded. "I have to double-check the Mediterranean arrangements we made for Phoenix's extraction with the 'package.' It's nice to be able to tap the resources of larger groups like the Agency, but coordination is a nightmare."

"Let me know if anything goes wrong," Price said.

Delahunt nodded, then turned and began to walk back across the floor toward the connecting door to the Annex's Communications center, her fingers punching out a number on her encrypted cell phone.

Price smiled.

She could feel the energy, the sense of purpose that permeated the room, flow into her. Out there in the cold, eight men on two teams were about to enter into danger for the sake of their country. If they got into trouble, if they needed anything, they would turn to her and her people.

She did not intend to let them down.

She made her way to a nearby desk where a light flashing on the desktop phone let her know a call was holding. She looked over at Kurtzman and saw the man returning a telephone handset to its cradle. He pointed toward her.

"It's Hal on line one," he said.

"Thanks, Aaron," she answered.

She set her coffee and paper down and picked up the handset. She put the phone to her ear.

"Hal, it's Barb," she said.

"I'm holding for the President on the other line," Brognola said from his Justice Department office. "Are the men up and rolling?"

"As we speak," Price answered. "Tell him both operations are prepped to launch."

"All right. Let's hope this one goes by the numbers," the gruff federal agent said.

"As always," she agreed, and hung up.

"All right, people," she announced to the room. "Let's roll."

# CHAPTER ONE

*Lost Parish, New Orleans, Louisiana*

The men hung from chains.

Gabriel Gonzales turned his blindfolded head and spit blood from his mouth. His lips were swollen and his teeth loose from where the Zetas gunmen had smashed a rifle butt into his face. His nose had been broken, so the act of spitting left him breathless. He quickly sucked in air, trying not to choke on blood. The air was stale and tinged with the harsh chemical smell of spilled oil.

His arms screamed in their sockets, and Gonzales pushed his toes against the concrete floor beneath his feet to give them some relief. Around him he heard the moans and shuffling of the two other men hanging next to him. He didn't know who they were, as they had already been bound and blindfolded in the back of the Lincoln Navigator SUV when he'd been picked up.

*Let them have gotten my call,* he prayed silently.

The sound of vibrating corrugated metal reached him

as a door slammed. The noise echoed in hollow tones and Gonzales realized he had to be inside a large structure, such as an abandoned factory or, more probably, an empty warehouse. He heard the sounds of boot soles striking the floor as a group of men muttering low in Spanish moved closer.

He heard Lagos and his heart sank. The man was speaking rapidly, and after a moment Gonzales realized he had to be on his cell phone because he was talking to his mysterious patron, the Frenchman "Henri."

*This is going to hurt,* he realized, and felt hopeless tears well up in his eyes behind the filthy cloth that covered them. When Lagos got off the phone with Henri, violent things always followed. There was a snap of hard plastic as a cell phone was shut. A snarling baritone growled an order and suddenly the blindfold was ripped from his eyes.

Powerful headlights snapped on, burning into his eyes and keeping him blinded. Gonzales tried to turn his head away from the painful, high-intensity beams. He didn't need his eyes to recognize the voice in command: Lagos was here and Gabriel Gonzales realized he was going to die. There was no doubt anymore, he was a dead man. All that remained was the suffering.

JACK GRIMALDI BANKED the Hughes 500MD Scout Defender hard in the darkness. The helicopter settled down into a hover some ten feet above the dark ground. All around the veteran pilot the devastation of Hurricane Katrina spread in a broken tableau of ruin and debris years after the storm had struck.

Behind him acres of swamp stretched toward the tide

tables nestled against the sea, while in front of him mud-caked rubble in geometrically spaced piles marked where houses and stores had once stood along roads. It looked like a war zone, even in the yellow moonlight, a ghostly boneyard of destruction and destroyed lives.

Reconstruction had passed this Parish by. The residents had been too poor, the neighborhood too peripheral to the campaign aspirations of politicians. This was an area the hurricane could keep as New Orleans fought its way back from the devastation.

But power abhorred a vacuum. The Zetas—former members of the army who had gone over to the dark side—had come to claim the forgotten place for themselves. The hard-core drug smugglers had found little in the way of opposition when they had first arrived. All of that was about to change.

The three men of Able Team leaped from the hovering helicopter and entered the stifling heat of the Louisiana night.

LAGOS SNATCHED GONZALES by the hair and twisted his face around. Ignoring the pain, Gonzales stared dully into the eyes of the former Mexican army special-operations soldier. The eyes stared back at him, black and empty like the dull, lifeless eyes of a shark. Devoid of emotion. What was happening was just business.

Lagos leaned in close to the sweating Gonzales and behind him the bound man could see the hulking forms of Lagos's men, all of them wearing balaclava hoods and holding weapons. Gonzales rolled his eyes around to try to get a better look at the men hanging with him, but Lagos held him firmly. His breath smelled like cigarette smoke.

"Was it you?" Lagos whispered. "Did you betray us?"

"No, I swear—" Gonzales began lying.

Lagos released his hold on the hanging man's hair and stepped back. He lifted his arm and backhanded Gonzales across the face, cutting off his protests. Lagos was a powerful man fuelled by a daily cocaine habit. The blow hurt.

Gonzales's head rocked back and he winced at the sudden, stinging pain. He stumbled backward, toes barely in contact with the ground, to the end of his chain and then was unceremoniously swung back toward his abuser.

Lagos stepped in close as Gonzales stumbled forward, planting his fist in the hanging man's midriff. Gonzales gasped and the muscles of his diaphragm spasmed painfully. He sucked in a breath, and Lagos snapped the top of his hand, extended in a flat blade, into Gonzales's vulnerable groin.

Agony stole Gonzales's sight. He moaned low as the sharp pain was almost instantaneously replaced by a dull, spreading ache.

*God help me,* he thought. *It's just beginning.*

CARL LYONS HELD UP an arm and then sank down on one leg, resting on his ballistic armor knee pad. Behind him the other two members of Able Team, Rosario "Politician" Blancanales and Hermann "Gadgets" Schwarz, copied his stance.

Lyons let his automatic shotgun hang from the strap over his shoulder and pointed out toward the team's twelve-o'clock position. Through a break in an acre-size lot of soggy timber, busted concrete and twisted rebar sat the low squat shape of an undamaged warehouse. Parked in front of the building, which spilled brilliant white halogen light through its cracks, were a dark, 1970s Dodge van and an H3 Hummer with a shiny black carapace.

"There they are," Lyons said quietly. The six foot two, two-hundred-pound man turned his attention back to his target.

Clutching a Steyr AUG bullpup-designed assault rifle, Schwarz moved into position closer to team leader Carl Lyons. Behind them Blancanales leaned in to hear their conversation as he covered the periphery with his H&K MP-5 SD-3 submachine gun.

Blancanales put a finger to the communication piece in his ear. "We're on-site and doing initial recon."

"Copy," Barbara Price answered. "Our coverage of local police channels put friendlies way outside your area of operation. Over."

"Roger. Able out," Blancanales murmured.

"Two vehicles," Schwarz muttered, scanning the structure. "But big vehicles. Anywhere from five to ten guys. All former Zetas."

"Sounds about right," Lyons said, nodding.

Their briefing on the last-minute search-and-rescue operation had given them little to go on other than a target—Gabriel Gonzales, CIA confidential informant—and a location gathered by triangulating the man's cell-phone signal. As part of his payment, the CIA had provided Gonzales, a former Mexican border patrol agent turned narcotic trafficker, with a state-of-the-art cell phone. The CIA had also added the location tracer buried in the body of the lightweight device.

As valuable as Gonzales might have been to drug-enforcement agencies, the CIA had turned a blind eye to his narcotics profiteering to concentrate on his anti-terrorism capabilities. It was a Faustian arrangement made common by the necessities of a post-9/11 world.

Gonzales granted the U.S. intelligence community a much-needed window into the realities of the growing, solidifying world of narco-terror. Organizations such as the former Mexican special-forces group turned drug runners, the Zetas and the violent international MS13 gang had begun to overlap with the intelligence agencies of Venezuela and the heroin syndicates of Southeast Asia and the Middle East.

Wherever there was illicit money to be made, there was an opportunity for black funds to flow into the operational coffers of terrorist organizations. It was a situation that Able Team had faced more than once.

"Let's move in closer," Lyons said. "But first scan with your optics. If there are sentries outside, they may well have night-vision gear. We'll exploit the range of your sniper scope."

"I see all," Schwarz whispered as he shuffled forward.

Schwarz raised the Steyr AUG A3 to his shoulder. The A3 was the carbine configuration of the classic bullpup assault rifle with a shortened 16-inch barrel. The standard factory-mounted sighting optics had been replaced by Stony Man armorer John "Cowboy" Kissinger with a Picatinny mounting rail upon which he placed a 1.5X-telescope containing a circle aiming reticle.

A low, full moon hung over the scene, providing enough ambient light for the three-man special-operations team to operate without night-vision equipment.

Schwarz flinched once as the 1.5X magnification qualities of his sniper scope suddenly presented him with vision of a huge rat running lightly along an exposed section of plumbing until it disappeared into the open mouth of an overturned toilet.

He settled back, ignoring the pungent stench of the flood area. The humidity was stifling and the Able Team commando sweated freely under the black smears of his camouflage grease paint. He scanned the target building in vectors, his brain reducing the activity to simplified angles and precise geometric patterns.

"Nothing outside," he said. "At least not from this angle… Wow, hold on." A bright set of headlights suddenly appeared out of the ruins on the far side of the building.

Schwarz turned his weapon toward the new threat stimulus and dampened the passive feed on his scope even further.

"Holy crap," he whispered. "It's a McLaren F1!"

"I know I'm going to be sorry I asked, but what's a McLaren F1?" Lyons asked.

Without preamble, and in the hushed tones of a small boy describing a cherished toy, Schwarz rattled off the car's specks. "The F1 was the fastest production car ever made, and they only made one hundred of them. It's got a 6.1-liter BMW S70 V12 engine, and it'll go over 230 mph easy, without turbo or supercharges. Price tag? Well north of a cool million, my man."

"Who the hell would drop that kind of money on such a classic supercar and then drive it into *this* mess?" Blancanales asked.

Schwarz shook his head as the metallic-silver supercar pulled in next to the SUVs and the bat-wing doors rose like something out of a science-fiction movie. "Anyone who'd do this is a bad, bad person. I think we'll have to kill them all."

"Suits me," Lyons answered. "I freakin' hate Zetas."

Schwarz let out a low whistle. "Does she look like any Zetas you've ever seen?"

A tiny, delicate foot in a wraparound stiletto heel emerged from the darkness of the McLaren F1 and came to rest on the damp gravel. The leg attached to the thousand-dollar shoe seemed to go on for miles. Even in the poor light and across the distance, Able Team could see it was a million-dollar leg.

The young woman emerged from the McLaren F1. A sheer white blouse was knotted below her full breasts just above her red plaid miniskirt. Her hair was raven-wing black and hung in long, loose curls over a heart-shaped face.

"Oh. That's very Britney Spears," Schwarz breathed. "Very 'I'm Not So Innocent.'"

"Please," Lyons said. "It's 'Oops...I Did It Again' and it's so 2001 it makes me laugh."

Blancanales's head snapped around to stare at the Able Team leader. Schwarz removed his eye from the sniper scope, his mouth hanging open in shock.

"Um, you into pop princesses?" he asked.

"Shut up. She's been all over the news, that's all," Lyons snapped.

Schwarz turned his head toward Blancanales. He could see the stocky Latino preparing a sarcastic riposte and felt his own laughter bubbling up in his throat.

Then the screaming began.

GONZALES BEGAN to shiver in fear.

Lagos moved between the men hanging from the ceiling like slabs of meat at a slaughterhouse. He lit a cigarette. Beyond the lights the hulking figures of his men were reduced to nondescript shadows.

The man hanging on Gonzales's left started to mumble a prayer to the Virgin Mary in rapid Spanish. There was the sudden sharp, acrid smell of urine as one of the men let his bladder go. Lagos chuckled and blew out a blue cloud of cigarette smoke.

"The people," Lagos said, "they don't understand that what we do is hard work. They think moving product is like being a rock star. You bang models and party all the time. Sometime you have to be like, uh, the Tony Soprano and use your gun. Right?"

Lagos moved around to stand in front of Gonzales. He regarded the hanging prisoner like some insect he'd found crushed on the sole of his shoe. He blew smoke into Gonzales's face, then reached up with one hand and snatched the informant by the chin. Lagos locked eyes with his prey.

"But we know the truth, don't we?" Lagos gritted. "We know it is hard goddamn work making our money. And the ladies aren't the only things we bang, eh?"

From behind Lagos his men chuckled. To the terrified Gonzales it sounded like hyenas regarding a wounded gazelle. He was close enough to Lagos to see the black clogged pores of the man's nose. There was a tiny residue of white powder around the edge of one of his cavernous nostrils. The man's eyes blazed as bloodshot as a rabid dog's. Gonzales squeezed his own eyes shut and tried to turn away. Lagos's fingers were like steel bands on his face, and they burned his flesh with his intense body heat.

"One of you bitches knows about Bellicose Dawn." Lagos released Gonzales's face and stepped back. "None of you should know about my Bellicose Dawn. Before I am finished, the one who knows will tell me what he knows. But since I will kill that person, I don't expect anyone to volunteer the information. So we were talking about hard work again, right? Getting the one of you to confess will be hard work. Just as keeping my woman happy can be hard work."

Lagos turned his back on the hanging men and walked past the halogen lamp setup. With his back to the men, his voice rolled across the warehouse away from them, echoed off the thin metal walls then bounced back, ringing evilly in their ears.

"So I… What do the gringos say? Yes. I can kill…I can kill two birds with one bush. Or get two stones in my palm. Something. Fuck it. My woman, she likes to hurt people who've disappointed me. For *her* it is not such hard work."

Lagos turned and faced the men, now a faceless shadow behind the lights that blinded them.

"It gets her very worked up, if you understand what I mean." On cue, his thugs laughed. "So I win. I don't have to do the work. I get my information. My lady is happy. Then she makes *me* happy. See? Everybody wins, yes?" Lagos paused and his dry chuckle trailed off. "Well, I am guessing not everyone. Not you, eh, bitches?"

From behind Gonzales one of the other two men began to scream.

"LET'S MOVE IN," Lyons said.

He rose off his knee and swept up the 12-gauge shotgun. Behind him Blancanales and Schwarz stood in smooth unison, their weapons sweeping up and tracking toward the danger zone.

In well-practiced motions the team approached its objective. Lyons raced forward several yards, then took cover behind some debris. He brought his drum-fed shotgun up, providing cover as his teammates jogged quickly past him. Twenty yards up, they dropped to their knees behind solid piles of junk and covered Lyon's bunny-hop motion. Able Team repeated the maneuver three more times before coming to the last bit of cover—an overturned and waterlogged Ford Taurus.

Lyons scanned the area around the building and saw no sentries. He made a *V* out of his index and middle fingers and gestured toward his eyes, then pointed toward a window on the side of the building.

Immediately, Schwarz rose, Steyr AUG up, and ghosted across the muddy gravel toward the four-pane window. He crouched beneath the opening, then slowly straightened until he was peeking inside. He remained motionless for nearly a minute, soaking in every detail.

From inside, there was the sound of a little gas-powered engine and the screams had turned to shrieks.

"Jesus," Blancanales muttered. He lifted a finger to the cell attachment in his ear. "Stony Base, Able is about to make entry."

"Copy," Price answered, her voice still cool. "Jack, go ahead and bring the Little Bird in over site."

"Roger," Grimaldi answered.

From out over the swamp Able Team could suddenly

pick up the whir and hum of the Little Bird helicopter. It formed a rhythmic droning punctuated by the shrieks of the torture victims.

From the window Schwarz turned back toward his unit. He held up his hand and spread the fingers. *Five.* He closed his hand into a fist, then opened it again. *Five more.* He closed his hand once more then held up three fingers. *Thirteen total.*

Lyons nodded once, his head moving sharply.

"Let's roll," he said.

# CHAPTER TWO

*France*

THOMAS JACKSON HAWKINS sat in the lobby of the Marseilles hotel. His com-link earpiece as inconspicuous as the newspaper he pretended to study in the crowd of EU powerbrokers. He read the story about a Venezuelan named Sincanaros connected to the improper campaign finances of a Maryland senator with genuine disgust. Underneath the rest of his paper, thrown casually to the lobby side of his little café table, was a parabolic mike designed to look like a cell phone.

The electronic device pointed toward the front desk and the pickup fed directly into the modified microphone Hawkins wore in his ear.

The Phoenix Force commando sipped his espresso and idly scanned the page of newsprint in his hands, searching for good news and killing time until the mark showed herself. He was the point man on this snatch operation.

A Joint Special Operations Command task force had

pulled a prepaid cell phone off the corpse of a Chechen master bombmaker during a black op in Karachi, Pakistan. The redial option had revealed a Luxembourg prefix and number. Intrigued, JSOC had passed the information on to their CIA counterparts.

Electronic and computer analysts had managed to track the number to a satellite phone purchased by a Saudi Arabian construction company specializing in the sale of heavy equipment and suppression of oil-well fires in Africa and Southwest Asia.

The only representative of the company in Luxembourg during the appropriate time frame had been one Nayef al-Shalaan, who had turned out to be a very interesting person. He drew a generous salary from a construction company that was owned by one of the currently eight hundred Saudi princes. A prince who also happened to be al-Shalaan's father.

Al-Shalaan had a degree in communications from Jordon College in Oxford and a master's degree in finance from Princeton University. He enjoyed diplomatic immunity as House of Saud royalty, and he was an expert at brokering deals around UN mandates. Though a great deal of animosity had existed between Saddam Hussein's Iraq and Saudi Arabia, al-Shalaan hadn't allowed that to get in the way of profit, and he had managed to wed up several companies connected to French politicians with the Jordanian representatives of the Iraqi oil ministry during what would come to be known as the UN Oil-for-Food scandal, taking considerable amounts in money and favors in broker fees from both sides.

His connections with Sunni intelligence agents of the

Special Republican Guard had continued after the U.S. invasion, and he'd grown rich channeling the finances of the Ramadi and Fallujah insurgents through Damascus and out to global points. Al-Shalaan was the very definition of a high-value target. The black bag surveillance specialists rolling out of Langley had gone right to work.

In short time the frequency for al-Shalaan's personal cell phone had been ascertained, triangulated and captured. Once his personal communications were cracked, a whole world of intelligence had opened up to U.S. agencies.

Then al-Shalaan had started transferring funds for men believed to be the bodyguards of Ayman al-Zawahiri, al Qaeda's number two. Al-Zawahiri was an Egyptian doctor and important figure in the radical Islamic Jihad group founded there, and was tied to many acts of terror designed to weaken and overthrow the secular North African state.

Suddenly the CIA had a problem. The Pentagon's Defense Intelligence Agency had put in a daily intelligence estimate that al-Shalaan, a prince of an important ally in the war on terror with diplomatic immunity, had suddenly come to the attention of another important ally: the brutal Egyptian GDSSI, or General Directorate for State Security Investigations. If al-Shalaan was going down, then the U.S. wanted him all to themselves.

Coordinating the intelligence cross-pollination, the DNI had gone to the Oval Office with his take on the situation. Al-Shalaan had to disappear. Taking the matter out of CIA hands, the President had gone to Stony Man.

Al-Shalaan was going to be pulled out of his Marseilles penthouse suite one step ahead of a black-ops squad of GDSSI agents. The resources available were scant. The time frame was ridiculously tight, the potential operational blowback a PR nightmare. Kidnapping a Saudi prince was unthinkable, even one that was a known facilitator of terror.

Phoenix Force got the job.

One number on al-Shalaan's phone had unfailingly come up in connection to his stay at the five-star Marseilles resort—the number to a very high-priced, very exclusive dominatrix for hire.

The Langley profilers had been nonplussed by the revelation that al-Shalaan liked to be spanked and humiliated. And submissives like the Saudi were willing to pay large sums of money to secure a professional dominant.

Monica Bellucci was such a woman.

Hawkins sat up in his seat, then studiously turned his attention to his paper. Bellucci had walked into the lobby. The Phoenix Force commando nonchalantly reached under his folded newspaper and turned up the volume on the parabolic microphone. The smooth technology fed the passive signals into his earpiece so well he might have been standing at the woman's shoulder.

Her voice was a smooth, husky alto, the kind, Hawkins thought, that would cause a man's heart to race when it whispered into his ear.

The concierge gave her a sealed envelope and a key card. Turning, she strode across the lobby toward the gilded doors of the elevator with more grace than an Italian runway model.

The concierge, an effete, overly trim man, stood

there looking slightly stunned, then his face regained its normal polite impassivity and he turned to help another guest.

Hawkins snorted to himself as he clicked the parabolic mike. His finger touched his throat mike. "We've got the room number," he said, standing.

IN THE ROOM, BELLUCCI went through her ritual. Her overcoat came off, revealing the strapless black rubber dress beneath. The garment fit like a latex glove over a body that could easily pull it off, and there was no doubt that she wore nothing underneath. A black ribbon was tied in a choker around her throat, usually a sign of submissiveness in the bondage and domination world, but just part of her costume in this case. She set down her designer bag and reached inside, removing a coil of soft cord, a riding crop and a prescription pill bottle. Leaving the implements behind her on the entrance table where her customer would notice them immediately upon entering, she took the pill bottle over to the suite's bar.

Her eyes already glassy, she washed down three Oxy-Contin tablets with two ounces of Bombay gin.

Though she spoke French flawlessly, the stunning blonde was German by way of Switzerland. She had always been drawn to older men, established men with influence and financial means. She had learned in her first year at the exclusive Paris university that married men of the jet set treated their mistresses *very* well.

She had accepted her first assignation—Bellucci did not turn tricks—at twenty. Her current lover, an assets manager with the World Bank, had come to her frantic.

Somehow a South African intelligence agent had gathered evidence of his insider trading involving relief funds going into Liberia.

Desperate enough to offend his beautiful mistress, he'd pleaded with her to get into the man's suite and steal the documents, knowing full well what it would require of her. The thrill that had shivered through her body when she felt the weight of the envelope containing the equivalent of ten thousand U.S. dollars—and what that money was buying—had been unforgettable.

She wore out the overweight, middle-aged South African government agent then rummaged his embassy-provided suite at her leisure and obtained the documents. Making copies for her own, soon-to-be-growing personal files, she'd promptly demanded another ten thousand before turning them over to her lover.

Realizing the potential of the situation, Bellucci had turned professional for the diplomatic community. Soon after, she quickly learned she liked her sex rough and her little black book, actually a PDA database, was filled with men, occasionally their wives and often their full-time mistresses, as well as a handful of female clients, who craved the release of a mistress with a capital *M*.

Almost immediately she had come to the attention of Henri Galli upon the recommendation of a powerful Venezuelan businessman named Marcos Sincanaros. She knew little about the man except that he was tied to the government in some shadowy fashion and that he paid very well. Under his patronage her career had truly blossomed.

She brought the cut-glass tumbler to her full, surgically enhanced lips and sipped. The gin gave off a scent that reminded her of pine trees as it sparkled tart on her tongue. Setting her drink down, she opened her purse on the bar and pulled out a blunt.

She licked the end of the marijuana cigar until it was wet, then took a vial out of her handbag and sprinkled a liberal amount of cocaine across the moistened end. Bringing the blunt to her mouth, she used an oversize lighter to fire it up.

The pungent smoke and aromatized cocaine filled her lungs as she dragged and held it in. The blood from her pounding heart rushed to her head, making her dizzy, followed immediately by a wave of pleasant euphoria. She felt simultaneously mellow and keyed up. The feeling would continue as her body absorbed the primary agents of her OxyContin painkillers.

She left the smoldering blunt in a fine crystal ashtray and wandered deeper into the suite, looking for the stereo system.

HAWKINS ENTERED THE ROOM on the fifth floor of the resort, some seven floors down from al-Shalaan's penthouse suite. Inside, the rest of Phoenix Force was going over its last-minute preparations for the operation.

Calvin James sat on a chair in front of the wrought-iron-and-glass coffee table situated in the center of the room. With quick, efficient motions he was securing the glass vials of Versed and succhyil chlorate into the loading chambers of the pneumatic injectors each of the team would carry in addition to a personal backup pistol.

James, a former medic with the U.S. Navy SEALs, had explained the drug in detail to the team prior to deployment from Stony Man. Erring on the side of safety, for his team, James had calculated doses for a 210-pound male. The pistol-shaped injectors made sharp clicking sounds as he set them down on the glass tabletop.

He looked up as Hawkins entered the room. "What's up, T.J.?"

"Everything's still good. I waited around until al-Shalaan showed up to confirm the numbers on his entourage. We're still five-by-five for our sitrep."

James nodded, then spoke into his throat mike. "T.J. confirms sitrep," he said to the team leader, David McCarter. The ex-SAS commando was the team member with by far the most driving expertise on the team. He was waiting in a H3 Hummer converted into a stretch limousine downstairs across the street from the loading dock at the back of the five-star hotel. The vehicle was perfect camouflage in the upscale setting.

James listened to the reply for a second, a grin growing larger on his face. "Copy. Out," he said.

"Let me guess," Gary Manning said from across the room. The big Canadian was attaching a sound suppressor to the specially threaded barrel of a Glock 17 pistol. "David's still pissed he's not cracking skulls on this one."

"Oh, you know how you alpha males like your skull cracking." James laughed.

Manning snorted. "If that anesthesia works half as well as you say, there shouldn't be any skull cracking going on."

"It'll take a minute," James admitted, and set the last injector down. "But with the adrenaline going, their hearts'll push the drug through their system just fine. They'll be out of commission even before they go under."

Rafael Encizo spoke up. "I've told Barb we're about to go live."

The stocky little Cuban walked into the central living area from the master bedroom. Like Manning, he wore a shoulder holster holding a silenced Glock 17. He shrugged on a leather jacket to hide his shoulder rig and tucked the tail of his short-sleeved shirt into the back of his faded jeans.

Manning stepped forward. "Okay, Rafe," he said. "You lost rock-paper-scissors, so you're the drunk."

"It's bullshit, you know," Encizo answered, crossing to the bar. "If anyone should be the drunk, it should be T.J."

"This is subterfuge," James said. "Not real life."

"I'm right here," Hawkins complained. "I'm standing right here."

"You want to be the drunk?" James asked, his voice dry.

"No. I'm good, thanks," Hawkins said.

"Not the vodka," Manning said as Encizo picked up a bottle of clear liquor from the suite bar. "It doesn't stink enough. Use the Beefeater gin."

The Phoenix Force pro upended half a bottle over himself. Instantly the room stank of pine needles over the abrasive smell of grain alcohol. Hawkins and Manning quickly backed up to keep from being splashed. Encizo kept a grip on the bottle and grinned at them.

"Don't be shy, boys. I'm not heavy, I'm your brother."

Manning and Hawkins quickly took their auto-injectors from James and tucked them into the small of their backs. Encizo put his arms around the shoulders of the two men, prepping for his role as incoherent drunk.

"This is all very Nancy Drew," Hawkins muttered.

"Nancy Drew used to pretend to get drunk?" Manning demanded, incredulous.

"She wore disguises and stuff," Hawkins said. "Besides, Rafe's really more of a Bess."

"Bess?" James asked from behind them. The team began to move toward the door to their room. "Who the hell is Bess?"

"She was Nancy's fat friend."

"Hey!" the stocky Encizo protested.

"They always said she was pretty, though," Hawkins said quickly.

"I am pretty," Encizo agreed as Manning pulled the door to the room open.

"Why do you know so much about Nancy Drew? Is there something you aren't telling us?"

"Don't ask, don't tell." Hawkins fired the standard U.S. military quip right back.

James fingered his com link. "We're rolling," he said.

"Copy," McCarter answered from the vehicle.

"Copy," Price echoed from Stony Man.

Phoenix Force moved down the hall toward the elevator.

## CHAPTER THREE

Gonzales felt his heart sink. He watched Marta, Lagos's woman, stroll into the warehouse through the door and walk into the light of the halogen lamps. At twenty, the former call girl and Mexico City porn star was a sight to behold. Her nails were painted in blood-red and her left hand held a lollipop she worked like a pro.

Her big, brown eyes widened in mock surprise as she regarded the hanging men. Her pink tongue lathed the head of the lollipop.

She giggled.

Lagos moved up behind her and whispered something into her ear. She reached up and traced her hand down the angular line of his face. If the violent drug kingpin had a weakness, it was this young female prostitute.

Despite himself, Gonzales's eyes were drawn to the smooth line of her flat stomach where a tiny gold hoop had been inserted in her navel. She wore no bra, and her nipples poked hard against the sheer fabric of her blouse. The skin on her body was flawless.

Gonzales felt his stomach turn queasy.

Her perfume, something heavy and expensive, rolled into his nose, momentarily overpowering the stink of body fluids and terror that surrounded him. His mind recoiled from his terror, his thoughts rebounding like a rubber ball in an empty room. He thought about his little girl and his wife. He flashed on images of the bodies of people he'd seen who'd suffered at the hands of the Zetas.

He felt tears welling up in his eyes and he used the last vestiges of his pride to blink them back as Marta, at once sadistic and seductive, glided forward. She leaned in close, her beauty a blunt instrument, her breath hot and sweet against his neck, the crush of her heavy breast hard against his stomach. When she spoke, she purred, but her voice was the singsong soprano of a little girl.

"You were naughty," she chided. "So naughty, and now you must be punished. I remember you from that restaurant in Cancún. Do you remember, Gabriel?"

Gonzales nodded. He'd worn a wire designed to passively boost the conversation for the CIA surveillance team's parabolic boom mike. Lagos had met with a Venezuelan moneyman named Sincanaros and a representative of FARC, the Colombian Communist insurgent army and largest narco-military in the world. Marta had been there, dressed in a stunning little black dress that cost about as much as a U.S. union plumber made in a year. She'd cooed and rubbed her thighs together throughout the meeting, flustering even the experienced Colombian guerrilla commander.

"I remember," Gonzales said, his voice hoarse.

"Lagos wanted me to act naughty that night," she said. Her expression was coy, childlike. "Do you remember me being naughty? How I touched myself while everyone watched?"

Gonzales closed his eyes. He felt his gorge rising and from his churning, fear-cramped stomach, acid bubbled up and burned the lining of his esophagus. He winced in pain.

Marta's tiny little hand found Gonzales's crotch. He flinched. "I think you were excited that night," she said. "I was so naughty." She let go and stepped back. "Tonight is going to be a little different."

From the small of her back the young woman produced a pearl-handled switchblade. She held it out and Gonzales closed his eyes again. He heard the greasy click as the tightly wound spring released the knife. He opened his eyes and saw the 5-inch blade wildly reflecting the light of the halogen lamps.

"Let's see what's going on with Gabriel," Marta giggled.

She dug the point of her blade into the denim fabric of his jeans at his fly. He winced as she poked the soft skin of his inner thigh, and he felt blood trickle down his leg. Marta worked, grunting softly with the effort, to cut away the fabric around his crotch.

In seconds his penis hung exposed. The crushing weight of his helpless vulnerability slammed into him all over again. Only the thought of his wife and daughter kept his tongue still.

Marta stepped back and slid the still-open switchblade behind the buckle of her wide, black belt. The pearl handle rested against the smooth, brown stretch of her flat abdomen.

She turned her head and barked a command. A short, squat gunman stepped forward.

Gonzales's eyes bulged from his head, and he moaned out loud despite his efforts to stifle the sound. Marta giggled again.

"No, don't start it," she snapped. "I want to start it."

"*Sí,*" the man said. He stepped back, handing the orange-and-black power grass trimmer to the slight young woman. The muscles of her arms stood out in vivid relief as she mastered the weight. The long orange extension cord trailed out behind her, disappearing into the dark beyond the halogen lights.

The grass trimmer sprang to life in her hands, the 18-volt power tool screaming as the hard plastic cord spun at 7000 revolutions per minute. Gonzales realized the device would tear his clothes from his body, then flay his flesh open in a techno-modern version of the ancient Chinese "death of a thousand cuts." His throat closed in his fear.

Marta grinned. "This is my favorite weapon. Its trademarked system uses centrifugal force to advance the line automatically as I need it."

The twisted Lolita rattled off the grass trimmer's specs in English with obvious enthusiasm, the way the proud owner of an American muscle car or an Italian Ferrari might talk about their automobile engine. *Goddamn you, Yankees,* he cursed his involvement with the CIA who had left him to die after his service.

Gunning the motor, Marta stepped forward. Her expression was twisted now, her grin so wide it threatened to split her face in two. Behind her, Lagos and his men had shuffled forward, their laughter almost muted by the high-pitched whine of the grass trimmer's 7.1-liter engine.

Still Gonzales didn't talk. He thought about it. If he did so, he might spare the other two men hours of torture. They were all dead, but maybe the other two men would be granted a quick coup de grâce if only Gonzales spoke up now.

Then he thought about his daughter and his wife. If he didn't remain silent, they'd be raped, then they'd be tortured.

No.

Gonzales offered up silent apologies to the other men and then bit down so hard on his tongue to keep silent that it bled.

Marta stepped forward and the spinning plastic cord whipped into his leg just above the knee. The denim split like paper and his flesh was lacerated so deep into the flesh of the vastus medialis that blood splattered at 7000 revolutions per minute, spraying across the walls like a Jackson Pollock painting.

Gonzales screamed, then screamed again. White-hot lances of agony surged up through his body in bullet trains of anguish.

Engulfed in the shrieks and the screams produced by the little grass trimmer, only two of Lagos's men, the ones nearest the door, heard the window breaking.

Marta stepped in again and thrust the grass trimmer forward. The spinning plastic cord bit Gonzales's inner thigh. Blood splashed her face in streaks like tiger

stripes, and unconsciously her slick pink tongue darted
out to taste the hot fluid smearing her lips.

There was a scramble of bodies behind her shoulder
as one Zetas gunman tried to shout a warning, then a
flash like a sun going nova and a bang so loud it split
eardrums. In the snap of a magician's fingers Gonzales
felt the concussion roll into him like the wind, punching him into motion on the end of his chains. He was
blind. He was deaf. He was dizzy and bruised, confused and battered, as a second and then third flash-bang
grenade went off.

The halogen light setup was knocked clear of its
moorings and crashed to the floor, plunging the room
into heavy shadow as a single brilliant lamp, now face-
down, continued to burn. Men shouted in pain and confusion and anger as the front door of the building was
smashed open.

Gadgets Schwarz thrust the barrel of his Steyr AUG
through the smashed window glass and saw a dark shape
pulling itself up off the floor, a long weapon in its hands.
Schwarz squeezed the trigger and put a 5.56 mm round
into the figure, then fired three more.

The figure went down and Schwarz pivoted smoothly,
spotting a cluster of shapes directly behind the tangled
mess of the halogen lights. He held back on his trigger
and snapped the shortened barrel in a tight Z-pattern,
burning a short burst into the crowd. Bodies hit the floor.

Carl Lyons entered through the warehouse door, his
Atchisson autoshotgun testing the strength of his thick
arms. The selective fire assault shotgun was fed with a
20-round drum magazine attachment and Lyons kept it

tucked in close against his body, firing from the hip in such tight quarters.

He saw a balaclava hardman jump to his feet directly in front of the door, an old-fashioned Ingram MAC-10 in the grip of a fist covered by black, fingerless gloves. A sound suppressor as long as the weapon itself preceded the weapon like a black wand.

The Atchisson boomed in Lyons's grip. The weapon recoiled smoothly into the ex-LAPD officer's hip. The 12-gauge fléchette round discharged into the Zetas's upturned face from a distance of less than three feet.

The tiny steel darts ripped through the flesh on the right side of the ex-commando's face and drove mercilessly into the man's skull. The back of the Mexican drug soldier's head erupted, and the man's body followed the momentum of his pulverized skull.

As blood spilled out of the ruined body, Lyons moved into the room. Behind him, Blancanales peeled off to the right, the H&K submachine gun up and ready in his hands.

Able Team moved in a tight configuration, a well-rehearsed ballet of trajectories and overlapping fields of fire. No motion was wasted as Schwarz anchored one section of the fire triangle and Blancanales another, letting Lyons and his autoshotgun move up the middle.

Blancanales tucked the folding stock of his submachine gun tight into his shoulder, the sound of Lyons's booming shotgun ringing in his ears. He saw the silhouette of a man holding a Kalashnikov and cut loose, a burst of rounds striking the gunner high between the shoulder blades and punching through his neck.

The narco-soldier tumbled, and, in the light of the single halogen lamp burning facedown on the warehouse floor, Blancanales saw three men hanging from chains. A man he instantly recognized as Humberto Lagos pulled a Beretta 92-F pistol from a shoulder holster and put it to the temple of one of the bound prisoners. The Able Team commando snapped the sights of his submachine over the man's head and his finger tightened on the smooth metal curve of his trigger.

A slight figure stumbled out of his periphery, coming between him and Lagos. To his surprise Blancanales saw that it was the young woman from the car. He leaped forward and grasped the noncombatant by the arm, still holding his weapon up in his hand. He caught a flash of beautiful brown eyes as he held the woman close. His stomach clenched as he saw the hanging prisoner jerk like a fish on the line as Lagos put a bullet through his head.

The former Mexican commando turned to face Blancanales and the Able Team operator caught a sudden flash of a scar across the man's neck. It was ugly, the tissue raised so that it looked like a piece of red licorice.

Blancanales pulled the trigger on his weapon, the 9 mm Parabellum rounds chewing into Lagos like spinning lead buzz saws. The Mexican dropped straight down as his forehead was brutally cracked open.

Blancanales felt the panicked woman squirm in his grip with sudden violence, twisting hard against his hold. He heard her cry out and suddenly he felt an icy burn stab into his stomach. He gasped at the sudden agony and the twisting hellcat broke free from his grip.

There was a second impact down low and another

sudden burst of agonizing fire. He looked down and saw the woman snatch a knife from his lower abdomen. He looked up and she was snarling as she yanked the knife back to stab him again.

His knees buckled in surprise and he fell to the floor, striking the ground hard on his buttocks. He looked up. The woman rose above him with the knife swept up above her head in both hands.

Marta screeched and snarled as she slashed downward. Blancanales felt his conscious mind snap like the shutter on a camera. Gone was the young woman in slutty heels and too much makeup. Gone was blazing pain low in his gut. Gone was the booming of Lyons's shotgun or the chatter of Schwarz's assault rifle. Gone were the stumbling, dying Zetas.

All that remained was threat and response as blackness swarmed up to claim him.

The H&K MP-5 jumped in his hand as if of its own volition. But even then he couldn't bring himself to do what needed to be done. The MP-5 jumped as he used it like a blunt instrument, striking the young woman with rapid-fire jabs like a boxer in the ring, first in the kneecap to bring her down, then into the soft curves of her body. Her slight frame shuddered under the impacts and she fell backward as she dropped her knife.

His guts felt as if scalding salt water had been splashed in them, but his arm was like the lever on an oil derrick and he laid the muzzle upside her jaw with a sound like a branch snapping.

She tumbled farther backward and fell to her back. Her head made a low, dull sound as it bounced off the floor. The arteries running into the avulsions left by the gun sight spilled her young blood onto the concrete floor, mingling with the puddle already formed by the blood of Lagos's still-warm corpse. Marta's eyes rolled back in her head and her jaw hung slack in loose reflex as she was shoved into unconsciousness. Her lover's eyes remained fixed and open on the scene as Blancanales's closed into darkness.

# CHAPTER FOUR

*France*

"Yes, Henri," Monica Bellucci said into the phone. "I'll have copies of his cell-phone logs to you by the morning. You just get my money." She hung up the phone.

Bellucci carefully tapped out a small amount of cocaine from a gold phial onto a little silver spoon she wore on a Gucci chain around her neck. She put the spoon to her nostril and quickly snorted the bump. She heard the lock on the room door unlatch as the key card worked the electronic mechanism.

She set the phial on the countertop and leisurely turned toward the entryway. She spread her legs slightly on her outrageously high stilettos and the black rubber dress stretched tight across her narrow thighs. She felt the last bump of coke kick in. She was fully engaged in her role.

The suite door swung open and Nayef al-Shalaan stepped inside the suite. Behind him towered four burly bodyguards in dark suits. In contrast al-Shalaan was short, but his face was set in the harsh lines of a man used to getting his way.

His mahogany eyes fell to the table and widened in surprise as he saw what was positioned there, sitting in plain view. Bright dots of color appeared on his dusky cheeks as he realized his bodyguards could plainly see the coil of rope. The manacles. The riding crop.

"Outside," he snapped.

Immediately the crew stepped back, their faces impeccably passive. Al-Shalaan slammed the door shut and the lock engaged. His eyes rose from the accoutrements and devoured Bellucci. His hunger was naked and exposed, and he drank in the sight of her.

"You must be more careful—" he began.

"Shut up!" she snapped.

Al-Shalaan was paying for a dominatrix, and he was going to get his money's worth. As high as a kite, Bellucci stalked forward like a cat closing in on its prey. She slinked as she moved, almost crossing the line between sensuous and slatternly, but the razor-sharp edge of predatory energy remained.

"Shut your mouth," she repeated. Her voice had lowered from a bark to a hissing whisper. "You're late. You kept me waiting." She drew even with the table in the entranceway. "I'm not used to being kept waiting."

Al-Shalaan quickly set his attaché case on the table. Made from the finest Italian leather, it featured clasps in 24-carat gold. Not plating, but solid gold fixtures, right down to the tumblers on the combination locks. The Arabic power broker kept his voice contrite and his eyes down as he answered his mistress.

"I a-apologize, please, one thousand a-apologies," he stuttered.

His English came with an Oxford accent. She was near enough now for him to smell her perfume, a timeless classic. In her heels she was taller than him. Her heavily lidded eyes glittered like diamonds. With her left hand she reached out and pressed a fingertip to his lips, causing him to fall instantly silent. The nail was long and sharp and red as blood in a Baghdad gutter.

"No more talking," she warned.

She leaned in close so that her full lips were near his ear. Her breath was hot against the flesh of his face and he smelled the gin. He felt his crotch go tight and he shut his eyes, body trembling. Bellucci reached over with her hand and wrapped her long fingers around the leather haft of the riding crop.

"Strip!" she ordered.

She brought the riding crop down against the polished wood of the table with a sharp crack and al-Shalaan hastened to obey.

THE ELEVATOR DOOR OPENED with a tasteful, muted ding and the four teammates of Phoenix Force looked down the hotel hallway. Encizo sagged, hanging off the shoulders of Hawkins and Manning, the bottle still clenched in his fist. The four bodyguards in front of al-Shalaan's door turned their heads in unison. The choreography of the movement was particularly impressive given that none of them seemed to have necks.

From the back of the elevator James, in his overwatch position, whispered under his breath, "I should have used more drug." He stood behind a hotel wheelchair they had acquisitioned from a bellhop in trade for a generous tip.

"There're four of them," Hawkins gritted as Encizo pretended to stumble. "This wasn't supposed to be a fair fight. This isn't the goddamn Ultimate Fighting Championship, it's supposed to be an ambush."

"Grin and bear it," Manning said.

"Hey!" Encizo lifted his head and shouted at the bodyguards in carefully memorized French. He made his voice slurred and the liquor in his bottle splashed as he gestured. "What the hell are you fat pigs looking at?"

The crew moved down the hall. James, who had learned French while serving as a Navy SEAL, spoke up quickly. "Don't mind my friend, he's had too much to drink. You know?" He shoved the wheelchair away and off to one side, as if the group of drunks had stolen it then tired of playing with the item.

The four juggernauts did not reply. One of them placed his hand under his jacket in an automatic gesture. James, charged with overwatch, tensed. *"Parlez-vous français?"* he called out.

*"Voulez-vous coucher avec moi, ce soir?"* Encizo said suddenly in his affected stupor.

"Oh, Jesus," James moaned under his breath as he heard Encizo ask the bodyguards if they wanted to sleep with him tonight.

One of the bodyguards, a dark giant with a potato nose and a cell link in his right ear, snorted in laughter. He reached out a hand as large as a dinner plate and put a restraining hand on the guard who'd put his hand under his jacket. The big man muttered something, and the other three bodyguards laughed.

Manning could see the tension leak out of them, but the group remained vigilant as the four Stony Man commandos approached al-Shalaan's suite door. In fact, he could see that they almost looked eager. Pummeling some of what they thought were drunk French tourists was an activity they seemed not averse to. This fit into the team's plans perfectly. A brawl was fine. As long as the bodyguards didn't feel the need to draw their handguns from the start, the odds would shift quickly into the team's favor.

Phoenix Force moved down the hall, Encizo ranting in a slurred voice while Manning and Hawkins pretended to stagger under his weight. James began to drift out toward the edge of the group. Encizo started making gagging noises as if he were about to vomit.

The paneling on the walls of the long hotel hallway was of heavy wood, the pictures original eighteenth-century European cityscapes: Paris in autumn, London in the rain, Venice in the spring, Berlin at night. The carpet was thick, a burgundy laced with golden threaded patterns that matched the subdued wallpaper above the black walnut wainscoting. The resort was a beautiful, five-star hotel. In a detached way Gary Manning began to feel sorry for the grand old structure.

Phoenix Force had a tendency to wreak havoc.

As they approached the knot of the powerfully built, James rattled off a room number, addressing the bodyguards. "Where is it?" he demanded.

The dark giant, seemingly the senior guard, shook his head. "You're not even on the right floor," he snapped.

Encizo made a horrible retching sound and let a long line of saliva dribble out of his mouth and onto the carpet at the bodyguard's feet. "He's going to throw up!" James suddenly cried. Instinctively the four bodyguards stepped back, crowding them against the door.

Phoenix Force uncoiled. Gone was the comfortable banter. Gone was the easygoing camaraderie and tough-guy ball busting. No one was smiling. No one was laughing. The machine that was Phoenix Force had been initiated.

Manning stood closest to the guards, and he ducked out of Encizo's arm, twisting at the waist. His right fist snapped out like a whip popping in a knife hand blow that struck the guard in the Adam's apple while his left hand reached for the auto-injector positioned behind his back.

The bodyguard staggered, his hands flying up to protect his face in a boxer's cover-up motion. Pulling the auto-injector free, Manning used his momentum to dip his massive shoulder and drive hard into the man's body like linemen stopping a defensive back cold on the scrimmage line. The giant gasped as air was driven from his lungs and Manning's shoulder hammered into his solar plexus. The man stumbled backward.

Instantly, Manning was on him, placing his leading forearm across the man's neck and pinning him against the hotel wall. The man's eyes grew wide with surprise, then quickly narrowed in effort as the bodyguard leader began to fight back. However, the pain from Manning's initial neck blow had frightened and slowed the bodyguard's reflexes so that his hook into the burly Phoenix Force warrior's ribs was glancing and ineffective.

Manning brought up the auto-injector and shoved it roughly into the giant's thick neck. The gun cycled and the sedative slammed into the man's system. Manning wasn't sure he'd hit the artery he was aiming for, but the muscles of the neck were extremely vascular. The bodyguard's heart was now pumping wildly.

The man looked stunned, then panicked as he felt the air-jet of liquid medicine invade his body. He struggled to sit up, badly out of position, and Manning rammed an overhand elbow strike into his unprotected face, driving him into the floor.

James attacked simultaneously with Manning. He leaped forward and threw his right forearm hard into the throat of the bodyguard with a French Foreign Legion tattoo on his neck while his right leg simultaneously hooked behind the man's ankle. As the bodyguard tumbled back against the wall, James fisted the auto-injector and thrust it forward.

He was aiming for the neck as Manning had, but the ex-Legionnaire twisted at the last moment so that the muzzle of the auto-injector struck him in the corner of his face, back toward the ear where the mandible hinge joint attached to the skull.

The man gaped in surprise, then almost instantly lost control of his jaw. The muscles of his face went slack even as James pulled back. He saw the bodyguard's hand come up, slap ineffectually at the lapel of his blazer even as he finished sliding down the wall to the carpet in front of al-Shalaan's door. James spun, auto-injector in one hand while he reached for his silenced pistol in case events were unfolding in a dangerous way.

He saw Encizo hammering a much taller man with huge, looping hooks, his knuckles smashing into the sides of the man's face with rapacious energy. The bottle of liquor had bounced as it had been dropped and rolled away, spilling alcohol on the expensive carpet. Encizo stepped forward and grabbed the stunned man's suit jacket by the lapels and shoved them down to his elbows, effectively pinning them to his sides in a hockey maneuver.

Encizo ripped his auto-injector free as the fingers of his other hand wrapped tightly into the close-knit curls of his target's hair. He jerked once, swiveling from the hips, and the screaming man took a nosedive into the puddle of liquor soaking into the carpet.

The little Cuban dropped in a knee-led pile driver that slammed into the man's back between his shoulder blades, pinning him to the floor. The auto-injector made contact with the easy target of the man's pulsing carotid artery and he activated the device.

Encizo kept his weight pressing down on the prone bodyguard, crushing him into the carpet until the surgical anesthesia took effect. He felt the man's struggles suddenly turn sluggish and then stop. The huge body in his grip went noodle-limp.

Hawkins had known from the beginning that when Phoenix Force unleashed its close-quarters ambush that of all the men in the phalanx, he would have the farthest distance to cover to initiate his attack. It was a distance of only two or three yards. But with an alert and possibly well-trained enemy, that scant distance would give his target a valuable couple of seconds of reaction time that the other bodyguards wouldn't have.

If the man was competent, then Hawkins knew he could find himself in a stand-up fight instead of a surreptitious attack. When McCarter had set up the action plan, Hawkins had kept his face impassive as he listened to his assignment. Inside he had felt a sense of pride as he realized he had been given the position David McCarter would have taken for himself had his driving skills not been so imperative to the second phase of the operation.

As James drifted out around Manning's broad form, signaling the start of assault, Hawkins sprang into action. He stepped forward from under Encizo's arm and toward his man.

The bodyguard's eyes grew wide in surprise, identically to those of his leader. Hawkins crossed the two endless steps between them as the rest of Phoenix Force clashed with the team of bodyguards. He felt a sinking feeling in the pit of his stomach as he realized he might not make it. He went up on the toes of his left foot as he pulled his right knee back and up, almost to the level of his chin. His momentum carried him forward, and his leg lashed out as the black plastic alloy of the bodyguard's Glock 19 was pulled clear of shoulder leather.

The heel of Hawkins's low-cut boot slammed into the bodyguard's sternum, and Hawkins felt the jar of the impact shock travel up his leg like the vibration of a tuning fork. He heard the bodyguard grunt as he continued moving forward, driving his foot down from the impact zone.

Hawkins had missed his specific target of the forearm attached to the hand holding the Glock pistol. He had made a mistake. As his right foot drove through the kick attack and landed on the carpet, the Phoenix Force commando was already following through on his first strike. He clamped his hand around the wrist holding the pistol as he whipped his right elbow around in an overhead crescent strike.

The point of his elbow smashed into the man's face just below his eye and the bodyguard's head snapped back into the wall, but the man didn't go out. Hawkins dug inside himself and brought forth the aggression and anger and will that had served him for so long in such life-and-death struggles.

The bodyguard jerked his arm back, trying to clear the pistol for a shot. Hawkins squeezed hard, stymieing the movement the way an NBA guard stuffs a dunk attempt. The muzzle of the gun dug into the bodyguard's stomach, keeping the man from pulling the trigger.

The man grunted, then forced his hand up, and Hawkins had to face the bitter truth that the man was stronger than he was. Millimeter by millimeter the gun began to move. Hawkins snarled then, and cold, greasy shots of adrenaline splashed into his knotted stomach.

Goose bumps rose on his flesh as fear-energy coursed through his system. In the blink of an eye he felt energized, supercharged.

His fingers crushed the man's wrist. His elbow began to rise and fall with jackhammer rhythm, each impact of the sharp bone sending shock waves through the bodyguard's head to rap his brain against the side of his skull. Hawkins's strikes tore flesh open across the man's forehead near the temples and blood gushed in sudden torrents.

The man went limp and the pistol fell from slack fingers. Hawkins rose, pulled his auto-injector free and shot it into the unconscious man's neck.

He turned and saw the rest of Phoenix Force looking at him.

"What?" he asked, catching his breath.

"Nothing," Manning said with a shrug. "If you're through playing with your food, do you think we could continue?"

"Sure, no problem."

"Next time I'm not going to give you a fancy toy if you're not going to use it right," James said.

"Fuck 'em," Hawkins replied. "They work for scum. They're lucky the powers that be didn't want corpses on friendly soil."

"Let's roll," Manning said.

## CHAPTER FIVE

From his overwatch position Gadgets Schwarz saw Rosario Blancanales fall. He saw the incongruous figure of a schoolgirl stumble back, a bloody knife in her fist. He shifted the shortened muzzle of his Steyr AUG A3 toward the female as she stabbed Blancanales a second time.

The aiming reticle of his 1.5X power telescope filled with the young woman's figure as she swept her knife up. She staggered in his sight as he attempted to put a 5.56 mm Teflon-coated round through the left side of her rib cage.

But the close-quarters battle exploded into a frenzy of activity as one of the Zetas gunslingers recovered his composure on Carl Lyons's flank and stepped into Schwarz's line of fire. The man raised a Browning Hi-Power pistol and triggered a round into the Able Team leader's back that was soaked up by his Kevlar body armor.

Lyons staggered under the impact as Schwarz put the man down. The Able Team leader triggered his assault shotgun, and suddenly the warehouse echoed with the sound of the full automatic 12-gauge weapon.

Bodies spun and were flung like rag dolls from the impact of .440 stainless-steel fléchettes that ripped through flesh and shredded internal organs. Blood and brain and bits of bone struck the corrugated walls of the old warehouse, and the metal structure rang as rounds punched through it.

Then there was silence.

From his position at the window Schwarz shifted his Steyr AUG, scanning the area. Nothing moved. He snapped the barrel to a different vector and found all still.

Carl Lyons stood at the point of the unit's triangle formation, his smoking shotgun pointed downward, his ears ringing from the booming of his own weapon.

For a second he couldn't understand Schwarz's frantic shouting, then his hearing returned well enough for him to make out what his teammate was hollering. Lyons spun, searching the floor for Blancanales.

He saw the unconscious Latino sprawled out, one hand still clutching his weapon, the other resting on an ugly mess of a wound leaking blood across his lap. Schwarz burst through the door and began checking Zetas bodies as Lyons made his way through the carnage toward his downed friend.

Blancanales's breathing was shallow and forced, his color obviously bad, even in the uncertain light. Blancanales himself often served as Able Team's field medic, so it was from his kit that Carl Lyons stripped the first-aid equipment.

He set down his shotgun and brought a soft, OD green plastic package to his teeth and ripped it open. He moved Blancanales's hand to the side and spilled the contents of the packet on his open wound. Instantly the coagulation powder went to work, clotting the blood around the puncture wounds.

Since Blancanales's breathing was uncompromised, if laborious, and there was no other obvious wound, Lyons dedicated his attention to that injury first. Behind him Schwarz kept his weapon in one hand and used his other to call in the team's helicopter.

"Help us," moaned one of the hanging prisoners.

"Shut up," Lyons snapped.

He finished securing a second pressure dressing over Blancanales's wound. The Latino's eyes fluttered open, glazed with pain, and Lyons could see the man struggle toward coherency through the force of sheer willpower.

"We good?" Blancanales asked.

"Yeah," Lyons answered softly. "Jack's coming. We'll have you medevaced in no time. I hear the chopper now."

"The girl?"

"She's out, buddy. You're lucky you're still spry for such an old fart."

"Screw you," Blancanales said. His teeth were gritted through the pain. "Help me stand."

"Negative," Lyons said. "You're bleeding internally. You try to walk, and you'll rip your guts open."

The big ex-cop put a heavy hand on Blancanales's chest, keeping the stubborn man down. As he did so, he noticed the man's abdomen pushing out and becoming rigid right before his eyes. The internal bleeding was bad, Lyons realized, rapidly filling the spaces between his internal organs inside his torso. The clock was ticking on the wounded man.

Blancanales winced as he sank back down and Lyons pulled a loaded morphine syringe from Blancanales's medic kit. As he prepped the needle, he called over his shoulder at the third member of the team. Outside he could hear the sound of Jack Grimaldi's chopper.

"How we doing?" Lyons asked.

"Good," Schwarz answered. Having made sure all the hostile personnel were down, he walked over to the hanging men. One of them was a dripping corpse. Brains clung to the dead man's shirt and blood spilled freely down his body from the gaping hole in his head, creating a growing puddle at his feet.

"Who knows Hart?" Schwarz asked the remaining two prisoners, using the CIA case officer's pseudonym. "Come on, who knows Hart? I hope to Christ it wasn't *this* guy." The Able Team commando gestured toward the corpse.

Gonzales turned his head. "Bellicose Dawn," he muttered. He felt exhausted, dried out like a piece of fruit turned to leather in the sun. "Hart wanted to know about Bellicose Dawn."

"Let's get you out of here," Schwarz said.

While Lyons gave Blancanales a shot to help him manage the overwhelming pain, Schwarz began undoing the manacles locked around Gonzales's wrists. The informant sagged onto his feet, fighting back tears of relief. He stripped off his sweat- and blood-soaked shirt and tucked it into his pants to cover himself. He felt a sudden urge to spit on the bodies of Lagos and the unconscious Marta, but restrained himself. A distracted part of his mind cataloged the vivid, ugly scar on Lagos's throat.

"Don't get bashful now," Schwarz warned. "I got a hurt brother, and you're coming out to help me get one of the stretcher benches attached to my chopper."

"My family—" Gonzales began.

"Covered," Schwarz cut him off. "Your boy Hart already arranged that. Now let's move."

"What about me!" the last prisoner demanded, his voice frantic.

"Don't worry. You'll only be hanging a few more minutes. We'll call the locals and tell them they have a cleanup on aisle ten. You'll be fine."

"You can't leave me hanging here!" the man cried.

"People judge you by the company you keep, asshole," Schwarz snapped. "Now shut up or I'll leave you like your friend. At least he's quiet."

The bluff worked and the man fell silent.

In minutes the wounded Blancanales was loaded onto the stretcher and then the Little Bird as Carl Lyons coordinated with Stony Man control on local response and emergency medical treatment for the wounded Able Team operator.

Gonzales was loaded onto the helicopter, and the Little Bird lifted off as the first units of the NOPD were making their way to the scene. The incident would remain an official mystery with its own PR story for the press.

The lid was off Bellicose Dawn.

# CHAPTER SIX

Gary Manning used his key card override on the door. The electronic indicator light flashed red, then amber, then green. The automatic lock snapped back with an audible click, and he turned the lever handle. The door swung open under his touch then stopped as the chain caught

Manning growled like a bear and put his shoulder to the door. The chain popped loose with a sharp sound and the door flew open. Hawkins rushed in, his silenced pistol up and ready.

He used the weight of his body to keep the door to the hotel room open as Encizo rushed into the room hard on his heels. Manning followed.

Phoenix Force stopped and stared.

Her rubber dress pushed up above her thighs, Bellucci straddled the nude al-Shalaan like a cowgirl on her pony. In one hand she held the end of a corded rope fashioned into a choker around the Arab powerbroker's neck. With her other she used a riding crop to urge the hopping man into continued motion. From the welts and livid red marks on the man's buttocks the dominatrix had not been shy about using the whip.

With each buck Bellucci hopped, causing her augmented breasts to bounce wildly. Al-Shalaan was barking something as the woman struck him. Phoenix Force's dynamic entry caused the pair to snap their heads around in shock.

Bellucci screamed as she saw the men rush in. Al-Shalaan threw himself straight to the floor, squeezing his eyes shut against the vision of four sound suppressors bearing down on him.

Manning blinked, stunned by the incredulous imagery before him, then training took over and put his conscious mind in the passenger seat.

"Freeze!" he shouted in French. Then added, "Secure the room."

Hawkins and Encizo immediately stood and pushed deeper into the suite, methodically clearing the room as James rushed toward the intertwined sex partners under the unwavering cover of Manning's pistol.

"Don't shoot!" the woman shrieked in terror, using French as Manning had.

"Stay down!" James snapped, and shoved her clear of al-Shalaan.

The featherweight woman tumbled off her partner's back and slid across the marble tile of the floor. Her riding crop went spinning away. She curled into a terrified ball. James slid his pistol back into its shoulder holster and reached down with his free hand to snatch the loose end of the rope wound around al-Shalaan's neck.

He jerked the man to his feet, pulled the auto-injector

clear and jabbed it into the side of the terrorist facilitator's neck. A second dose went straight into the man's bloodstream. James shoved the man against the wall and let him slide to the ground.

"You want to dose the woman?" he asked Manning.

"Clear!" Encizo and Hawkins called in French from deeper inside the room.

"Yeah," Manning answered.

The Canadian holstered his pistol as Encizo and Hawkins came back into the entranceway. Drawing his auto-injector, he moved toward the cowering prostitute. She tried to scramble away from him, but he was too quick and too strong for her. He pinned her against the bar. Her arm swung desperately, knocking a tumbler of ice and gin to the ground where it exploded into glass shards with a pop like a gunshot.

"I'm sorry, this won't hurt," Manning said in French, finding manhandling the woman a distasteful task.

Mission first.

He leaned his weight against her body and applied the auto-injector into the soft, smooth flesh of her neck. The woman's heart was racing in terror, and the drug affected her almost instantaneously. He lowered her to the floor, avoiding the spilled liquor and broken glass.

Manning rose and surveyed the scene. James was using a tactical folding knife to cut the ropes from around the neck of the unconscious al-Shalaan. Hawkins was quickly shoving the Saudi prince's attaché case, cell phone and laptop into a black nylon gym bag. Coming across the man's suit jacket lying on the floor, the Southerner lifted the man's leather wallet from the inside pocket and threw that in, as well.

Encizo was at the open door, scanning the hallway for witnesses and bystanders while covering the slumped bodies of the guards. He had collected guns from every man and dropped them inside a waist-high ceramic vase set beside the entrance to the room. Manning was satisfied that the operation was unfolding as smoothly as could be expected.

"We've picked up our uncle and we're coming home," he said into his throat mike.

"Copy," McCarter and Price echoed.

"Get the wheelchair," Manning said to Encizo.

Encizo disappeared around the edge of the door as he darted down the hall. Manning turned and crossed the room's foyer to help James hoist al-Shalaan's limp body off the floor. Behind them Hawkins had methodically made his way around to the woman's purse, dumping the contents out onto the bar.

He let out a long low whistle as he shifted through the mess. "Jeez, how much drugs does this woman have?" He shook his head as he pulled up the menu on her phone and read some numbers, quickly scanning for prefixes that might be important. "Nothing."

"You got everything?" Manning asked.

"Yeah. All we have time for. I haven't found the room safe, but it wasn't on our op plan anyway."

"Let's go," James said.

Encizo came back into the room, pushing the wheelchair ahead of him. Without preamble James and Manning slung the unconscious body of al-Shalaan into the seat. The big Canadian stacked the man's loose clothing on his naked lap. This was a discreet hotel. If a VIP was being escorted dead drunk and naked to a waiting car by his entourage, then it was best not to make the situation hotel business.

Phoenix Force moved out of the room and passed the sprawled bodies of al-Shalaan's guards. They turned down the hallway opposite the elevator bank. They moved quickly in a quintessential VIP protection pattern.

"Let's go, guys," McCarter said in the earjack. "The valet is giving me grief."

"Pay him off, we don't need the heat. The package is naked."

"Whose fault is that? Just hurry. This fussy little man out here has numbered days if he blows that goddamn whistle at me one more time," the ex-SAS commando said.

"I believe him. We'd better get moving," Manning said.

"It's nice to know cooler heads prevail," James muttered.

Phoenix Force reached the end of the hall and opened a door set off to the right of the stair access entrance. They stepped into an Employees Only area where the hotel maids kept their cleaning carts and the bellhops cached folding trays for room service. A freight elevator stood to one side of the long, narrow staging area.

They moved quickly to the elevator, and Manning pulled a firefighter override key from his pocket and called the lift straight to the floor.

The elevator door opened with a pneumatic hiss and Encizo pushed the wheelchair inside.

McCarter's voice came over the com link. "I've got sirens."

"Copy," Manning said. "We're headed to the lobby now."

The doors sealed shut and the elevator jerked as it started its descent. The inside of the freight elevator was deep and wide, big enough for a small forklift to fit into. The walls were dented and painted a flat, institutional white above metal plating that ran about halfway up the sides. It smelled like cleaning products.

McCarter spoke into the com link. "I'm moving to Route Bravo. The first gendarme has arrived."

"Copy," Manning acknowledged.

The elevator slowed, then halted and the door slid open. A rail-thin bellhop with slicked-back hair looked up in surprise.

Manning stepped forward in the manner of an arrogant bodyguard and brushed past the man. "Move!" he snapped in German.

Behind him Phoenix Force rolled out of the elevator and began to navigate the warren of halls behind the hotel's lobby, heading toward the loading docks. They caught some stares from janitors and building workers, but no one said a word to the hard-eyed men.

They hit the back dock moving briskly. As if taking a cue from some off-scene director, McCarter pulled up into the loading bay. He was driving the stretch Hummer as part of the cover, right down to the chauffeur's uniform. He locked up the independent disc brakes and jerked the heavy vehicle to a stop. Manning heard the sound of the automatic locks disengaging and quickly jerked open the back door on the big vehicle.

Hawkins and Encizo put their hands under al-Shalaan's arms and catapulted him out of the wheelchair as James pulled it away, thrusting him through the open limo door. There was a shout from behind them, but the team ignored it as they leaped after the unconscious man and into the vehicle.

McCarter slammed his foot to the gas pedal before Manning had time to pull the door closed behind him and the big vehicle hurtled out of the loading dock and onto a side street.

"What'd you do?" McCarter demanded.

A Fiat suddenly appeared in front of him and he jerked the stretch Hummer into the other lane to avoid a rear-end collision.

In the back, the Phoenix Force commandos rolled up against the side of the vehicle with the sudden sharp swerve. They struggled to get the unconscious Saudi into a seat and a safety belt around him. James managed to click the buckle just before McCarter slammed on the brakes.

James was thrown backward, bouncing off the granite mass of Manning and landing on top of Encizo. The men scrambled to fit themselves into seat belts as McCarter slalomed the gigantic stretch Hummer in and out of traffic.

"This is bollocksed!" McCarter snarled to no one in particular.

"Let's just get to the jetty!" James called back. "It'll take them a while to shift the pursuit to the water. By that time we'll have scuttled the boat and be gone."

"That's what I'm doing, mate," McCarter agreed.

He tapped his brakes, snapped the steering wheel to the left, gunned the gas and zoomed past a black four-door sedan, then he cut the wheel back to the right. Behind him a single siren and flashing light bar became three.

Hawkins crawled over the barrier between the backseat and the driver compartment through the open glass divider. He swung down, twisted and slid into the shotgun seat. McCarter darted around a heavy diesel truck stacked with crates and the motion threw the former U.S. army commando up against the passenger door. Hawkins snatched hold of the handle above the window to steady himself.

"Let's use the improved clearance on this thing," Hawkins said. "Cut through something, drive over something. Those patrol cars are low-slung."

"I'll see what I can do."

Hawkins looked at the NSA field version of the vehicle's navigation device and watched their GPS coordinates speeding through the map display of the French city. He saw a series of switchback turns coming up on the road ahead toward the team's exfiltration point.

McCarter burned through an intersection against the light. Horns blared in sudden panic, and the Hummer rocked on its suspension like a boxer avoiding jabs. They crested a rise and through a break in the buildings, and the Briton could see empty black under a dark sky. Behind them a police cruiser gunned forward and tried to pull parallel. McCarter swerved to cut him off and bullied the cop back with the superior weight of the stretch Hummer.

"Up ahead. Take that alley," Hawkins barked, "drive across the parking lot and down the hill. There's no way the cops'll follow us in their cars. It'll buy us minutes as they try to navigate the switchbacks down to the shore."

"That's crazy!" McCarter shouted. "We'll flip for sure." He jerked the wheel in a tight, 180-degree spin then let it flip back around. "Hold on!"

The Briton reached down and flipped off the all-wheel drive, switching the custom setting to front-wheel control. He tapped the brakes and the rear wheels of the Hummer locked up, screaming in protest as McCarter just managed to slide the rear end around.

The knobby front tires of the sliding vehicle clawed at the asphalt. They met the curb of the sidewalk and bucked up into the air. The rear wheels caught hold and as the front of the Hummer bounced back down McCarter snapped the vehicle back into all-wheel drive.

"Who dares wins," McCarter gritted.

THEY SPED INTO THE NARROW alley Hawkins had indicated. The former SAS commando struck a pair of garbage cans with the stretch Hummer's heavy bumper. They bounced up into the air, spilling trash across the windshield, then bounced off the hood and flipped up over the vehicle's roof. McCarter snapped the wheel to avoid a larger, industrial-size green garbage bin and scraped the wall of the alley. There was a shower of sparks, then the screaming of metal peeling away from metal as his sideview mirror was snapped off.

"Oh, we're having fun now," Hawkins said.

The stretch Hummer rocketed out of the narrow alley and shot across the street. McCarter lay on the horn as he cut across two lanes of traffic. A forest-green Audi locked its brakes as the Hummer suddenly loomed in front of it. The little coupe turned sideways, its rear end fishtailing.

The Hummer's front wheels struck the edge of the sidewalk and bounced up again. McCarter wrestled the massive vehicle over a parking divider, uprooting a sapling as he did so. He weaved in and out of sitting vehicles as he crossed the parking lot. A middle-aged couple in evening dress appeared at the edge of his headlights.

The woman screamed and the man had the presence of mind to jerk back. McCarter turned his wheel, kissed the side of a parked Fiat and shot past the terrified couple.

"Sorry!" he yelled, knowing they couldn't hear him. He glanced at his sideview mirror to see how close the pursuing patrol cars were, and then remembered he'd ripped the driver-side mirror clean off the body frame. His eyes darted to the passenger-side mirror. He saw spinning lights emerging from the alley across the street.

He turned his gaze forward again. A thick hedge of arborvitaes formed a wall at the rear of the parking lot. He cut his eyes toward Hawkins, then back toward the wall of foliage. He never slowed.

The bucking of the vehicle as it hit the curb rattled their teeth hard. Then the heavy bumper struck the arborvitaes like a battering ram and the Hummer slammed through and out the other side.

For a second McCarter couldn't see anything but the rubbery, fanlike needled leaves. The Hummer hurtled through a shoulder-high fence of 4x4 planks and turned them into splintered kindling.

Then there was nothing.

The Hummer hovered for a moment out into open space and Hawkins had an absurd, momentary flashback to his childhood and the television show *The Dukes of Hazard*. The Hummer tilted as they hovered and they could see the lights of the city plunging down the steep hill below them.

# CHAPTER SEVEN

Jack Grimaldi put the nose down of the Scout Defender helicopter and ran for the open water, putting the devastation of the forgotten New Orleans ward behind Able Team like a bad dream.

Below them roads stretched out in geometric patterns like gray scars on black skin. The mounds of rubble stretched out, then gave way before a wall of trees that delineated urban buildup from bayou as sharply as a fortress wall.

In the cramped space of the cargo bay, Gadgets Schwarz and Carl Lyons worked feverishly to keep Blancanales alive. The former Black Beret had often served as the primary team medic, but all of Stony Man's attention had received combat medic training. They may not have been as skilled as James, or even as skilled as Blancanales, but they knew enough to keep a man alive during a rapid transport. They hoped.

Schwarz tore the stethoscope from his ears and let the air bleed out of the blood pressure cuff he had wrapped around his unconscious teammate's arm. He looked over at Lyons.

"Pulse racing, BP dropping," Schwarz said. "Narrowing pulse pressure—he's at ninety-eight over ninety."

Lyons nodded, his face grim. "His heart's beating faster to try to compensate for lack of volume in his blood vessels because he's bleeding out so fast. The increased heart rate is dumping more blood out to bleed internally so it's a vicious cycle. If he doesn't get under a knife soon he's done, Gadgets."

"IVs?" Schwarz asked.

"Yeah." Lyons nodded. "All we can do is try to slam enough volume in there to keep his heart from running dry and seizing into cardiac arrest."

Schwarz was already pulling 1000 ml bags of clear saline solution from the medic box set in the bulkhead of the helicopter. Lyons snapped some latex tubing around Blancanales's arm to try to get a vein to rise.

"Jesus, I can see his abdomen filling up with blood," Gonzales muttered. "It looks like a balloon."

"Shut up. Don't speak unless spoken to," Lyons growled. Then he turned and looked at the Mexican informant. "I know you're hurting, buddy. That's one nasty gash. You've got to put pressure on it, understand? Get the dressings out of the kit at your feet. We didn't save you to have you bleed out on the way home."

Gonzales nodded, and Lyons could see the man was edging into shock. He kept an eye on the Mexican as he prepped the emergency medical equipment he was using on Blancanales. The man's hands were shaking as he applied the pressure dressing to the ragged, seeping wound in his leg.

The aqua-green light of the tactical bulbs inside the cargo bay cast the huddled men in the same, strange quasi-illumination as night-vision goggles.

The Able Team leader secured the needle into a vein on the inside of Blancanales's arm, then ran the tubing out and spiked it into the bottom of the saline bag held by Schwarz. Schwarz had another 1000 ml bag dangling between his teeth, and he promptly began to squeeze the bag Lyons had just hooked up, forcing fluid into Blancanales's leaking vascular system.

Lyons shifted position and began to start an IV in his friend's other arm. He repeated the process with methodical, almost automatic efficiency. Blancanales would die if he screwed up.

He might die anyway.

Lyons spiked the second bag and gently squeezed, pushing the liquid out. He looked down at the face of his unconscious teammate, and in the uncertain light of the helicopter cargo bay the veteran's skin was ashen gray.

Schwarz looked out through the windows and saw tangled delta bayou give way to the black waters over the coast. He turned his head and called out to Jack Grimaldi in the pilot's seat.

"We close?" Schwarz yelled.

"How's he doing?" Grimaldi shouted back.

"Not very good, Jack!" Schwarz answered.

"Then we're nowhere near close enough," Grimaldi replied.

"I KNOW," PRICE SAID. Her voice was flat, emotionless. "I understand, Jack. This is part of the game." Steel threaded itself into her voice. "I understand how bad he is. I have a flight medic crew with the 160th Special Operations Wing coming to meet you at the rendezvous. They have a flight surgeon, two flight nurses and a paramedic. They'll get him to the secure wing of Bethesda Naval Hospital."

She stopped talking and dots of color grew on her cheekbones. Sitting near her, Carmen Delahunt and Akira Tokaido quickly looked down at their computer screens. They could hear Grimaldi shouting into his com link through the speaker of Price's encrypted sat phone.

"Can it!" Price snapped. "I *know* he could die. There is no way I can justify jeopardizing the Farm to risk you setting down at a civilian hospital. End of story! The NOPD is all over that warehouse now, and what do you think the survivors are telling them, Jack? You think a bunch of men-in-black can just show up at a major metropolitan trauma center and frighten an emergency room full of people and a surgical team into keeping quiet?"

Price lowered her voice and the emotional exhaustion was just as evident as her resolution. "Stony Man is more than just a single operative. You want to save him, you fly your ass off. Stony Base out."

She clicked the end button and set the phone down. Her face was a flat affect as she turned toward her office. She heard the soft sounds of wheeled tires and turned as Aaron Kurtzman rolled toward her.

She managed a smile as she took another mug of coffee from his beefy hand. "You didn't make this pot, did you?"

"Nah, you're safe," he replied. "Cowboy made it." He paused, watching her take a sip of the strong brew. "Hal is en route to where Able Team is taking Gonzales."

Price nodded. "You give him the rundown on Rosario?"

"I did." Kurtzman looked her in the eye. "Just so you know, he concurs with your assessment about keeping Pol out of a civilian hospital." He stopped. "Even if…" He let the sentence trail off.

"This is the world we live in," Price said. "Rosario knows it better than anyone."

Kurtzman nodded and Price turned away. She put a hand on Carmen Delahunt's shoulder as she worked a computer screen, a headset over her red hair.

"What's the word on Phoenix now?" Price asked.

"Unpleasant," Delahunt answered. "They haven't initiated communication since informing us they were forced to escape and evade the locals. They haven't made contact with Charlie Mott at the rendezvous coordinates yet. I have no idea if they're waterborne or still driving."

Price turned toward Akira Tokaido, who had his earbuds down around his neck for once. He was working two keyboards and muttering into the microphone of his own headset. His finger tapped the enter button on one of his keyboards and the screen of his G5 laptop began to scroll information.

"What's the word on the local law-enforcement response for Phoenix?" Price asked.

Tokaido didn't turn his head. His gaze jumped back and forth between his screens and his lips mouthed words. He struck the space bar with his thumb and the scrolling screen froze. First the encryption-decryption software translated the signal, identified the language and then routed it to the proper translation program. The result was a rolling screen that looked like a digitalized version of a court recorder's transcript.

"They have three patrol cars on the pursuit now. They've called for backup and six more shift patrolmen have responded. They asked for a helicopter, but we caught a break, as the air unit was tied up with something else. The locals haven't informed any other agency of the chase—so they must not realize Phoenix is going to go waterborne and exit the country."

Tokaido looked up and smiled. "Apparently, David's driving scares the hell out of them."

"Well, it scares the hell out of me, too," Price replied, her voice wry.

CARL LYONS SET A BOTTLE of spring water in front of the silent Gabriel Gonzales. The informant looked grateful and snatched it up. He opened it and chugged down several long swallows. The special-operations medic had left only a few minutes before, leaving behind some white, oblong pills in a paper cup for Gonzales's pain.

The medic, dressed in an OD green flight suit bereft of name tag or any identification markers, had done his primary survey, dressed the man's wound, hooked up a slow IV drip to replace the blood loss and deemed him "fit for questioning" before leaving the pills.

Having obviously done this before, he addressed Lyons's primary concern even before the ex-LAPD detective could ask it. "Don't worry," he said, after coming out of the room. "The pain meds won't keep you from questioning him. They may, in fact, help him a little, loosen him up. He won't be inebriated or too stoned to remember details."

The man reached down and picked up his green canvas medic bag and left the building to where an unmarked Ford Explorer was waiting. At no point during his interaction had the medic asked who the hurt man was, or who Lyons and Schwarz were or who they worked for. He'd simply done what was required of him without unnecessary comment and then left. The hard-nosed Lyons was impressed, almost in spite of himself.

He watched Gonzales take his pills and then wash them down with the water. The informant sat in a straight-backed chair in front of a small metal table in a nondescript room. A black lamp with a flexible neck and a powerful bulb sat turned off on the table. There was a tablet of lined paper and a ballpoint pen on the table in front of the man.

Lyons reached over and turned on the lamp. Gonzales blinked against the sudden harsh illumination. Then the big ex-cop turned to where Schwarz was waiting beside the door, and nodded once. Schwarz reached over and turned off the overhead lights in the room.

Now the hard light of the lamp provided the only illumination in the room. It cast a sharp-edged white pool that plunged the rest of the room in deep shadow. Just beyond the reach of the lightbulb Lyons pulled up a chair and sat opposite Gonzales.

Behind him the door next to where Schwarz was standing swung open, revealing a dark hallway. Hal Brognola, his face cloaked in shadow, entered the room, closed the door behind him and took a seat against the wall.

"Gonzales. Excuse the setup," Lyons said, his voice neutral. "It's for your own protection."

"Yeah, sure," Gonzales replied. In his mind's eye the Mexican informant was seeing the burly blond-headed man sitting across from him as he had been in the New

Orleans warehouse—the automatic shotgun booming, Zetas bodies being thrown around by the impact of the 12-gauge rounds. "Where's my handler?" he asked. "Where's Hart?"

"You'll see him in a bit," Lyons replied. "He's taking care of your wife and daughter. I know you're worried about them, but they're safe. We pulled you free of that warehouse, and my very good friend took a knife to the stomach to get you out. So, now, in return, you will fill us in on the missing pieces."

"I don't know much that I hadn't already passed on to my handler," Gonzales replied. "I only knew something big was coming. I thought it was a drug deal."

"This Bellicose Dawn," Brognola said.

He was a faceless voice in the shadows. Gonzales instinctively looked up toward the sound and was immediately blinded by the glare of the lamp. He held his hand up, blinked, then looked down. He nodded.

"I passed that much on," he said. "Then I tried to find out more and somehow Lagos knew that information had gotten out. I was supposed to meet them for a dinner. I wound up hanging in that warehouse instead."

"What'd you find out?" Lyons asked.

"I only know bits and pieces. It doesn't make sense, but it doesn't sound like a drug deal." Gonzales paused and drank more water. "It sounds like an assault, an attack or something."

"A terrorist attack?" Schwarz demanded.

"Maybe," Gonzales replied. "I mean, that seems the most likely. But these are Zetas, you know? Former commandos, so maybe it was a takedown."

"A robbery?" Lyons asked. "Why would they switch

from multimillion-dollar drug deals to strong-arm holdups?"

"I don't know," Gonzales said. "I overheard Lagos. What I got was that he was supposed to set up a cache and rendezvous point in New Orleans. I gathered the launch point was Puerto Lobos on the gulf coast of Mexico—a fishing village and resort town north of Mexico City."

"You been there?" Lyons asked.

Gonzales shook his head, but then said, "Yes." He paused, swallowed. "Puerto Lobos has a regional military commander, regular Mexican army, and also a police chief. Neither of them are averse to narcotics money as long as trouble stays out of their backyard. I was on a fishing trawler converted for smuggling that stopped there once. The Zetas have a way station, mostly for the Colombians, they run there. Airstrip and docks. It is run by Montoya Aslargo. He's the one I overheard Lagos talking to."

"Tell me about Montoya Aslargo," Brognola demanded.

Gonzales shrugged. "I've never met him, I stayed on the boat. I know only that he used to be a unit commander in the Mexican border patrol, before I worked for them. Then one day he shows up in a million-dollar hacienda in Puerto Lobos, keeping things running smooth between Lagos in the north and a guy named Reyes running the show in Mexico City." Gonzales shrugged again. "He loves Celine Dion."

"What?" Schwarz burst out laughing.

"I don't know, that's all I know. Lagos used to make fun of him for listening to her all the time…" Gonzales trailed off. "I'm just saying… Besides…"

"Besides what?" Lyons demanded.

Gonzales shrugged, took a drink from his water, then started picking at the crystal-blue label. "Just rumors, gossip. Stuff I overheard Lagos telling that psychotic bitch of a girlfriend he had, about Aslargo."

"Just tell me," Lyons said. "You're not on TV for Christ's sake."

"Just that Aslargo hadn't really come out of the border patrol like everyone thought."

"Then how'd he get enough juice to get away with paying off the army *and* the police? How'd he get the job being the go-to guy?" Lyons snapped.

"He was working for Reyes," Gonzales answered, his voice very soft.

"Reyes?" Lyons asked. "You said he was the guy running the show in Mexico City."

"Reyes is Cisen," Gonzales said, meaning the Mexican National Security and Investigation Center.

"The Mexican CIA?" Lyons demanded.

"Yeah. And this Bellicose Dawn thing? Maybe it doesn't come from just Zetas in Mexico City. Maybe it doesn't come from the Colombians. Lagos told *la chicka loca* that maybe it came from *them,* from Cisen." Gonzales shrugged. "This is all I know, man."

"Okay," Lyons said. "We have a name and a location. We've done a lot more with a lot less." He reached out one heavily muscled arm across the desk and pushed the pen and notepad closer to Gonzales. "Tell us again. From the top. Write down the names, give us dates."

Behind them Hal Brognola rose and left the room. He had calls to make, deals to cut, oaths to uphold. Able Team had stumbled onto something and he was going to use every resource available to Stony Man to find out what.

IN VENEZUELA, MARCOS Sincanaros could feel the frustration rising in him. He stood at the window in his villa's master bedroom, watching the stream that cut across his property.

He could not raise either Reyes or al-Shalaan on their cell phones. That French bastard Galli hadn't returned his calls in almost thirty-six hours. This close to execution of the plan, that was completely unacceptable.

His mistress slid up behind him and ran her hands across his torso. She leaned forward and breathed into his ear. "Come to bed, baby," she whispered.

Her insipid clinging angered him and he shrugged her off. He gave her a taste of his knuckles, and the slap echoed in the room as she fell on the bed. He looked down at her and saw the blood running from the cut near the corner of her lip.

"To hell with them," he snarled, and threw down his phone.

His hand stung where he had struck the woman and the sight of her blood excited him. His hand dropped to his belt buckle and he moved toward the cowering woman. He needed something to take the edge off, he decided.

# CHAPTER EIGHT

*France*

The stretch Hummer slammed into the ground and even that vehicle's heavy-duty suspension groaned in protest. The right side of the vehicle popped up into the air, and Hawkins was tossed across the front seat toward McCarter.

McCarter snapped the wheel against the sudden tilt and Hawkins was thrown back the other way to bounce off the passenger door. Ornamental hedges and carefully laid gravel was decimated by the lumbering vehicle as it plunged down the steep hill.

"Put your seat belt on!" McCarter yelled.

Hawkins fought to regain his balance and then felt the grip of the tires beneath give way. The Hummer slid down the hill as McCarter fought to regain control. The back end of the vehicle looped around until they were sliding down perpendicular to the hill's sharp incline. Hawkins jammed one hand up against the ceiling and the other against the dash. His legs were locked tight as he pressed them as hard as he could against the floorboards.

"David? David!" he shouted.

"I'm on it! I'm bloody well on it!"

The stretch Hummer plunged off the hillside sideways. It hopped over the curb and tore great gouges into the earth set between the switchback of the hills. McCarter spun the wheel again and the big, knobby tires bit into the ground, spinning up great rooster tails of dirt.

He brought the front end around and fought the racing monster of a vehicle back under control. They roared off the hillside and cut across an empty street, barely missing a lamp pole and then rocketing over the edge of the hill again. The car bucked and kicked violently, bouncing back and forth, the vibrations of the impact hammering through the bodies of the passengers with brutal energy. Hawkins looked into his sideview mirror and realized he couldn't see the patrol cruisers anymore. McCarter's desperate plan seemed to have bought them some time, a modicum of breathing room.

Hawkins looked back and the dark expanse of the Mediterranean spread out below them, the reflection of the city lights twinkling on the undulating waves. Then the headlights of the Hummer illuminated the patch of sidewalk directly across the road from them.

The old man wore a vest and a slouch hat. His arms were thrown up in shock and terror as McCarter plunged off the hillside and hit the street. The old man tried to turn and his feet tangled up in themselves. Hawkins saw he had a beard and hair as thick and white as a Macy's storefront Santa Claus. The old man tripped and hit the sidewalk hard, his head snapping, and he didn't get up. His face, twisted in fear, turned toward the on-rushing Hummer.

*We're going to hit him,* Hawkins thought, his horror taking over his adrenaline rush like water extinguishing a flame.

"Damn it!" McCarter snarled.

For the final time that night the Briton cut the wheel on the stretch model Hummer. The headlights were jerked off the sprawled body of the old man. The front tires hit the curb at an angle and popped up, Hawkins felt himself rolling out toward his door, then the back wheels struck the curb and the auto frame bucked awkwardly.

The Hummer shot safely past the downed old man and plowed over the edge of the hill on the final incline before the road fronting the quay began. The angle was sharp and as soon as the tires rebounded Hawkins knew they were going to spin.

He felt the Hummer leave the ground and seem to float up into the air. Then the world turned in a carnival Tilt-A-Whirl ride and he felt himself come out of his seat. There was a shuddering impact and the windshield filled Hawkins's vision.

Instinctively the Southerner threw up an arm to protect himself and then he felt the impact as if from a million miles away, almost as if it was happening to someone else. His body shot forward like a missile as McCarter slammed on the brakes to try to regain the crashing vehicle's center of balance.

Hawkins struck the windshield and lost consciousness as his body twisted into the night air some ten feet above the ground. He slammed into the dirt of the hillside with near-lethal velocity and bounced, rolled, struck the ground again and began to slip down the hillside.

The rolling Hummer tumbled after him, gouging huge chunks of earth from the ground as it rolled along like a boulder. Hawkins's foot caught on a tough bush and his spinning body snapped to the right just as the rolling team vehicle bounced over the same spot. He sprawled out and came to a rest, his face a mask of blood.

Then he stopped breathing.

The Hummer rolled onto its top and began to slide down the hill like some gigantic version of a child's sled. It came off the hillside and skidded onto the asphalt of the narrow access lane fronting the ocean quay. McCarter jerked up hard against his chest restraint, and while the vehicle was rolling he felt his lower rib snap under the pressure. He gasped in pain as he was thrown against his harness again and again, then he felt his left collarbone simply snap with the same final sharp stab of pain as his rib.

As McCarter hung inverted in his harness, he reached out to grab the wheel and the air bag suddenly exploded in his face. His left hand was thrown against the Hummer's driver's window hard enough to crack the bullet-resistant glass, and he felt the bones in that hand break, as well.

*I'm bloody well fucked,* he thought.

He moaned softly at the pain and reached down to undo his safety belt. He dropped the last few inches to the roof, landing awkwardly on his shoulder. He grunted as pain lanced through his body from every direction, then carefully reached across his bruised body and opened the door.

He tumbled out into the street, still confused and disorientated from the tumbling roll he'd just survived. His first thought was for his weapon, but then he remembered where he was and he looked for his teammates.

He saw the back door to the stretch model Hummer kick open and Encizo emerged unharmed. The veteran Phoenix Force commando saw that McCarter was down and rushed to his side while James and Manning muscled the still-unconscious al-Shalaan out of the wreckage. They could hear the police sirens approaching in the distance.

"Can you move?" Encizo demanded as he knelt next to McCarter.

"I'm banged up good, but I can move," McCarter said. "Help me up."

Encizo complied, ducking his shoulder under the taller man's arm, supporting his weight. Each breath McCarter took sent waves of pain coursing through him from the damaged rib and his broken hand and collarbone.

Manning looked around, and he and McCarter asked in unison, "Where's T.J.?"

James suddenly cursed and pointed up the hillside. McCarter felt his heart drop away as he saw the crumpled figure of his teammate sprawled across the hillside.

"Jesus," he muttered, and tried to move forward, but Encizo held him back.

The sirens were louder now as the patrol cars hit the beginning of the switchbacks on the road. The members of Phoenix Force had seconds, and they knew it. James shoved the unconscious al-Shalaan toward Manning and without hesitation the big Canadian shouldered him in a fireman's carry.

James knew the truth even as he raced up the hill. He knew what was going to have to be done even before he dropped into the dirt beside the still form of Hawkins and realized the man wasn't breathing. He plunged his hands into Hawkins's hair and ran them down the back of his neck, looking for obvious spinal injuries before he began CPR.

Above them the spinning light bars of the racing police patrol car began to illuminate the scene in staccato flashes. James looked up and met Manning's eye as he cleared Hawkins's airway with a jaw thrust maneuver designed to save a potentially damaged spine from any further trauma.

"Go!" James yelled, the smell of Hawkins's blood overpowering. The man was covered in it. The ground was soaked with it. "He can't be moved, or he'll die!"

Manning seemed torn. The police cars were flying down the switchbacks and incredulously, the tires of the Hummer were still spinning.

"You'll be arrested," Manning said. "Can't we evac him to the boat?"

"No!" James snarled. "He's dying, he will die. He needs surgery. He has to stay behind. We have no choice."

Manning swallowed. Then McCarter spoke up, still the group leader despite his injuries. "Leave him, Cal! The cops are coming, and the paramedics have to be close. They must have seen us wreck."

The pain of saying that stabbed McCarter deeper than any wound he'd ever suffered. Hawkins wouldn't talk, and this was France. Price and Brognola would figure something out. It was leave him or let him die, Mc-Carter realized.

James breathed into Hawkins's lungs, saw the chest rise in response. He lifted his head as he shifted to start his chest compressions, breaking several first-aid rules in the process. "I can't leave him, goddamn it! He can't breathe. He'll die by the time the cops get here."

"We can't have two lost—" McCarter began, hating the sound of his voice.

"Negative," James said. He worked Hawkins's still heart for him, pushing down on the sternum and circulating the artificially oxygenated blood through his system. "Carry out the mission. I'm staying behind."

That's what Phoenix Force did when things turned sour. No matter how painful the decisions, Phoenix Force always carried out the mission.

End of story.

McCarter cursed as the police cars appeared on the hill directly above them, then looked over his shoulder. The jetty with the boat was a quarter mile down the access road. He could smell the sea and hear it lapping at the rocky shoreline even over the sound of the police sirens. He smelled dripping gas from the ruined Hummer.

Time seemed to stretch out beyond itself so that each heartbeat lasted for an eternity. He looked up the hillside and met James's eyes as the ex-SEAL performed chest compressions on their fallen comrade.

"Let's go," McCarter snapped. "We'll find you," he shouted to James, but the combat medic had already turned his complete attention back to saving Hawkins.

"This is crap!" Encizo gritted. "We don't leave people behind."

"He dies if Cal doesn't stay, Rafe," Manning replied, his face ashen in shock at the sudden turn of events. "Let's go." He turned with al-Shalaan over his shoulder and began to run down the road.

Encizo turned, the badly injured McCarter leaning against him for support. They began to jog down the road. Each step was a lightning bolt of agony for McCarter but he pushed himself harder, forcing more pain into himself, trying vainly to drive out the feelings of guilt he felt as James and Hawkins receded behind them.

He felt a hot poker deep in his chest and suddenly the back of his throat was filled with blood. Nicked a lung, he thought. He drove his legs harder, tried to lean less on Encizo. The little Cuban turned his head toward his team leader and saw the frothy, pinkish blood bubbling out of McCarter's mouth, realizing instantly what that meant.

He skidded to a stop and folded into McCarter like a wrestler going for a double leg takedown. McCarter tried to protest, but it turned into a hacking cough as he choked on his own blood. The world spun for him as Encizo shouldered his weight.

*We're screwed,* he thought before the world went black.

JAMES CONTINUED WORKING on Hawkins's broken body. He heard the hysterical shrieks of the police sirens above him and the sudden squeal as brakes were locked up. He didn't bother to look up as he heard car doors slam. More sirens raced past the parked police vehicle and tore around the end of the final switchback in the hillside road.

He realized the rest of the team hadn't had too much of a head start. The distance to where they'd stored the boat for exfiltration was short, but McCarter had barely been able to stand when they'd left and Manning was packing an unconscious body. The odds against them grew with every step they took, James knew.

He heard someone screaming at him in French as he gave Hawkins another round of rescue breathing. He lifted his head and shouted, "Get an ambulance," in French. He was pushing so hard on Hawkins's chest he felt the snap, crackle, pop of the man's ribs bending to the breaking point, cartilage coming loose from bone.

The French policeman screamed for James to show him his hands but the ex-SEAL ignored him. "He needs CPR!" he shouted in French.

Below him on the access road next to the water, the first of four police cars swerved past the overturned Hummer and shot down the road. James felt dirt clots and loose gravel strike his back as the police officer above him began his descent.

*At least he didn't shoot me,* James thought. "Ambulance! Ambulance!" he cried.

He felt a stunning blow across the back of his neck as the police officer kicked him hard. James let himself topple forward, concentrating on not striking the busted-up Hawkins as he rolled with the blow.

He couldn't show any resistance, couldn't fight back. The police would be too tuned up by the chase, too angry. In the dark James's black features might get him confused with an Algerian by the responding police and that could get him killed in the south of France.

"I give up! I give up!" he called as he landed on the dirt below Hawkins. "Please, please! This man needs help! He needs an ambulance!"

The partner of the first police officer knelt by Hawkins as the other cop covered James with his pistol. The cop, a gray-haired veteran with a face like a basset hound and steely eyes, whistled low as he looked down at the injured Hawkins. He reached up to the mobile mike attached to his shirtfront and James almost wept with relief as the man called for an ambulance.

"Please," James said. "I don't have any weapons. He needs CPR."

The cop covering him glanced over at the bloody Hawkins, then to his partner, lifting a brow inquiringly. The older cop cocked his head to one side, considering the situation, then spit as if he had a bad taste in his mouth. "Yes, do it. I want him alive so he can go to prison."

ENCIZO GRUNTED AS HE RAN under McCarter's dead-weight. Just ahead of him Manning was running full-out down the public jetty. Waterfront restaurants and villas with million-dollar views lined the quay while an ancient lighthouse cast bars of yellow illumination onto the Mediterranean waters. Behind them he heard the wailing of police sirens pulling closer, and he began to wonder if they were going to make it.

There was a bitter taste of ashes in his mouth as he thought of James left behind, pumping Hawkins's chest up and down in a desperate attempt to make the man's cardiac system respond.

He left the narrow access road and stepped over a low-slung chain hung between two concrete pillars and then thumped out onto the dock. McCarter made no sounds on his shoulder, though Encizo knew each step had to be excruciatingly painful for him. That had to mean that the big Brit had lost consciousness. A cruiser locked its brakes behind them and squealed to a stop. Car doors were thrown open.

Just ahead of him Manning raced up to the *Boston Whaler* and unceremoniously dumped al-Shalaan into the watercraft. The terror facilitator slumped to the bottom of the boat with the wet slap of flesh on flat metal. The boat made a hollow thump as the man's head bounced off its side.

Behind them Encizo heard the police shouting at him in French. The twin outboards on the vessel roared to life under Manning's steady hand. Encizo, knowing what was coming, dived forward.

The sharp reports of handguns exploded behind him as he made the boat. The air split and hummed and whined around him as bullets burned past him. He leaped up and landed in the vessel, trying hard to soften the impact for the gravely wounded McCarter.

There were dings and whines as rounds burned off the metal gunnel and slapped the water. Encizo was thrown backward as Manning goosed the power and the sleek craft picked up its nose and sprinted out for open water.

Pushing himself up, Encizo looked past Manning's determined face, back toward the shore where more police cruisers were pulling up. Encizo's gaze hunted the landscape, looking for where he knew James and Hawkins had to be swarmed by the French police.

But Manning cut the boat hard into the ocean and out toward international waters and the lights and shadows of the coastline blurred as they receded.

# CHAPTER NINE

Barbara Price put down her sat phone. She turned to stare at Hal Brognola, and she had the look of someone who'd just been punched, hard, in the stomach. She lifted a hand and tucked a stray wisp of blond hair behind her ear.

As she did so Brognola could see the Stony Man mission controller set her jaw, saw the color flood back into her features. She sat at the conference table across from the man from Justice. She carefully set down the encrypted communications device.

When she started her situation report, her voice was solid and steady. She was an accountant crunching numbers, a lawyer giving a brief on tax law, a mathematics instructor running down an inconsequential equation.

"Charlie Mott got Phoenix off the ocean without a hitch. Al-Shalaan is now incommunicado at Diego Garcia. The boys from the CIA's backroom are talking to him. David was moved to the U.S. navy hospital ship in the Gulf of Oman. He's sustained a lot of injuries and nicked a lung, so he's out of action, but he'll recover."

Brognola grunted his understanding. His hands automatically began running down his pockets with the habits of decades, looking for one of the cigars he'd given up some time ago. Fresh out.

"Pol's the same," he said. "He'll pull through just fine, but he'll need time to recover before he can operate again. T.J.…?" He let the question trail off, as if he were afraid of what he was going to hear.

"Rafe and Gary say he was bad. He's fallen down a deep, dark French hole and since Phoenix is such a black operation I've had to circumvent normal channels to try to ascertain his status."

"As long as we know he's alive," Brognola said.

"He's alive. If he wasn't, the news reports would have said so. The French government isn't keeping this under wraps much. Apparently they haven't sweated much out of Cal as the most prominent theory being floated by the French news is that this was kidnap-for-ransom by foreign mercenaries."

"The State Department will be no help with the French. Kidnapping a Saudi diplomat on French soil isn't something that gets explained away 'back channels.' In fact, I've kept everything out of my briefings, just focused on the fact that we got al-Shalaan."

"We know where Calvin is. I've transferred funds to a civilian law firm in Paris. I think our best plan at the moment is the simplest. We get Cal out on bail, then get him out of the country," Price stated.

"He's a foreigner. The prosecution is going to deem him a supreme flight risk—and rightly so."

"He's sticking to his cover story as a journalist who was interviewing al-Shalaan when the attack came.

Since the Saudi's bodyguards are already out of the country, all the police have is the witness reports of him moving through the back of the hotel. No one's dead and our Paris law firm is good—for now it seems like the most prudent course of action."

"We've never had both crews this depleted at the same time before," Brognola said. "Not like this anyway. We may need to roll them over into each other. Make a single four-man team. Able still has to follow up on that information they got from Gonzales out of New Orleans."

Price nodded and reached for a cup of Kurtzman's coffee. She made a face at the bitter taste but felt the rush of liquid caffeine course through her system. She set the cup down.

"Gary managed to snag some things from the Company boys. Cal was supposed to be part of the interrogation team, handling the chemicals, but obviously that didn't happen. Now the Agency is playing very close to the vest with what they're getting. I thought Aaron was going to cruise down to Langley and add some stars to their wall," she said, referring to the wall of honor for CIA agents who had fallen in the line of duty over the years.

"Gary managed to palm al-Shalaan's PDA. The Agency got the laptop and the phones, but he was able to get that much out. Hunt's looking at it with Akira right now."

Brognola nodded. "If anyone can crack it, it's those two. We'll see if it ties into anything else we have, but our priority right now is this Bellicose Dawn situation. I'll need to roll Gary and Rafe in with them. I'll handle the situation with T.J. and Cal personally. I'll need to use Carmen, if you can spare her."

Price nodded. "Let her start helping Hunt and Akira bust the encryption on al-Shalaan's PDA, then she's all yours."

"Oh, happy day," Delahunt said from the doorway. The redhead breezed into the room. "Talk about serendipitous. I thought I felt my ears burning." She walked over to where Brognola and Price were sitting at the table and threw down a sheaf of loose papers. "Akira is a boy wonder," she stated. "He cracked that Saudi intelligence code like an egg. Once he had the inspiration, Hunt created a binary code on the spot that converted the test."

"I expect no less from them." Price nodded. She reached over and pulled the papers to her. "Anything juicy?"

"Oh, yeah," Delahunt stated. "Very juicy. So juicy it's scary."

"What do you mean?" Brognola leaned forward.

"Al-Shalaan sent a text message to a server used by Saudi intelligence in Amman, Jordan. The server shuffled it off and we weren't able to track it past that. But we do know what the message was," Delahunt replied.

"And?" Price asked.

"It was a reply to a message that stated 'Initiate Bellicose Dawn.' Al-Shalaan's reply was simple and straightforward—'Bellicose Dawn initiated.' We can tie the date of that reply to a money transfer he made to a bank in Sudan from an account in Venezuela."

Brognola stood. "Get Able and Phoenix together in the War Room. We need to roll on Able's lead yesterday. I want to know what Mexican *narcotraficantes* have to do with Saudi intelligence and a terrorist middleman like al-Shalaan.

"Carmen, come with me. We've got to figure out how to find T.J. and get him home." He turned to Price, who was rising from her seat. "Let me know how far your Paris lawyer gets with Cal. If we need to go to Plan B, I want plenty of heads up."

PAIN WOKE T. J. HAWKINS.

A hard light burned in his eyes, blurring his vision. He hurt all over, and he didn't understand what had happened. As he blinked, he tried to orientate himself. He remembered getting into the stretch model Hummer with McCarter. He couldn't remember anything else.

He went still as he heard voices speaking French. That wasn't a good sign. He tried to slow his breathing but the pain kept growing, signals converging on his brain from everywhere in his body, the signals increasing in strength with each passing moment.

A hand came down on his leg, and Hawkins jerked upward as pain exploded through his body. He realized he was tied down as his limbs thrashed against the soft restraints binding him to a hospital bed.

He screamed, then bit the scream off. Around him he saw a nondescript hospital room. He was attached to monitors and an IV stand. There were three figures in the room with him: a slim man with glasses, in a business suit, a female in green medical scrubs wearing a surgical mask over her face and a bulky male with a ponytail, in casual street clothes. The slim, well-tailored man gently shook Hawkins's leg again. The former U.S. army commando felt the ends of his broken bones grind together and he hissed his pain through clenched teeth.

"You may call me Henri," the man said. His French

accent was thick but his English was flawless. "I am very displeased."

Hawkins began to mentally prepare himself for suffering.

"PISS UP A ROPE," Price told him.

Gary Manning stepped back, his face wearing an almost comical mask. His brow furrowed and he leaned slightly forward, his eyes narrowing. Price stepped right up into his face.

"What?" he asked, his voice cool.

"I said, piss up a rope, Gary," Price repeated. "That's what it would be like. Pissing. Up. A. Goddamn. Rope. We don't know where T.J. is. And we aren't going to send you and Rafe into a French federal prison to rescue Cal. We have a plan. We're working the plan. I don't need you and Rafe in my plan—at least not yet. However, Able *does* need you. Therefore, Gary, I'm putting your two teams together."

Manning stared at Price. Their eyes locked; neither one blinked. The muscles along Manning's jaw worked until they stood out like steel cables. The mission controller could see him struggling hard with his inner demons, struggling to keep from lashing out. She knew a great deal of that wild energy came from his own intense feelings of guilt for having to leave his brothers in the first place. She put a hand out and rested it on the massive pillar of his arm. When she spoke again, her voice was softer.

"Gary, there's nothing for you to do, at least not yet. All you can do is make sure that Cal's sacrifice isn't wasted. You got al-Shalaan out. We discovered his connection to the Zetas. *That*'s where we need you now. You have to see that."

Manning nodded. He turned away and walked over to the conference table, pulled a chair out and sat beside Rafael Encizo, who passed him a cup of coffee. Manning took the coffee. He lifted his head and stared across the table at Carl Lyons and Gadgets Schwarz.

"Nothing personal," he said. His voice sounded tired.

Lyons shook his head, negating the big Canadian's apology, and held up his hands, palms out. "I understand, Gary. If I was you, I'd be pitching a bitch, too." He shrugged and looked at Price. "But she's right."

Manning nodded again and Encizo spoke up, smoothly transitioning the group back to the task at hand. "What's the plan? Until Akira is able to follow up on more information from al-Shalaan's PDA, it seems like this dude Montoya Aslargo and Puerto Lobos are the next stop. At least until we can figure out exactly how this Reyes in Mexico City is tied to al-Shalaan."

"Oh, yeah," Lyons said. "Pol's lying in a hospital because of the friend of a Mexican intelligence agent. Now T.J.'s lying in a hospital because of someone with ties to Saudi intelligence. Those intelligence operatives have connections with jihadist terror cells and Mexican drug gangs. Something here stinks, and we're going right to the garbage heap."

Manning looked up and smiled.

"That's what I wanted to hear," he said.

"Good." Schwarz nodded and leaned forward. "Let's come up with a plan."

Price kept her own smile off her face. She stepped forward and hit the intercom button on the admin phone sitting on the conference table. "Aaron," she said into microphone.

After a moment the burly head of Stony Man's cybernetics team answered, "Go ahead."

"Can you bring those workups you've done on Puerto Lobos to the War Room now?"

"I'm on my way," Kurtzman grunted in response.

Price looked up from the phone and into the faces of the four men seated in front of her. "Puerto Lobos has been on the DEA's radar for a long, long time. Working through the Directorate for National Intelligence, they managed to get the National Reconnaissance Office to do a satellite survey of the built-up areas and the surrounding geography. We have a pretty good workup on the area. Last year SEAL Team Four did a hydro-topographical reconnaissance and beach survey as a high-speed training mission before redeployment to Iraq. The results were given to the Coast Guard, and the Justice Department got a copy. Hal dug them out of the computer library there and passed them on to Aaron."

As she looked at the serious, almost eager faces of the Stony Man team, Price realized a hellish storm was about to descend on the Mexican drug haven. Someone out there, in the geopolitical world, had launched a plot against the United States, and the mission controller intended to see that they paid dearly for their audacity. And sitting in front of her at the conference table with barely concealed bloodlust in their eyes were the perfect tools.

It was enough to make her smile.

MARCOS SINCANAROS snatched up the cell phone. He looked at the caller ID and recognized the number instantly. He had been waiting for this call. He felt anger rising up in him. He did not like to wait.

"Henri," Sincanaros snarled. "It's about time you called."

The Frenchman was unflappable. "We have a problem."

*France*

THE CORRECTIONS OFFICERS brought Calvin James into the visitation room handcuffed and shackled. The American went with them passively, his face a careful neutral mask. His eyes darted around the little room, taking in the sparse details and noting the furnishings before settling on the only occupant.

James recognized the man as a lawyer immediately. He seemed the worst example of the breed, and French. But the Hugo Boss suit the man wore was too expensive for him to merely be court appointed, which meant that, through some roundabout fashion, he was from Stony Man.

The Phoenix Force commando really didn't like what he saw, which might mean the lawyer was good. Expensive Italian loafers to go with the navy-blue power suit. A designer watch, gold cuff links and a leather attaché case that probably cost more than James's first car. The man's grooming was impeccable. Each strand of his fashionable "bed head" haircut had been carefully gelled into place. The lines of the man's face were pointed, with high cheekbones, a sharp nose and thin, bloodless lips. His fingernails were manicured and buffed to a high gloss. The Monte Blanc pen in the man's long, slim, almost effeminate fingers tapped as the man displayed his impatience. He looked like he was being forced to smell some offensive odor.

In fact, James realized, the smell in the room was offensive. The unpainted walls and bare, concrete floor smelled like industrial disinfectant. But underneath that there was the stink of European cigarettes, unwashed bodies and…guilt, he guessed.

James shuffled forward to the seat across the table from the lawyer and carefully lowered himself into the chair. He greeted the fussy-looking man in French.

"Please," the lawyer answered in perfect, clipped English. "Please speak English. Your French is like so-called American cuisine—that is to say…atrocious. My English is outstanding. We will speak in English, then. Yes? Okay."

"Sure," James said. "Whatever. Can you tell me about the man who was injured? Where is he? Is he okay?" As part of his deception James had made the decision to deviate from the cover story originally conceived by Stony Man—that of being a journalist—and instead pretended to only be passing by when the wreck had occurred and then gone to help. The story was thin, but it was in line with his espionage tradecraft: admit nothing, deny everything, demand proof.

"Questions? Questions? Please, I am the one to ask the questions. I have not been hired to represent this 'injured man' you speak of. I have been hired to represent you. You were staying at the hotel, no? You decided to take a walk because Marseilles is beautiful. You wanted to go and see the Mediterranean by moonlight, no? Of course you did. You saw crazy men driving off the road, they crashed. One was hurt so you helped him. You were what? A Good Samaritan. This was stupid. You are stupid. Don't help people. Look what it got you. You should have had some wine. They make wonderful wine in the south of France. Why did you not do this instead? And prostitutes. The prostitutes in Marseilles are excellent!" He tapped the pen on his notepad for emphasis. "Please, they are excellent." He whirled and jabbed his pen at the corrections officer standing like the Sphinx near the door to the room. "Is that not so? Are not the prostitutes in Marseilles excellent?" he demanded of the guard in machine-gun French.

*"Oui,"* the guard agreed, shrugging a pair of shoulders as big as cannon balls. "They are indeed very good."

The lawyer whirled back toward James and jabbed his pen at him. "You see? They are excellent. Not at all like the ones in Dijon. So this is what you should have done. You should have had some good wine and bought a prostitute. Instead you try to be a, as you Americans say, 'good guy' and you see what this gets you. The magistrate has your passport. You are no flight risk. I will get you out in two hours, yes?"

James sat back in his chair, feeling as though he were sitting in a small boat on a large lake after a hurricane had just passed. He felt windblown, nearly over-whelmed and just a little bit relieved. "Sure?" he said finally.

"Sure?" The lawyer sounded incredulous. *"Sure?* You are correct. Sure."

"Um," James broke in, "I understand that some witness claims to have seen me with the kidnappers in the hotel."

"What?" The lawyer looked like he'd been slapped.

"What?" James knew the man was saying "what," but it sounded like "shit" even though the two words shared none of the same syllables. "What? 'Some witness saw you at the hotel with the kidnappers'? Please. This is racism." The man waved a hand, dismissing the notion of "witnesses" as ridiculous. "They think they saw you because they saw a black man. To these people all black men look alike. The bourgeois bastards! I will not put up with this! They are racist pigs!" He turned his head and spit twice on the floor of the interview room, then turned back toward James. "You are black? This is correct? Yes?"

James nodded, keeping the smile from his face. "Yes, yes, I am. Have been my whole life."

"You see!" the lawyer shouted, triumphant. "You are black! This means only one thing in France, in Marseilles. It means you are Algerian! And everyone knows those provincial buffoons in Marseilles think *all* Algerians are terrorists. You are black, therefore anyone who accuses you of a crime is racist."

"Okay."

"I have you out in the morning." The lawyer began collecting his effects from the table. "We go before the judge in his chambers with the prosecution. I tell them next time you get a prostitute, you don't stop to save lives. They keep your passport so you are no flight risk. You get out. Simple. The end. Goodbye." He rose. "I see you in the morning. Please shower." He turned toward the corrections officer. "I am done. Open the door." He turned toward James as the big French police officer complied. "Tomorrow." Then he breezed out of the room, leaving behind only the scent of his cologne.

Still feeling windblown, or a little like Dorothy when

she realized she wasn't in Kansas anymore, James stood. He looked at the corrections officer standing beside the open door. He shuffled forward to be led back to his cell for the rest of the night.

"Your lawyer is very good," the uniformed man said.

"Yes," James answered. "Isn't he?"

# CHAPTER TEN

Hal Brognola breathed in the fresh mountain air and looked around the Farm from the door of the main farmhouse of the Stony Man compound. He rarely had time to appreciate the sheer beauty of this valley. Every time he flew in from Washington there was always some crisis brewing, some emergency he had to take care of. The big Fed sighed deeply. Today really was no different.

He reached into the pocket of his tailored but now wrinkled slacks and pulled out a half-finished roll of antacid tablets, popped a few into his mouth and chewed them.

He ran a hand through his graying hair. He was tired and had been for a long time now. He put his unlit cigar back into his mouth and glanced at his watch. He was still early, which was good because after he set this part of the mission into order he had to return to the beltway for a meeting with both the Man and the director of National Intelligence.

Plausible deniability, he thought. The phrase, Stony Man's very watchword, was thick with meaning, he realized, and not for the first time. In many ways it stood for the desire of the government to have its cake and eat it, too. Governments wanted to be able to do what they wanted to do and, quite often, they didn't want to have to be accountable for it if it went wrong. Or, sometimes, even if it went right. Plausible deniability meant an avoidance of political embarrassment. But it also meant operational security, a way to get things done that needed doing because what was popular wasn't always what was right and, conversely, what was right wasn't always popular.

A side effect of the kind of activities that required plausible deniability was that the men and women tasked with performing them were expendable. The operatives, agents, commandos, operators, soldiers and government officers who volunteered for those kinds of missions understood that.

Brognola forced his mind off such a pessimistic musing. Price was on the French situation, so it could be in no more capable hands. Out there, beyond the borders of the U.S., a shadowy cabal was gathering resources for some kind of a strike against America. It was a well-known situation for the Stony Man team—one they spent their careers and lives fighting. They would uncover the truth and punish those responsible. Hal Brognola believed that very deeply. He sighed; it was something he had to believe.

He heard the rumble of a big block engine and turned to see the head of Stony Man site security, Buck Greene, driving a black Chevy Blazer up from the airfield. Greene pulled up next to Brognola and the big Fed heard the automatic locks pop open.

Brognola reached out, jerked open the Blazer's door and nodded to the driver. "What's up, Chief?" he asked as he slid into the comfortable leather interior of the SUV and pulled the door closed.

"Not much. I was overseeing the blacksuit detail you wanted to serve as an op-force for the boys when I got your call."

Brognola nodded. While he and Price's operational support personnel had begun setting things in motion for the next phase of the operation, Price had directed the combined team of Phoenix Force and Able Team to begin a series of short training exercises and immediate action drills to help the merged crew coalesce. A detail of Chief Greene's blacksuits had been tasked with providing oppositional forces for the field training exercises.

"That's where I need to go, Chief," Brognola said. "I have to pull Rafe out and get him rolling downrange. Things are starting to move fast."

"Don't they always?" Greene asked.

He touched the send button on his secured com link. "This is Bravo Sierra Six," he rasped.

"Six, this is Two," a deep male voice answered. "Go ahead."

"Pull Rafe out of the FTX," Greene ordered. "Tell him they need him at the big house."

"Copy. Two out."

In minutes the Blazer pulled up to a bend in a dirt road running along the perimeter of the farm. Rafael Encizo emerged from a thicket of tangle vines set behind a row of fruit trees at the edge of the remaining orchard. He smiled as Brognola lowered the window, and walked over to the Blazer.

The Phoenix Force commando was sweating freely as he approached the vehicle. He wore faded jeans tucked into hiking boots. The straps of a small field pack dug into his shoulders through the nondescript khaki of his button-up work shirt. The long sleeves had been rolled up, revealing forearms encased by ropes of muscle. An H&K MP-5 SD-3 submachine hung from a black nylon strap around his neck.

"Hey, boss. What's happenin'?" Encizo said as he climbed into the back of the Blazer.

"Not too much, Rafe, not too much," Brognola allowed. "How's the exercise going?"

Greene nodded once at the Phoenix Force commando and pulled the Blazer back onto the gravel road. He drove at a sedate pace back up the track toward the main house.

"It's going well," Encizo answered. "We've worked together enough to combine pretty seamlessly. How's our French situation shaping up?"

Brognola felt his stomach twist into an involuntary knot. He frowned to himself and inhaled through his nose, dragging in the strong smell of the unlit cigar in his mouth. "Barb's on it. Cal's going to be fine if the French judicial system plays out the way it's supposed to. She's still got Carmen running down T.J. Apparently a request to match his fingerprints was made through Interpol and our State Department."

"Too bad for them he doesn't exist," Encizo noted.

"Yeah, too bad. Of course Aaron is going to have to hack both Interpol and State when this is done to remove the copies but more than likely the local French jurisdiction will retain a hard copy. Akira is going to backtrack the request to try to pinpoint which department or group is holding him and, hopefully, where."

"The units on our ass that night were National Police."

Brognola nodded. "Akira was able to verify that easily enough through our intelligence intercepts."

France had two national police forces. The National Police, controlled by the Interior Ministry, were responsible for enforcement inside the country's larger towns and cities, including the Mediterranean port of Marseilles. In addition, there were the Gendarmerie, controlled by the Ministry of Defense and tasked with jurisdiction over the remainder of the country and all overseas territories.

"We think, because of the circumstances, that control of T.J. was ceded to one of the Gendarmerie's counterterrorism units. We'll find him, Rafe. Leave it to us," Brognola said, closing that line of conversation.

"I know, Hal," Encizo said. "What's up?"

"Puerto Lobos."

"Puerto Lobos," Encizo echoed.

"Our analysis is too spotty. The situation is too confusing at the moment. It's not readily apparent that Aslargo's running the town out in the open or more covertly. Are the police turning a blind eye to the drug activity or are they openly involved? How is the military armed? Same goes for the military unit in the area. Is it ignoring things or providing security in the countryside? How are they armed? What kind of things do they respond to and how do they interact with former Zetas, et cetera. How 'bout the local population? Are they all pretty much employees of Aslargo the way villagers in a Colombian cartel coca-growing hamlet would be, or are they simply fishermen and farmers intimidated into silence? How are strangers treated? Are they actively harassed by local authorities or simply bullied, or even ignored? Plus, we need better intel on Aslargo's movements. We can't be sending you guys in without being sure the kingpin's where we think he is, how's he guarded and the like. We need a point man, a facilitator to run a pathfinder operation."

"So I'm going in?" Encizo deduced. "Go in and do the preliminary intelligence support? Carl, Gary and Gadgets are too obviously Anglos."

"Exactly."

"What's my cover?"

"You're a journalist for a travel magazine doing a story on Mexican coastal towns. You wander around taking some photos, chatting up the locals, drinking in the bars, eating in the restaurants. We'll see what the response is to you. In the meantime you'll need to do a beach reconnaissance for the rest of the team's infiltration. You'll need to set up the electronic interdiction equipment to tap into Aslargo's communications," Brognola told him.

"How we going to get that kind of equipment to me if we're worried about me being harassed?"

"You'll do some hiking. You find a good spot for an aerial drop and we'll send in Charlie Mott. It's risky, but less so than a police checkpoint stopping your car and finding spy gear in the possession of a travel writer.

"I'm going to have Aaron and Akira bring you up to speed on the equipment you'll be using and set up a secure communications system for you while the rest of the guys practice helocast operations with Jack Grimaldi. Then tomorrow afternoon, late, you'll fly civilian airlines out of Dulles to Brownsville in Texas. Barb has a vehicle waiting for you and you'll drive across the border and south to Puerto Lobos," Brognola stated.

"Sounds good, boss," Encizo replied.

It was the answer Brognola had expected. A can-do attitude was the hallmark of any elite trooper, and Rafael Encizo was no exception. The road map of scars and old wounds on his body was proof enough of that.

Despite his high level of skill and vast experience, the situation was still ripe for exploitation by that bastard Murphy and his immutable Law, Brognola realized. Encizo would be going alone, under rather flimsy cover to a nonpermissive environment to prep the way for a covert operation raid on a well-armed and justifiably paranoid drug kingpin. The odds against it ending well seemed astronomical.

Astronomical odds, Brognola mused. He bit down on his now well-chewed cigar. Sounded about right.

*France*

EVEN BEFORE JAMES ENTERED the little room off the main hall leading toward the building's courtrooms he smelled the cigarette smoke. He squinted as he walked through the door. This room was bland but much less stark than the interrogation cell where he had first met his lawyer several days earlier.

Pierre Lejeune sat in a chair on the other side of a dark wooded conference table. The heavy glass ashtray at his elbow held several crumpled cigarette butts, and the French lawyer puffed away on another, a smug look on his face. He was chatting in what James thought was Dutch on a cell phone.

James stepped forward to take a chair, surveying the room further. There was a Monet print on the wall, a fern in a mahogany-colored floor vase and a black landline telephone on a nondescript filing cabinet. On the table in front of Lejeune's attaché case was a second, less expensive briefcase and a single sheet of paper.

*"Oui,"* the lawyer murmured into his cell phone, switching to French.

He said something else that James didn't catch as he was sitting down, and then the lawyer snapped the cell phone shut. He slid the phone into an inner pocket on his suit jacket and took a long drag off his cigarette. He squinted at James through the haze of blue-gray smoke.

Lejeune reached out with a long, slim finger and tapped the single sheet of paper lying on the table. He looked at the National Police officer standing just behind James's shoulder.

"You don't know what this looks like? You haven't seen one before?" he snapped.

The policeman, with the air of one long used to tedious suffering, grunted and moved forward, his keys jingling in his hands. James offered up his wrists and the uniformed man undid his shackles.

"I'm free?" he asked in French.

Lejeune bobbed his pointed chin sharply and then ground out his cigarette. He carefully pushed the full ashtray to the side and reached out and pulled the second briefcase to him. He regarded James with a shrewd look while the National Police officer left the room and closed the door behind him.

*"Oui,"* Lejeune said. "You are free. Let me explain

something to you. In France, unlike America, our justice system is very old, very civilized. It has certain...redundancies, shall we say, built into the structure. One of these redundancies is our judicial investigations."

"Judicial investigation?" James repeated. He rubbed his wrists, grateful to have the cuffs off. He had a certain, sneaking suspicion that the man sitting in front of him would have been able to teach the late Johnny Cochran an item or two about overly clever and more than slightly shady attorney tricks.

"Yes. A judicial investigation. What? I am maybe talking to myself?" The lawyer sighed and lit another cigarette. "Please. We speak English, okay? Your accent is killing me!" He sat back in his chair and blew out a cloud of smoke. "After the initial police investigation—which in your case determined that you had to be working with the kidnappers from the resort—there is a second, separate investigation run by the Judicial branch that builds on the first and decides if a case should go to trial or be dismissed."

"And in my case the judge decided...?" James trailed off.

"Louis is a very sensible man. He decided that it was obvious that you could not be the man from the hotel, therefore making the only reasonable explanation that you were simply a Good Samaritan trying to help the victim of a car crash."

"How's the press going to react?"

The French attorney waved the hand holding the cigarette around his head, like a man batting at an annoying fly. "It is inconsequential. Tomorrow a minister will be found in bed with some boy, or a TV actress will be found with cocaine after being pulled over while driving drunk. The press in this country is like a man's mistress…" Lejeune seemed to be looking for the appropriate word.

"Capricious?" James offered.

"No! I was going to say 'as unconcerned with the truth as a priest,'" he snapped. He dragged on his cigarette, let out the smoke, then cocked his head to one side as if considering James's words. He shrugged in the quintessential French way. "I suppose capricious works as well," he finally allowed.

"Thank you for your help." James tried to change the subject. "I'm free to go now?"

Lejeune leaned forward and tapped the second briefcase on the table. "This is for you. From your benefactors." He reached into the pocket of his suit jacket and pulled out a small gold key. He placed it on the briefcase and carefully slid both items halfway across the table.

James rose and pulled the briefcase toward him. It was heavy. He took the key and settled into his chair again. "I think it best if I open it in private," he said.

Lejeune again dragged on his cigarette in a languid fashion. He gave James an effete smirk. "My law practice is very successful." He uttered the non sequitur as casually as if he were remarking on the weather outside.

James looked up sharply. "I assume my 'benefactors' have already addressed your retainer."

"I am not speaking now of money, but rather, of experience."

James remained silent, regarding the French attorney.

He didn't say anything. Lejeune continued through the awkward, pointed silence, smirk firmly in place.

"Last year, for example, I helped defend a civil servant in the judiciary—our friend on your case, the judge Louis, surprisingly enough."

James frowned. He was beginning to understand where this was going. He was surprised the rail-thin French attorney was being so bold as to connect the dots so openly. He wondered idly if the room was bugged. He remained silent.

"Or, perhaps, not so surprisingly," Lejeune continued. "What I find curious is that my good friend the judge had his own fees augmented once it became clear the Ministry of the Interior was going to pull out all stops on that case."

"Pierre," James said evenly, "do you have a point?"

"Oh, *oui,* only that it was the same courier who provided the retainer from my office. A courier who I later met at a party." Lejeune paused, so obviously for dramatic effect that James couldn't help but smile. "A party at the American Embassy."

"I would suggest," James offered, "that if you would like to be invited to any more parties that you exercise, how do you say…discretion?"

Lejeune sat back in his chair and snorted. He crushed out his cigarette and for the first time since he had met the man James detected a genuine smile.

"Please," the French attorney said. "I, *monsieur,* am French. French lawyers are the very epitome of discretion. Granted, we are not Swiss, but still."

"That's good to hear, Pierre." James smiled. "That's very good to hear."

CARMEN DELAHUNT WATCHED the rotors of the civilian Bell JetRanger helicopter turning. She could see Charlie Mott had worked through what she knew was his final preflight check, and knew he was just going through the motions and already prepared for liftoff; he was just waiting for her.

She raised a steady hand and ran it through her red hair. The ex-FBI agent was a competent veteran, had been a very experienced field agent when the man sitting next to her in the Chevy Blazer, Hal Brognola, had handpicked her to come to Stony Man. Since that time she had heard more, seen more, done more than in all her years in federal law enforcement combined.

Her experiences in Myanmar with the man she knew was Mack Bolan had been a vivid, visceral example of how different the world at Stony Man Farm was compared to the one she had left behind at the FBI. Now she was being asked to go out again, being asked to do things more espionage than police, more commando than cop—even if only in a support capacity.

She felt her nerves twisting inside her stomach, tying it into knots with merciless effect. She felt her fear but was not immobilized by it. Everything was brighter, clearer around her.

The sunshine coming in through the windows was hard and bright. She thought it was a beautiful day and she felt a smile, just as hard and just as bright on her face as she nodded to what her boss, Brognola, was telling her. She repeated it back to him.

"Charlie takes me to Shreveport. The blacksuits with Marine FAST platoon backgrounds are already there with the yacht, an eighty-seven footer. They sail the boat and provide security. I handle the communications and satellite relay equipment inside. We put in off the coast of Puerto Lobos to provide commo support to Rafe and a logistical staging area for Gary and the boys when it's time for them to go in. We stay out at sea unless circumstances completely fall apart. We do not tie up in Puerto Lobos. We avoid other boats and ships in the area. We stay in international water. If Mexican police or military naval units approach us, we run. Our code for U.S. Coast Guard force protection patrols loitering in the area is a single burst transmission already hard-coded into the appropriate com units."

Hal Brognola grunted as the redhead rattled off the information for the fortieth time. Repetition was a safety feature hardwired into operational planning. He wasn't worried. If he'd given Carmen Delahunt a bottle of tequila and a New York City telephone book and told her to drink the first and memorize the latter he knew she would pull it off.

The off-site communications relay mission Delahunt headed was vital. They were looking for a digital needle in an electronic haystack. The equipment Rafael Encizo had smuggled into Mexico with him was powerful and high-tech, but necessity had required, for his cover, that it remain small and unobtrusive, thus eliminating the most sophisticated and powerful units available. By providing an offshore communications relay platform tied by NSA satellite to Stony Man Farm, Encizo's signal intelligence capabilities had been pumped full of techno-steroids.

"Perfect," Brognola said. "As usual." He reached behind him into the backseat and pulled Delahunt's flight bag forward. He handed it to her. "You know how Barb is," he said gruffly. "Real mother hen, that one. Why don't you call ops once you touch down in Shreveport and then when they get the yacht under way?"

Delahunt took the bag and got out of the vehicle as Brognola spoke. She turned, one slender hand on the heavy door. She looked into the vehicle cab and met Brognola's eyes. "Barb." She smiled. "Yeah, right."

"Knock 'em dead," Brognola said.

"I'll leave that to the boys, if you don't mind," she retorted, smiling, and slammed the door closed.

Brognola chuckled as he watched the woman cross the yard, head down against the rotor wash of Charlie Mott's waiting helicopter. She climbed inside and as Brognola eased the Blazer away from the airfield he heard the engines begin to scream as the bird lifted off.

## CHAPTER ELEVEN

Rafael Encizo splashed some rum into a tumbler of ice and cola. He lifted the cut glass to his lips and sipped his drink. He stepped out onto the terrace of his hotel suite and felt the breeze of the gulf in his face.

Puerto Lobos was deceptively beautiful.

It was also simply deceptive, as a multimillion-dollar cancer was thriving under the watchful eye of a cynical marriage between elements of the Mexican National Military and a criminal syndicate comprised of former antinarcotics commandos: the Zetas. A marriage Encizo had come to be convinced was under the stewardship of elements of Mexico's intelligence service, Cisen.

The players of the Puerto Lobos cartel believed they were immune to interception because even if their cellphone conversations were being monitored, the phone network was encrypting the transmissions as part of the digital signal structure, making it impossible to understand them.

However, the interception system Encizo had brought

to Mexico did not need to decrypt the transmissions. On a typical network, and this was certainly true of the limited Mexican service, it was the base station that controlled the encryption. The hyperassertive multichannel digital receiving system Encizo had set up in his seventh-floor hotel room replaced the single base station operating on the somewhat isolated Mexican coast.

It relayed those signals through computerized digital feed equipment under Carman Delahunt's control on the yacht offshore. First the signals in Puerto Lobos were swept as computer algorithms hunted for keywords and phrases such as names, activities or items. Those specific channels were then entrapped and triangulated, providing location. Then they used the base station's control link signal to simply turn the desired cell phone "active" in a passive mode. They turned Aslargo's cell phone, and those of his main lieutenants, into bugs.

Within seventy-two hours of arriving, Encizo had plucked a needle from a haystack. He had then used the triangulation of the signals to provide him with locations. His tactical reconnaissance had been sent through live digital feed to the station in his hotel room and then out to the ship where it was prepped, packaged and bounced off a secure low earth orbit satellite where it was delivered to the waiting Barbara Price at Stony Man Farm.

*Doom on you,* Encizo silently toasted the Mexican kingpin.

IN THE WAR ROOM at Stony Man Farm, the amalgamated team gathered for a briefing. The men had just showered after returning from a navigation exercise utilizing their Zodiac assault rafts in heavy surf off the Virginia coast. Over the past seventy-two hours the men had congealed into an excellent small boat crew.

It had been ironic, Gary Manning thought, that the two most experienced maritime operators, Calvin James and Rafael Encizo, should have been there but were unable to help in the surf evolutions and helocast operational drills.

The downtime was weighing heavily on the men as they waited for some word about T. J. Hawkins and the intelligence Encizo was gathering, without backup, in the operational area. Carl Lyons in particular was beginning to chafe at the bit. Not a follower by nature, he had done his best to meld under Manning's direction, but despite their consummate professionalism, the blending had not been without friction.

Hal Brognola entered the briefing room, followed by Aaron Kurtzman. The gruff, barrel-chested man greeted the assembled commandos with a nod. They returned his greeting with good nature as they waited for Barbara Price to join them.

"I almost hate to ask, but any word on T.J.?" Carl Lyons asked once she had arrived.

"We'll address that momentarily." Price lifted her eyes to catch Brognola's. "We think Wethers has found our link. We're having Cal check it out now."

"The professor?" Schwarz smiled. "If Hunt is on it, you'll have your boy back in no time." He slapped his hand out and clapped Manning on the shoulder.

The Canadian nodded. "That's good news, Barb."

Price smiled at him. "Well, Rafe's on the line and I

think he's got the news you've been waiting for. The beach is prepped and we're ready to roll on Puerto Lobos."

*France*

THREE HOURS LATER the phone rang in southern France.

The sound of the ringer jarred James out of his reverie and he let the heavy curtain fall across the window. He picked up the encrypted sat-com unit and punched the activation button.

"James."

"Cal, Barb," Price said. "How you doing? How's the house?"

"House is good. I'm outfitted well, as long as the encryption unit holds, we should be fine. Of course the fact that they can't pick up our signal or crack the code is going to tell the French something anyway," the ex-Navy SEAL pointed out.

"But that's why it's called plausible deniability. They know. We know they know. They know we know—but everyone pretends they don't know."

The television was on in the background. He reached over, picked up the remote and hit the mute button.

"I understand that, Barb." James's voice was tight. "This isn't about that. I'm sitting in France with a blown cover. I think I'm being watched. If I'm under surveillance, then how can I help T.J.?"

"You ID your shadows?"

"Not ID, just notice. I can't say if they're spooks or cops."

"How good are they?"

"Well, I noticed them, but they seem professional. I assume all this means that Stony One is unavailable to help?"

Price sighed on the other end of the line. Even with the laser-clear connection she still sounded three thousand miles away. James felt very alone. On the television screen a smiling brunette with a dazzling smile held up a bottle of laundry detergent. James didn't recognize the brand. The television program cut to a news feed showing the split-screen images of the disgraced Maryland senator and the Caracas tycoon Marcos Sincanaros.

"Stony One is out of contact at the moment," Price said. "We can't send him. We can't send anyone else. I have Phoenix and Able working the southern angle. It's a potential attack on the U.S., Cal."

"Can't we go outside Stony?" James asked.

He moved to the window again and looked outside. He saw dirty European cobblestone slick from the falling rain, grungy streetlamps with weak yellow "environmentally friendly" lightbulbs, and Peugeots, Yugos, Audis and BMWs cruising past his location in staggered patterns of random traffic. Nothing unusual.

Price was silent on the other end of the connection. James looked up. The cloud cover was close, claustrophobically so. He felt smothered by the gray shrouds. He refused to speak first despite Price's hesitation; he knew what he was asking.

"That's not going to happen, Cal," she said finally. "Not on a hostile extraction in France. It just won't fly. Officially we don't kidnap people from sovereign countries. Especially ones that are supposed to be allies. You're it, cover blown or not. You're all I can spare and you're all the Man is willing to spare. They were happy to have al-Shalaan tied up in a neat little package, but they're never going to admit they worked to get him. End of story."

James bit back a harsh laugh. "He survived 'the Mog' to get nabbed in Marseilles of all places?" he said, referring to Hawkins's experience in Somalia.

"T.J.'s survived a lot more than just Mogadishu, and so have you," Price answered. "I'm not saying we're giving up, you know that, Cal. I'm saying we're small, we're clandestine, we're expendable. I know you can do this. Akira has got something I want you to check out. Are you ready for your instructions?" Price's voice was mechanically smooth and detached.

With a flick of an internal switch James put aside everything else and became a field operative.

"Go ahead," he said. "I'm listening."

JAMES STEPPED OUT into the street. He was wearing a raincoat over his clothes, but he had neglected to bring an umbrella against the weather. He would be needing his hands free. The streetlights reflected off the oil puddles of rainwater, and the headlights of passing cars caused him to narrow his eyes against the glare. The drizzle cut into the exposed flesh of his face and neck as he crossed the sidewalk to his vehicle.

As he walked, he kept his head up and his lookout sharp. He moved through hourglass-shaped areas of darkness spread between the pools of light. Behind him, standing on the narrow stone steps in front of a brownstone-style tenement, a man in a rain slicker lit a cigarette. The flame briefly illuminated his face in red light.

James hadn't left the country after the incident and

despite the Machiavellian skill of his lawyer he knew his actions had caused him great scrutiny by French antiterror units. He would be followed, but he couldn't let the realization descend into paranoia.

He pulled his keys out of his pocket and pushed the red button on the fob. The alarm system on his rental car chirped and the parking brakes flashed twice in quick succession. He could smell the salt of the ocean in the rain and taste the brine on his lips as he slid behind the wheel of the Saturn Outback.

The engine turned over smoothly as he started the car. He checked his window and rear mirrors carefully, then pulled into the light traffic. He was two blocks down when he saw the headlights of a car flash on and then the vehicle pull out into traffic behind him.

Nothing sinister about it. It happened a thousand times a day in every major metropolitan center in the world. Ten thousand times.

He had one operational hope. If the police had simply put a single unit on him, designated to tail him, then he could lose it. If a task force had been assembled, then plainclothes sentries would be stationed in leap-frog patterns around his route of travel and he'd have to go to ground all over again.

James kept his speed down just below the posted limit, taking into account the rain-soaked streets. He remembered the feeling of floating he had felt before the stretch model Hummer had crashed back down to earth and he'd been slammed around in his harness. It had not been a pleasant sensation. He made a conscious exercise of willpower and suppressed the thought.

He continued to head in the opposite direction of

where Price had said the French government currently kept his teammate. He ran a yellow traffic signal, and saw a set of headlights that had been tailing him three automobiles back suddenly surge forward and do the same thing.

It was official: he was being followed. But by forcing their hand he'd confirmed his suspicions that he was being followed by only a single tail and not a team of tactically positioned officers. That was something. He had a plan now.

James turned the wheel sharply and cut down a secondary road off the main thoroughfare. His tires hummed on the wet pavement and behind him the chase vehicle kept pace. He had carefully studied the street maps of the old city while he had waited for Price's instructions, expanding considerably on the topography he had previously memorized in support of the initial mission.

Once he had decided on his course of action he went about it with unflappable detachment. He touched a splay-tipped finger to his wireless headset. He heard the digital dial tone chirp out its arranged signal. His trained ear could detect the security shunts and the change in pitch from his in-unit encryption hardware.

There was an almost mechanical click as the connection was routed through. "Congratulations! You have reached the A-Man! The A-Man is now speaking," Akira Tokaido announced.

"I'm shaking loose an extra set of eyes as we speak. You get any official chatter like before?" James said without preamble.

"Negative," Tokaido replied. "Not on these police

freqs. Could mean an intel unit but it could just be a small detective op, as well."

"Copy. I'll be in touch. Out."

He drove for ten more minutes then, without using his blinker, cut into the multistoried parking garage of the city's main rail station. He entered the structure and shot up two levels at random, moving fast and almost reckless as he cut down narrow aisles lined with sub-compact econo-models of European cars. He ran up ramps and darted around turns. Spotting a space, he zipped in and killed the car engine.

Getting out of the vehicle, he slammed the door behind him and began to briskly walk toward the elevator bank set at one end of the parking level. Taking it down to the main lobby, he stepped out into the milling crowd.

Over the next hour he began a simple series of maneuvers designed to lose his shadows. He paid for a ticket on the next train heading out of the city center. He boarded it, drinking good coffee from a vendor, then got off at a random stop. Following that, he chose and got off at another arbitrary stop, raced across the platform, shifting in and out of the crowd, and boarded a second random train as it prepared to pull out of the urban station.

He rode for a half hour, then repeated the process, this time heading back into the city proper. He got off, stole a car and began driving to where Stony Man thought the French government was keeping Hawkins under wraps. He simply had to infiltrate a major metropolitan hospital, find his subject, who was gravely injured, more than likely sedated and under heavy guard, and then extract him.

## CHAPTER TWELVE

The ramp of the CH-46 Sea Knight began to lower with a screaming of hydraulic gears. Warm gulf air rushed into the back of the helicopter and pitch-black darkness from an overcast sky stretched beyond the opening. Below the hovering aircraft, whitecaps curled and split as the gulf current pushed against the stiff sea breeze.

As Stony Man pilots Jack Grimaldi and Charlie Mott worked to keep the helicopter steady just yards above the tossing ocean, the three Stony Man commandos picked up the F470 Combat Rubber Raiding Craft—CRRC—and began to jog with it down the back of the cargo hold.

They cast it out the back and immediately followed, single file out of the hovering helicopter and into the water. The drop was short and the impact sudden as the men descended into the ocean. As soon as Mott had cleared the back of the aircraft, the ramp began to rise and Grimaldi brought the CH-46 up off the surface of the water.

Gadgets Schwarz felt the waters of the Mexican coast, almost blood warm, envelope him in a liquid womb. His momentum and the weight of his gear dragged him below the surface immediately. He snapped the cord on his life vest and felt it inflate, then kicked out strongly for the surface, following the buoyancy of the vest.

He saw a softening of the darkness above him and began to let air escape his lungs as he pushed for the surface. His head broke through the waves and he took a deep breath, filling his lungs and treading water for a moment, casting about for his bearings. He picked out the CRRC bobbing on the surface immediately and kicked out for it.

Schwarz reached it in ten hard sidestrokes and grabbed hold of a gunwale. He pulled himself over the side in a movement so practiced in the training leading up to the insertion that it was now second nature. Three heartbeats later Gary Manning flipped over the opposite edge and into the raft.

"Where's Ironman?" Manning demanded.

As he asked the question he was moving toward the stern of the CRRC to where a wooden transom served as a mounting platform for the watercraft's twin 55-horsepower, two-stroke engines.

"Let me see," Schwarz replied.

Schwarz shifted up the center of the raft toward the front where secured bags contained the team's equipment and weapons. He lifted his head up and scanned the ocean. He saw Lyons kicking hard for the side of the boat. Leaning over the edge, he reached out a hand and grasped hold of Able Team's leader.

Lyons's face was twisted in pain so apparent it was obvious even in the limited visibility. Worried, Schwarz hauled him over the side. Behind them he heard Manning start the engine. The sound of the pumpjet propulsor with its shrouded impellor, instead of a traditional exposed propeller, was modest and muted against the white noise of the surf and wind.

Lyons hissed once and Schwarz could see a livid red mark like the lash of a bullwhip across his right cheek and down the exposed skin of his neck. The welt was raised and ugly.

"You okay, man?" Schwarz asked.

"I swam up into a jellyfish!" Lyons snarled. "I'm lucky it only got hold of me for a moment."

"You want me to pee on the sting?" Schwarz asked, his voice earnest. "That's supposed to help."

"Piss on yourself," Lyons replied, forcing himself into a sitting position.

The big blond man leaned back against the 6-gallon fuel bladder set next to the storage bags and began to root around in one of the cargo pouches on his leg. "I'm fine," he muttered. "Get the bearings for our 'coxswain,'" he said.

"Don't worry, Carl," Manning called. "You'll feel better once you shoot someone."

"Oh, they're going to pay for this," Lyons agreed.

Working alongside Manning, Schwarz checked his handheld GPS and then shot a westerly azimuth with his compass. While they compared readings, Lyons began to smear an antiseptic cream across the sting. The muscles of his face felt slack and numb now, despite the pain. The situation could have been very dangerous.

He'd received only brushing contact with a trailing tentacle of what he thought was a Man-o'-War. If he'd come up within reach of more of the tentacles or been more fully engaged by the one he *had* come in contact with, he could have easily drowned. Even with a less severe outcome he could have been blinded or too badly stung to continue the mission. Despite his pain Carl Lyons was happy for it, because it meant it wasn't something worse.

"We're good," Schwarz answered, agreeing with Manning.

"Hold on," the big Canadian said, and grabbed the tiller arm.

The pitch of the engine's whine changed as he goosed it. The speed skags under the boat began to push down against the waves and the CRRC took off hard for the over-the-horizon objective following their navigational bearing.

While Lyons gave himself first aid and Manning guided the raft toward Puerto Lobos on an almost due west bearing, Schwarz moved forward and began breaking into the waterproof storage sacks. The boat skipped across the surface like a stone hurled from a muscular arm, shooting out like a laser along its azimuth.

Taking a pair of night-vision goggles out of the gear, he quickly pulled them into place and cinched them down tight. The rubber straps bit into his head as he secured them and the weight of the NVDs bore down on the bridge of his nose.

The smell of the sea and the humid wind clogged his nostrils. He paused to turn his face into the breeze and felt himself grin like a boy despite the situation. He felt powerful and nocturnal, like some swift, amphibious predator. Adrenaline coursed through his veins like some illegal drug.

Schwarz looked northward, and as Manning skimmed over a roll of waves he saw the blinking infrared signal from Carmen Delahunt's yacht. He turned back and found Manning in the monochromatic wash of the goggle.

"We've established visual with Water Witch Six," Schwarz said. "Mr. Coxswain," he added, deadpan.

"Good, go ahead," Manning instructed him, ignoring the good-natured gibe, and Schwarz could here his own laughing exhilaration mirrored in the big Canadian's voice.

Removing an emergency beacon from the bag, Schwarz took it in his hand and found the selector switch on the side. The US A/N-4 Mission Specific Light Beacon was a smooth cylinder in his grip. He clicked the indicator over two positions and an irregular light began to pulse in the ghostly green illumination of the IR spectrum.

He held up the light for several seconds above his head. After a moment the IR running lights to his north blinked twice in rapid succession and then switched out. Immediately, Schwarz powered the A/N-4 off and stowed it.

Protocol finished, he turned to see if Lyons needed assistance. Putting a hand down against the bottom of the boat, he carefully maneuvered himself into position and leaned in close to the big ex-LAPD detective.

"You good, man?" he asked, raising his voice above the engine.

Lyons nodded and grimaced. The right side of his face seemed slower to respond, but Schwarz could see the dramatic red the sting had first held was more sub-dued now. "I'm fine. This stuff Cal told us to pack works pretty good. By the time we hit the beach I'll be ready to go."

Schwarz nodded and gave Manning a thumbs-up. "You stay here, then. I'll start handing the weapons back once I check them."

Lyons nodded and Schwarz moved back into posi-tion. Out on the horizon he could detect nothing but more water as the CRRC raced across the ocean. He checked his watch, depressing the glow feature and reading the time. If they were on schedule, it would be another two-and-a-half minutes before he would be able to see the lights of Puerto Lobos on the horizon.

Schwarz ignored the heavy pull of his wet fatigues. Already he was starting to feel cool despite the muggy temperature. He removed the NVDs, then opened the zippers on the satchels all the way up and began assem-bling the unit's weapons. For the requirements of the mission they had decided to forgo favorite personal choices in arms and streamline the ammunition and magazines they carried down into identical loads.

Each Stony Man operative would utilize a 5.56 mm M-4 carbine and a 9 mm Beretta 92-FS Elite pistol. While they were signature U.S. military weapons, they were also extremely ubiquitous in the Western hemi-sphere for exactly that reason. Each man would carry a combat load of two hundred carbine rounds in 30-round magazines and five 15-staggered-round magazines for the pistols. The pistols themselves sported Pachmar grips and shortened but heavier slides than the more traditional models. Each one had been outfitted with a specially threaded muzzle and a 4-inch sound suppressor.

Moving with practiced efficiency, Schwarz first locked and loaded a carbine and pistol each for Lyons and Manning, then handed them back. After arming some for himself he loaded his own web gear and began handing back clusters of magazines that were, in turn, quickly secured by the two other men. Finally, Schwarz prepped the weapons and LBE-harness pouches for Rafael Encizo.

To the weapons Schwarz added an assortment of nonlethal grenades: flash-bangs, smoke, CS gas and several rubber ball grenades, each one packed with 840 hard, rubberized pellets. If forced to extract Montoya Aslargo from a crowd of noncombatants, as Encizo had indicated was a probability, then the Stony Man unit was prepped for that eventuality.

Out over the bow of the CRRC the modest skyline of Puerto Lobos blinked into view. The multitude of lights were stretched in a north-south procession along the black line of the horizon. Manning saw them appear and immediately rechecked his azimuth while Schwarz double-checked the GPS display.

Manning shifted the arm on his tiller, and the boat responded by instantly cutting across the rolling surf like a scalpel through skin. The rubber raft shot off two compass degrees toward the southern edge of the lights. Manning ran full-out for ten minutes, then brought the boat in a degree to the north and ran straight on through to the shoreline.

Lyons slid forward and pulled a bulky pair of night-vision binoculars from a watertight pouch.

"That hurt like a mother," he finally admitted with a grunt. He leaned along the gunnel and began systematically sweeping the shore toward their LZ with the binoculars.

"I don't know why you're bitching," Schwarz replied. "I offered to piss on it, and you know G-man's got your back, as well."

"In your dreams," Lyons replied, intent on scanning the shore. "In your dreams, Gadgets."

Schwarz chuckled. The incident with the jellyfish had pissed off Lyons, and the man had used his furious temper on more than one occasion to drive him through situations that would have driven most people to the hospital. In a way Schwarz almost felt sorry for the people who were about to be on the receiving end of Lyons's consternation.

It, in fact, made him smile.

HAL BROGNOLA EASED BACK in the chair behind his desk. He sighed and looked out the windows of his office. The beltway scene outside was dreary, overcast and threatening rain. Out on the streets, cars were self-contained, anonymous worlds unto themselves.

He looked at his coffee, realized it had to have gone cold and grimaced. He punched up the security screen saver on his computer and made to get up and get another cup. His cell phone on his desk began to vibrate and, resigned, he sank back down into his seat.

The big Fed reached over and picked up his phone. He read the display and frowned. His cell phone was enhanced and when the display read Caller Unknown, as it did now, then it meant someone was using equally savvy tech.

Brognola leaned back and brought the phone to his ear. "Shoot."

"You've caused us some consternation." The voice was male, smooth and undeniably French.

"I'm sure I don't know what you mean, Henri," Brognola replied.

"You've been sending your garbagemen over to pick up our trash."

"While I don't know what you're talking about," Brognola said to his Groupe d'Intervention de la Gendarmerie Nationale counterpart, "I must admit to be sympathetic to conservation issues, in the general."

"You want to know how a counterintelligence agent works?"

"I never turn down free advice, but I usually get what I pay for."

"A good one works much like a detective. In fact, often *exactly* like a detective. I often take inspiration from the works of Sir Arthur Conan Doyle."

"Sherlock Holmes."

"Just so. If you eliminate the impossible, then whatever is left, no matter how improbable, is the answer."

"Sure, but coincidences happen."

"Not in our world," Henri said. "A hostile extraction like that—"

"Like what?" Brognola asked.

"Pretend you know about the Marseilles operation. Humor me."

"For an old friend like you? Sure."

"You get a snatch like that, you have to ask yourself some questions. Try to narrow your parameters. Who could pull off that kind of operation? The answer is too vague, but only technically. Quite a number of government agencies or the military employ personnel who could theoretically do something like that. The SEAL teams, Army Special Forces and of course the thirty or so intelligence agencies in the United States."

"Oh?" Brognola feigned confusion. "We're talking about the U.S.? I'm old-fashioned. I still prefer to blame the Russians for everything."

"You were going to indulge me?"

"Quite right, apologies."

"However," the voice continued, "while theoretically the list of potential culprits is quite numerous, in actuality the list narrows dramatically."

*Here it comes,* Brognola thought.

"The hostile extraction was done in an ostensibly friendly and allied nation."

"Yes, 'ostensibly,'" Brognola said dryly.

"This eliminates almost all of the special-operations forces from consideration. It is a clandestine, not a covert operation. Of the agencies, only the CIA's Operations Department is tasked with this, and of them only the paramilitary operatives of the Special Activities Division have ever been called upon to do this."

"Yes, I read a story about that once," Brognola said. "I think it was written by Ian Fleming."

"However," the voice continued as if he hadn't been interrupted, "we know that almost as soon as Naval Special Warfare Development Group and the Combat

Applications Group became active that the SAD has not been tasked to undertake hostile extractions on their own but rather always as a part of a joint task force."

Naval Special Warfare Development Group, also called DevGru, was what the navy and Department of Defense now called the legendary SEAL Team 6 just as CAG, or Combat Applications Group, was the official designation of what was once more popularly known as Delta Force, Brognola knew.

"Or any of the more esoteric units like the ones responsible for hunting down Milosevic, such as the Intelligence Support Activity, sometimes called Task Force Orange."

Idly, Brognola wondered about the long-winded approach and the potential it gave him to triangulate the call. He decided that Henri was being deliberately provocative. He was being "open" in a world of black secrets and Brognola knew that meant he was being sent a message. He began to feel increasingly uneasy.

"Those units working in conjunction with the CIA's Special Activities Division are the most likely culprits for what occurred in Marseilles," the voice stated. "But it wasn't them."

"You sound very sure of yourself," Brognola commented.

"We are. And we are prepared to act accordingly."

*Now we're coming to it,* Brognola realized.

He sat up in his chair, reached for his coffee then remembered it was empty. He frowned and sank back into his chair. Outside, rain began to fall harder. Drops pounded against his window like loose change.

"I see," Brognola said, his voice even, neutral. "I don't know what this has to do with me."

"Mainly in the fact that these rather infamous, well-publicized options from your JSOC and CIA are not the only ones available to your President."

Brognola closed his eyes. "I have dinner waiting. Is there a point to this?"

"Yes. There are rumors that you have 'connections.' Pull your active operative out of Marseilles right now. Forget about the one in the hospital. He is the price of doing business in our yard without our permission. Give him up. Try to rescue him, and we turn our information over to the press. Can you imagine? Hard on the heels of NSA wiretaps, Guantánamo Bay, Abu Ghraib, Extraordinary Rendition, you add mercenary commandos kidnapping Saudi diplomats on French soil, what do you think will happen?"

*A replay of the Church commission that neutered the CIA, a replay of the Iran-Contra scandal that weakened U.S. special-operations capabilities to the point of impotence—that's what I'll think will happen,* he thought. What he said was, "Since I have no idea what you're talking about, I'm sure I couldn't say."

"I know a 'hawk from a handsaw,' so good. We have an understanding." The line went dead.

"Don't quote Hamlet at me, asshole," Brognola said to the dead signal.

Cursing to himself, Brognola hit the end button, then he opened his menu. He clicked down to Speed Dial option #2 and hit Send.

In three rings Barbara Price picked up the line.

*France*

HAWKINS CAME AWAKE TO PAIN. They kept his pain medication low so that his suffering was constant and prevented him from getting any real sleep. Without true sleep he wasn't healing and he was becoming more exhausted. His mouth felt dry and as thick as cotton. He was desperately thirsty.

The door to his room opened and he managed to turn his head. The bastard Henri smiled at him, reptilian eyes glinting behind his glasses. Hawkins let his head sag back down onto the pillow. He began marshalling his resources to resist another round of questioning.

Henri snapped his suit cuffs in an impatient manner and strolled over to the bed. He pulled a Mont Blanc pen from an inner suit pocket and smiled grimly down at the wounded American.

"Can I sign your cast?" the Frenchman asked.

"Maybe later." Hawkins looked away.

"I've ordered your pain medicine to be increased," Henri said. "I just thought you should know. I'm taking you to a little…let's call it a 'chalet,' that I have out in the bay—well away from that nosy black man who's been searching for you so diligently."

"I have no idea what you're talking about," Hawkins said.

"Yes. And you're also just a tourist who took a wrong turn."

"That's the story," Hawkins replied.

Henri laughed and the sound came out like clear musical notes. "I've changed my mind. I think the facility transfer will be so much fun you won't want it dulled by morphine. We'll just hold off on that for now."

"Henri?"

"Yes?"

"Fuck you."

Again the laughter. "If you haven't figured out who's fucking whom by now, my friend, you're not half as smart as I've given you credit for."

The Mont Blanc pen came down on the mess of bandages wrapped low over Hawkins's stomach. His eyes bulged and he spasmed as the pain lanced through his body. Instantly his body was covered with sweat.

"What do you know about Bellicose Dawn!" Henri barked.

Hawkins closed his eyes. *Here we go again,* he thought. Lying helpless on the hospital bed, Hawkins prepared for the suffering to begin in earnest.

## CHAPTER THIRTEEN

Salt spray splashed Carl Lyons in the face, stinging his wound.

He grimaced and leaped over the bow of the CRRC. He splashed down into the Mexican coastal surf as Gary Manning and Gadgets Schwarz mirrored his actions behind him. Running out from the saw grass on the dunes above the beach, Encizo appeared and approached the group.

Stooping, Lyons snatched the strap handle for the raft and lifted it up in synchronicity with the rest of the combined Stony Man task force. They began jogging up the beach out of the surf, double-timing through the powder-fine sand. Encizo fell into place beside them and grabbed up a free handle.

"Jeez, Carl, what happened to your face, man?" Encizo asked.

"Jealous woman, Rafe. You know all about that, I imagine."

"Oh, yeah, Ironman. That's my area of tactical expertise. But I can't lie, man. That looks like a jellyfish sting."

"For Lyons that's the about the same thing," Schwarz replied.

"How's it going, Rafe?" Manning greeted his teammate. The reconstituted team raced up the beach and into the sea grass, following Encizo's lead. "What's the sitrep?"

"Everything is five-by-five," Encizo replied. "There's a party going on at the hacienda, but there's always a party going on at Aslargo's hacienda. We go in just like we planned once we take down the supply center."

Running over a short series of grass-covered dunes the team came up to where Encizo had parked his Excursion. Working quickly, the unit transferred their weapons and equipment out of the raft and into the SUV. Manning disengaged the engine and began camouflaging the raft, covering it up from the casual observer.

Once that was completed the Stony Man operatives climbed into the SUV and Encizo started the engine up. Each man rode with his M-4 in his lap, safety off. Encizo's intelligence had shown the Mexican army involvement to be largely passive. For generous fees passed down through the officer corps, the military patrols simply looked the other way.

The Puerto Lobos police were a different matter entirely.

The entire twenty-man force from the chief down to the last patrolman was on Aslargo's payroll as enforcers and security. They oversaw the loading and unloading of shipments at the port. They kept the townspeople in line and formed the first line of general defense around both Aslargo and his operations, tasked specifically with keeping the civilians in the village quiet and passive.

Rafael Encizo had found a population cowed and intimidated into silence while they remained forgotten and abandoned by their government, exploited by the forces meant to protect them, prey for men sworn to protect their safety. His cell-phone surveillance operation on Aslargo had confirmed suspicions already aroused by his urban reconnaissance.

Puerto Lobos's police force were *narcotraficantes,* murderous and heavily armed with a communications network tied directly into Aslargo's main operation.

"Stony One wheels up," Manning said into his com link.

"Copy," Delahunt said from her floating electronics platform off the gulf.

"Copy," Barbara Price acknowledged from Stony Man Farm.

Encizo put his foot down on the gas pedal and pulled the SUV out onto the dirt road.

*France*

AFTER HANGING UP on Brognola, Henri had made one other call. For more than a decade he had served as a covert liaison official for all back-channel relations between France and NATO members involving espionage activities. Henri had handled several quiet tasks on behalf of the U.S. government where they aligned with the interests of France, either active or tacit.

This time those interests had not coincided. Questions

of sovereignty had arisen. Questions of retribution, as well. And for Henri himself. His first task was damage control on his end. His second task was to earn the hefty retainer given him by Marcos Sincanaros.

The connection completed, Henri uttered his introduction to the Saudi prince on the other end of the secure line.

"I regret to inform you that there has been an incident involving your son, Nayef al-Shalaan. No, it did not involve French authority. It involved elements put into play by the cowboy Americans. But he is gone, perhaps Diego Garcia, perhaps Guantánamo Bay, maybe even Poland, we're not sure."

He paused, listening to the angry report coming over the line from the city of Dubai, where the prince kept two separate vacation palaces. When the prince paused, Henri smoothly continued, unruffled.

"No, we are not a source of support in this matter." It was time to disengage himself from any connection with the project. The prince was a powerful man, and it wouldn't do to have him thinking Henri had sacrificed his son to save himself. Which was, of course, exactly what Henri intended to do. "We are not pleased with how your son chose to use his diplomatic clearance. When I hang up this phone, France is no longer involved in this matter with you. But know this—wherever he is, they will make him talk. You have already lost valuable time. Whatever you were doing, change your plans. If those plans included dealings of any sort with a certain Venezuelan who shall remain nameless, then sever them immediately."

The man on the other end of the phone, a powerful

Saudi prince not used to being addressed in such a fashion, began to bark again, but Henri simply used the tip of one well-manicured finger to cut the connection. He sighed and wished his wife hadn't forced him to stop smoking "for the children." His mistress, both of them actually, enjoyed a cigarette still, so he could smoke there, but after being diagnosed with the ulcer last month he'd found himself persuaded into the sensibility of at least cutting back.

He picked up his platinum pen, a gift from his mistress, and began closing out his report. It would have been counterintuitive to think that a man in his position, existing in a vacuum of disavowal such as he did, would be making written reports to his superiors at all. But France was the country that had invented the word *bureaucracy* after all.

The Puerto Lobos night was muggy and close. The Stony Man unit rolled up the secondary road with their windows lowered and their weapons primed. The lights of the casino-resort out on the point were brilliant against the dark backdrop of the ocean. By agreement, Encizo knew from his surveillance, the casino security forces steered the tourists away from Puerto Lobos, and in turn the police force insulated them from the darker undercurrent of the narcotics depot. Money moved in both directions and both remained satisfied with the arrangement.

"How you feeling, Carl?" Encizo asked. "Jellies can be nasty mothers."

"I feel pissed off. Jumped out of a perfectly good helicopter into the ocean. I swam into a jellyfish. I'm a tough guy. But it hurt. That asshole Aslargo is responsible. If he hadn't felt the need to poison people for profit, if he hadn't potentially climbed into bed with a terrorist conspiracy to attack innocents in America, I wouldn't have had to jump in the ocean. If I hadn't had to jump in the ocean, I wouldn't have swum into a jellyfish. Therefore, Aslargo owes me."

Encizo guided the big SUV off the main dirt track and down into a narrow gully on the east. The tires bounced off the ruts and jarred the vehicle's occupants despite Encizo slowing the vehicle. He cut the headlights and braked long enough to slide the night-vision goggles into place. He began to ease the vehicle forward once again, crawling over the broken terrain between the cactus, scrub brush and scattered boulders.

They drove forward in complete silence as they made their final approach. For ten more minutes they wove in and out of low hills and arroyos, Encizo putting the 4x4 suspension through its paces. Up ahead, a sheer cliff face came into view and loomed above the vehicle.

The men from Stony climbed out of the SUV. Their weapons were primed, locked and loaded as the heavy perfume of colitas swirled into the muggy air around them. Faintly, from across the broken terrain, they could hear music coming from the casino out on the coast. Close by, they could hear the rush of ocean and the droning of night cicadas.

Above them, at the top of a sheer 30-foot bluff, Aslargo's distribution center commanded the landscape like a haphazard blend of freeway off-ramp strip mall and fortified gun bunker. On the eastern side of the complex a single dirt road, graded and primed with gravel to facilitate truck traffic, wound down the mesa and cut straight as an arrow six miles across the desert to connect with the major national north-south arterial. A Mexican army post served as a roadblock at the connection.

The compound was a consolidation point for all product arriving from process centers in central Mexico such as anabolic steroids and methamphetamine, as well as the cocaine and heroin from the Caribbean and South American ports of call. From there it was flown, trucked or boated through Zetas's controlled outlets to the north. A short, single-lane runway of fresh macadam had been revealed at the center of the warehouse groupings by satellite imagery provided by the NRO.

Two gun towers blocked in the compound. One sat above the gate entrance on the west side while one was set midway down the razor wire–topped chain-link fence. Each man inside the towers was armed with a drum-magazine mounted M-249 Squad Automatic Weapon, powerful binoculars for the day and a searchlight similar to door-mounted police models for night sweeps.

Encizo's reconnaissance had revealed a less than professional standard of readiness. With the army and police paid off, and the locals frightened, sentry duty had become a boring, punitive assignment in the organization.

Encizo had scouted the wire from all points of the compass and discovered another factor that contributed to the lackadaisical nature of the guards; the northern and southern exposures had been purposefully seeded with a carpet of prickly pear cactus out over the distance of an acre in a wide sweep. The cactus garden was supplemented by small lawn sprinklers fed through PVC-pipe irrigation running out from the compound. With the sheer bluff to the east, the compound security thought themselves well positioned.

That sense of confidence was about to be exploited. Aslargo was a major target whose operation pumped millions of dollars' worth of narcotics into the United States. Shutting down the distribution center had been deemed an important component in getting the President of the United States to sign off on the excursion after the fiasco in Marseilles.

While the other three members of the assault force provided security, Encizo first covered their vehicle in a patch of camo netting, then removed an air-pressured grapnel launcher. The grapnel was high-strength aluminum alloy capable of projection to a height of at least fifty yards and outward horizontally to a minimum of eighty yards while sustaining a weight of two thousand pounds once in place. A climbing ladder attachment could be elevated to just over twenty yards by the hand-held system, and it was in this configuration that Encizo deployed the launcher.

The Phoenix Force veteran held up the launcher in both hands like a jackhammer being used on an overhead projector and triggered the device. It made a heavy, pneumatic cough followed by the thunk of the release and a whirring sound as the line played out. The grapnel arced up and caught on the chain-link fence set back ten feet from the edge of the vertical rock wall of the bluff face.

Encizo dropped the sturdy launcher and hauled back on the line, ensuring it was seated. The tactical climbing ladder lay against the rock like stacked H's, dull in the low light. Carl Lyons stepped back away from the wall and swept the muzzle of his M-4 carbine up.

"Clear," he whispered.

Encizo scrambled up the ladder with the dexterity of a sailor in a ship's rigging. Schwarz watched the area of operation from the three-o'clock position to the six and Manning served security across the rest of their hasty position fighting perimeter. Each man kept his finger on the smooth metal curve of his carbine trigger.

At the top of the ladder Encizo moved into place and slid over the lip of the rock wall, pulling his M-4 carbine free. He tucked his broad, muscular frame into a tight curl down on one knee and swept the perimeter along the length of the fence. Lyons quickly shrugged into his rifle sling and pushed it behind him before starting up the ladder, climbing fast.

The team had drilled in the grapnel climb several times until each operative knew its choreography by rote and brute muscle memory. The rungs of the tactical rope ladder sagged beneath each step the heavy Lyons took, and he was breathing sharply as he powered his way up, the muscles of his thighs and shoulders pumped with blood from the explosive effort of the short climb.

He went over the side and took up a defensive position with his back to the crouching Rafael Encizo, the muzzles of their weapons pointing in opposite directions. Below them Schwarz turned as he rose from his crouch, ducking under the sling of his own weapon as he turned. He took three bounding steps and pulled himself up onto the ladder, exactly duplicating the motions and efforts of his teammates while Manning scrambled backward, his own weapon still pointed outward.

On top of the bluff Encizo watched the rear line of the compound with a sharp eye. He saw Quonset hut warehouses formed by corrugated tin and prefabricated structures. A narrow walkway was set between the back of the garages and storage buildings and the chain-link fence. The dried brown knots of tumbleweeds choked the back of the fence, interspersed with brightly colored paper, aluminum cans, plastic wrappers and other bits of assorted litter. The bright red eyes of a desert rat winked out at him before the little creature turned on its tail and scurried off.

Lyons heard the sound of muted voices coming from the far side of the structures, and from off to the south he heard the low hum of a generator. He was sweating freely in the muggy air under his uniform and body armor. Above them the cloud cover continued to obscure the sliver of the moon. A harsh male voice muttered something in Spanish, and several others laughed in response.

Schwarz slid over the top of the rock face like a snake gliding across a jungle floor. He shuffled forward, bringing his M-4 to bear just opposite the tightly coordinated positions of Encizo and Lyons. A second later the grapnel tangled in the top of the chain-link fence sagged against the wire loops as the heavy weight of Gary Manning eased onto the ladder.

After a moment the blocky shoulders of the big Canadian were silhouetted against the open sky behind them. Manning scrambled over the top and brought up his weapon, settling into position next to Schwarz. He looked around carefully. From their current position the flat roof of the northern gun tower could be seen just over the tops of the compound structures.

The searchlight on the top of the gun tower rotated in a counterclockwise motion, playing the narrow beam of illumination first out across the desert and then back over the fenced-in compound. The team remained motionless as the light skimmed through the air in a blunt bar four feet above their heads. The searchlight just caught the top of the chain-link fence and the interlocked diamond patterns of the wire loops briefly played across their faces in shadow.

Once it was past, Manning turned toward Encizo and nodded.

The little Cuban rose in a crouch and jogged forward to the fence just off to the side from where the grapnel had landed. He went to a knee and let his carbine dangle from his shoulder strap as he pulled a pair of wire cutters with rubber grips from a pouch on his web belt. Manning tapped Schwarz on the shoulder once.

Schwarz immediately rose out of his crouch and hurried forward, holding the M-4 carbine vertical by the pistol grip. He slid into place beside the hunched-over Encizo and reached down to curl his fingers around the edge of the fence at the bottom near the ground. He waited for the first snick of the wire being cut, then began to peel the loose edge upward.

Working with smooth economy, Encizo cut a 4-foot-high line in the chain-link fence while Schwarz continued peeling back the lower edge. Holding up one end of the fence, Schwarz reached down and slapped Encizo on the back.

Immediately the little Cuban replaced his wire cutters, took up his carbine and slid through the rend cut into the fence. Pushing himself through the loose thorns and paper trash, Encizo shifted down the inside of the fence line about two yards to where the edge of one building ended, and took up a defensive overwatch position flat on his stomach.

Schwarz turned and nodded and Lyons was through the fence in a flash, like a middle linebacker running a Hail Mary pattern. He put his back to the wall next to Encizo and kept his muzzle pointed in the opposite direction from the Phoenix Force shooter.

Manning looked toward the partially blocked gun tower, then got up and rushed over to Schwarz's position before sliding through the hole in the fence, as well. Once the big Canadian was through and into position, Schwarz turned and unhooked the aluminum alloy grapnel from the top of the fence and repositioned it through the wire at the bottom. He followed Manning through the hole, then carefully pulled the bent section of chain-link fence back into place. He turned back toward Manning and gave the dark-clad commando a thumbs-up.

Manning nodded. "Let's roll," he whispered.

# CHAPTER FOURTEEN

The hospital stood like a medieval fortress on the hillside with the waters of the Mediterranean behind it in backdrop. James surveyed it from the top of the parking structure next door while at the same time carefully monitoring his back trail to ensure he hadn't been followed. Five stories below him, in the narrow access alley between the garage and the hospital, two police cars were parked nose to nose, their lights off but engines running idle under the lackluster gaze of a bored officer in an immaculate uniform who stood between them with what appeared to be a cup of coffee clutched in his hands.

James looked up. The hospital rose two stories above the structure of the parking garage and the roof was dotted with HVAC units, exposed air ducts, satellite dishes and a forest of skeleton tree-shaped antennas. A phalanx of display lights were clustered around a large Catholic cross, highlighting it against the dark sky behind it.

James felt his cell phone vibrate on his belt, and he

stepped back into the shadows to answer it. "Go ahead," he said.

Barbara Price's voice was tense and clipped. "I need you to abort. Get out of the area and proceed to the secondary safe house. There's been a compromise." From the background noise it was obvious she was talking into a speakerphone.

"Have I been IDed?" James asked. He took a half step backward and surveyed his surroundings.

The roof of the parking structure was open to the air and dotted with cars, mostly two-door economy sedan models. The yellow lines delineating parking spots were bright against concrete as clean and white as a fish belly. Across the way, a ramp descended downward into the gloom of the building on the next level. Like trees with single branches, streetlamps rose out of the waist-high concrete wall encapsulating the roof, casing gleaming puddles of fluorescent light that reflected off the clean concrete.

Nobody moved and all the cars were dark and silent. From beneath him he heard a car engine as someone drove around. His pistol was a comforting weight in the small of his back.

"Yes, you have," Price replied. "You are no longer just under suspicion. Elements in French intelligence have correctly identified you as a paramilitary operative. They are going to react accordingly. We have to get you out of country, Cal. It's not the police after you now. It's heavy hitters determined to send a back-channel message to the U.S. government."

"What about T.J.?" he asked.

"We know he's been moved from your current location. We don't know where he is, but he's not at the hospital anymore. Things have gotten too hot. No more arguments, Cal," she said. "You have to return."

James began walking, frustration and paranoia dumping adrenaline into his system. "There has to be a lead, Barb. I don't want to have the same argument with you."

James rounded a line of cars and approached the automobile he'd appropriated for his mission. He thought briefly of taking a different one but decided to keep this one long enough to get away and into the city. He waited as Price paused.

Instead he heard Hal Brognola speak up. The big Fed's voice sounded tired and resigned. Like an exhausted parent who'd decided it wasn't worth it to keep fighting with a willful child. Beneath that, like the subtlest of seasonings in an otherwise bland dish, was a hint of grudging respect.

"I and Barb have done everything we can to convince you to save yourself, Cal. But that's what it is at this point—you saving yourself. The operation was exposed. If this was about Stony Man security I'd send Buck Greene and a team of blacksuits to bring you back. But it's not about that anymore. T.J. has been identified as an operative. You get to the safe house and get on a better encryption system than your field model and I'll give you what I have."

"I'll be in touch," James answered, and hung up.

HE WAS PULLING OUT of the parking garage when the first team came for him.

A jet-black Mercedes shot out from the street and pulled up broadside just as James put the nose of his car into the turn lane, trapping him inside. The windows on the Mercedes were blacked out and reflective, making it impossible to see inside.

James didn't hesitate. He smoothly shifted into Reverse, twisted hard in his seat to look out the rear windshield and floored the gas pedal. A tall dark-haired man with a face like a skeleton suddenly materialized in the passenger window of James's automobile, emerging from between two parked cars. A 9 mm pistol with the oblong shape of a silencer attachment appeared in hands so thin they seemed fleshless.

The man lifted his pistol, his eyes black and face an expressionless mask. James snarled as he jerked the wheel instinctively. Immediate Action Drills were a series of movements practiced by soldiers in response to common battlefield happenings. A core, foundational principle was that to break its lethal energy, an ambush was *charged*.

Instead of whipping the front of his car away from the pistol muzzle, James instinctively swerved into the attacker as he hit the accelerator. His vehicle engine roared as he floored the gas pedal and put the front tires on a wide, comma-shaped track.

Surprise appeared like a sunrise on the skeletal man's face and he jumped back, pulling his shot wide. He tripped and rolled across the hood of a dull green Chrysler with Swiss plates. From the opening of the garage, the rear window of the Mercedes powered down and the muzzle of an H&K MP-5 SD-3 submachine gun appeared. Keeping his foot pegged to the floor of his car, James threw himself down across the seat.

He couldn't hear the muted chugs of the submachine

gun over the racing of his engine, but hard chips of plasti-glass rained down over his head and shoulders as the Parabellum rounds shattered his windshield. He pulled his own pistol free and snapped his head up long enough to guide the wildly reversing French automobile around the barricade of two parked cars and toward the ramp rising toward the second level.

The fleshless, pedestrian assassin completed his roll across the hood of the Chrysler and landed on his feet. He seemed to pirouette, as graceful as a dancer, and flung himself belly-down across the hood of the car. The pistol was up and steady in both hands. It coughed, and he smothered the recoil with a strong grip as smoking shell casings were ejected.

James's left headlight exploded; a streak mark of scrapped paint appeared on his engine hood. The rear-view mirror exploded off its moorings and fell to the glass-covered dash. The Mercedes's tires spun and screeched as the kill-car driver brought it around and into pursuit.

Lead slugs buzzed past his head like steel-jacketed hornets and smacked into the backrest of his seats, tossing stuffing fibers like guts. He cut the wheel hard, playing out the corner on screaming wheels and a tilted suspension. The maneuver left his flank exposed as he motored past the ramp turn.

Instantly dimples appeared in a herringbone pattern across the door and his driver's-door window shattered, spraying him with glass like razor confetti. The subsonic pistol rounds failed to penetrate the car frame despite the heavy fusillade and he was able to cut around the corner and out of sight.

James's hands were slick with sweat on the steering wheel, and his heart was pounding in his throat. His eyes dilated like the lens of a camera, bringing things into vivid relief and sharp focus. His breathing increased as he flooded his bloodstream with energy-giving oxygen and cold shots of adrenaline squirted through his system and splashed into his stomach like raw liquor.

His lips curled back from his face in a naked snarl, and he brought up the pistol in his hand. The hospital parking garage was a long rectangle with the ramps between levels rising up from the exact center of the structure. James guided his car around the ramp riser in a loose diamond pattern, cutting sharply back then whipping a bootlegger maneuver until the nose of his car was pointed away from the pursuing gunmen.

His rear bumper kissed the side of a red Honda Accord, denting the main panel on the driver's door. "Sorry," James muttered as he shifted smoothly out of Reverse. "My bad." He shot forward, leaving twin skid marks like a massive equal sign on the scrubbed, bone-white concrete. The Mercedes powered around the corner, its own tires squealing like angry pigs.

As James surged forward he snapped off two quick, exploratory shots that blew out the window on his passenger door. One shot flew wide and gouged concrete in the wall next to a large blue number 1 painted next to the first ramp. The second skipped off the Mercedes's windshield like a rock off a flat lake, and he knew instantly that the black car was a diplomatic model with upgraded performance and defensive augmentation.

His car fishtailed slightly as he gunned it, and the rear windshield exploded as the submachine gunner in the rear tore off a tight burst. He shot around the far corner of the ramp housing, cut to the right and saw a pair of headlights suddenly flare out of the lane between parked cars.

Instinctively he raised the pistol, but prudence held his fire until he was certain the car was an opponent. In the sharp light of the overhead fluorescent bulbs he saw a heavyset, middle-aged man in a leather slouch hat gape at him, his jaw dropping open. James caught a vision of a pinwheel of sparks as the man's lit cigarette tumbled down his shirtfront. Then he was past and running for the front corner of the ramp housing.

His hand found the emergency brake set between the front seat, and he worked it as he power-slid around the final corner, bringing him 360 degrees back to the garage entrance. He saw the skeletal man in the dark trench coat standing ready with his pistol and they both lifted their weapons simultaneously. The man was snarling like a dog as he sighted down his barrel on James.

James saw the starfish pattern of the man's muzzle-flash even as his own unbaffled weapon barked. The handgun bucked with the recoil as he triggered three more shots and cut his car to the left, running it down the aisle and back toward the exit to the street.

He didn't have to register where the other man's bullets struck but he saw the gunner double over as if punched, and then fall away. Then James's vehicle bucked in his grip and fought to skid out of his control so that he was forced to use two hands to bring it back in line. The molded plastic of the steering wheel was slick with his sweat and his fingers threatened to slide from the grooves, forcing him to squeeze so tight his knuckles showed white with the effort.

He jerked the wheel back into obedience and stepped down on the accelerator. The echo of his screaming engine bounced back to him, filling the cab of his bullet-riddled vehicle. His eyes slid over to his driver-side mirror and he saw the black, shark shape of the Mercedes-Benz shoot out of the garage and onto his track.

His eyes cut across to the passenger-side mirror and he caught a brief glimpse of the wounded gunmen waving the Mercedes on with one hand while clutching his bloodstained stomach with the other. His face was twisted in an agonized grimace.

"I hope you fucking choke on it," James muttered.

CARL LYONS CAREFULLY surveyed the scene.

His M-4 was nestled in his hands, up and close to his body, his finger on the trigger. Adrenaline smoothly leaked into his system, feeding his reflexes, senses and capabilities like high-octane nitrous into a racing engine. He looked up and down the line of buildings. Each one had a single wooden door set in the center of the Quonset hut's rear walls under a single, naked lightbulb. Night bugs fluttered around the exposed illumination in twisting, darting clusters.

He heard the sound of footsteps coming down the narrow alley, then run to the south of the building they were backed up against. He snapped his head to the side.

From the ground Encizo held his arm up and closed his fist. This was the military hand-and-arm signal for "freeze in place." The Stony Man team became as still as statues. Lyons kept his gaze locked on the prone Encizo, the only unit member who could see the approaching threat.

The footfalls were obvious and unconcerned as they strolled between the buildings. Encizo's reconnaissance hadn't revealed regular patrols inside the compound wire; the approaching individual was a twist in their plans.

The footfalls approached the back of the building. A bit of cloud above them parted for a moment and a pale bone-colored light fell from a sliver of moon. Suddenly the shadow of the approaching figure exploded out of the gloom with distorted features and exaggerated size. Lyons saw Encizo's hand reach down and rest on the handle of the double-bladed Gerber fighting knife the Cuban kept sheathed on his waist. Reflexively, Lyons brought his left hand to the butt of his silenced 9 mm pistol.

Gravel crunched loudly under a boot sole. The clouds congealed above them again, and the stretched-out shadow of the figure disappeared. The man stepped forward into view, a Remington 870 pump shotgun hanging casually off one shoulder. He wore a yellow straw cowboy hat and a checkered shirt tucked into denim jeans. Besides the Remington, he wore a heavy-caliber revolver on his hip.

The man stepped to the edge of the building opposite the Stony Man infiltrators. He reached into a shirt pocket and produced a pack of cigarettes. He slapped one free, replaced the pack, then hunched his shoulders around a silver lighter. The infiltrators remained motionless, Encizo with his knife held half drawn. Lyons remained statue-still, his hand held carefully around the grip of his silenced pistol.

They heard the striker click and an orange reflection flared off the corrugated tin wall of the storage building. The lighter snapped out and the man released a cloud of cigarette smoke the color of milk. In a lazy fashion the man opened the fly on his blue jeans and began urinating on the wall in front of him.

The man's stream continued for an improbable length of time. The urine poured out of him and splashed off the building while he sucked in and blew out lungful after lungful of tobacco smoke without using his hands. The smoke curled up past his left ear in a long gray ribbon.

Finally the man finished, tucked himself away and then rebuttoned his pants. He took his cigarette out of his mouth and scratched his forehead under the cowboy hat with a blunt thumb. With a casual gesture the man tucked the butt of his cigarette into the corner of his mouth underneath a bristling black-haired mustache.

He shrugged the Remington 870 off his shoulder and tucked it under his arm like a man setting out for a stroll during duck-hunting season. He plucked the cigarette out of his mouth, dragged it across the wall of the building to extinguish it and dropped the butt to the ground. He ground the toe of his worn cowboy boot into the smoldering butt and then spit. Satisfied, he began to amble back down the narrow run toward the center of the compound.

Encizo let his knife ease back into its sheath. Lyons exhaled and released the butt of his silenced pistol. He turned and caught Schwarz's eye and grinned. The other Able Team member returned the smile. Schwarz shook his head slowly in bemused wonder at the close call with the oblivious sentry.

Manning looked at Encizo and held up an open hand: *Is it clear?*

Encizo gave him a thumbs-up in answer and slowly rose off his belly. He maneuvered himself into a crouching overwatch position and aimed the barrel of the M-4 down the alley.

"Go," he whispered.

Behind him the commando unit unfolded into motion. Like dark shadows they darted past Encizo and across the opening. Lyons moved all the way down the back of the next building where he dropped once again into a defensive crouch. Schwarz fell into position behind him, followed immediately by Manning. Once they were into position Encizo hurriedly joined them, taking up the rear security post.

Twelve hours earlier a shipment of crates large enough to fill the rear of two 5-ton military trucks had been unloaded by a small freighter in Puerto Lobos under the watchful eye of the municipal police and Aslargo's top three lieutenants. The plain wooden, rectangular crates had reminded Encizo suspiciously of armament rather than narcotic packing.

He'd radioed the name of the ship to Carmen Delahunt who'd, in turn, bounced it on to Stony Man where Hunt Wethers had backtracked its progression up the Caribbean from Caracas, Venezuela, after a transatlantic journey originating in Split in the former Republic of Yugoslavia. Encizo had hidden out in the desert and used a sniper scope to watch the Zetas cohort unloading the boxes into the warehouse from the far southern corner of the compound.

The Stony Man crew was going to get some questions answered before they knocked on Aslargo's front door.

## CHAPTER FIFTEEN

James cut the wheel of his car hard to the right and bounced over a concrete divider as he raced out of the parking garage. The jarring impact traveled up through the vehicle chassis to shake the steering wheel hard in his grip. He fought the speeding automobile under control again as the black Mercedes shot out of the garage's entrance.

He cut his turn so hard he heard his rear driver-side hubcap ping as it came free from its moorings and then clatter as it bounced across the asphalt street. His tires screamed in protest as he slid through a loose 90-degree arch then they clawed into the road, finding purchase and shooting forward.

Behind him the high-performance Mercedes-Benz took the corner like it was on rails.

Through his blown-out windows James heard the powerful growl of the V8 engine behind him, the mechanical roar overpowering the sound of his own much smaller engine. He caught a brilliant starfish flash out of the corner of his eye as the gunner in the backseat fired again, and he marveled at the hit team's audacity.

None of the bullets struck his car and a second later the Mercedes raced forward, overtook him and rammed him hard. His head shot forward on his neck cruelly enough to snap his teeth down on his tongue. The harsh copper-salt tang of his own blood filled his mouth, and electric jolts of pain caused him to gasp in surprise. He spit blood onto the floor.

The Mercedes surged forward and struck his car again. He gripped his steering wheel tight in both hands and tried to ride out the impact. He felt the blunt force push through him like a piston-driven wind and he spit another mouthful of blood out on the floor.

James couldn't outrun the faster car, nor could he out-ram it. He couldn't drive and shoot at the same time. His pistol had one-fifth the rate of fire as the hitter's submachine gun. They would run him down like pack dogs on a fox and rip him apart piece by gory piece, he realized.

"The hell they will," he growled to himself.

His hand found the emergency brake as he cranked the steering wheel. His car abruptly shot to the side, then snapped around almost perpendicular to the chasing Mercedes. He heard the other vehicle suddenly lock up as the enemy driver tried to anticipate his maneuver, and failed.

The nose of the Mercedes nudged the rear panel of James's car. He was standing with both feet on the brake as he snatched up his pistol. The impact slung him loose in his seat and he was thrown against the driver's door. His shoulder struck the already compromised window and knocked out the remaining glass.

The force of the Mercedes's impact rocked James's vehicle up on its frame. It tottered on the driver-side wheels for an improbably long second then crashed back down onto the road. The suspension sang out in protest and metal panels along the auto body crumpled. There was a loud bang as the rear passenger tire popped and then the stench of gasoline as furrowed metal punctured the fuel tank, dumping gallons of gas onto the ground.

James threw himself out of the vehicle and rolled across his shoulder and back onto his feet, the pistol up and in his fist. The driver's door of the Mercedes was thrown open, followed by the rear passenger door. The Phoenix Force commando dropped to one knee just past the trunk of his car as he leveled the pistol and let air escape through his clenched teeth.

A black-haired European in a stylish leather jacket and black, crew-necked sweater came out from behind the steering wheel of the Mercedes. As he reached into his jacket under his armpit, James gunned him down in a smooth, fast kill by the numbers.

The man's head jerked like a boxer taking a hook on the chin and a splash of crimson flew against the reflective window glass of the high-end car. The man's eyes showed only the whites as he sagged to the ground.

James sensed movement and tried to spin to face the second threat. The submachine gunner, impossibly tall and well-built beneath a tan windbreaker and red soccer jersey, laid the H&K MP-5 SD-3 down on the roof and triggered a burst.

James had come up, trying to get back to the nominal safety of his disabled vehicle when he felt twin hammer blows rock into his body armor center mass. He winced in pain and his rib cage seemed to groan on impact, but he absorbed the kinetic energy and completed his leap. He rolled into a wave of gas fumes and then popped up.

He and the MP-5 gunner triggered their weapons simultaneously. James felt hot lead knife the air between the curve of his shoulder and ear, and saw his own rounds spark off the hood of the Mercedes-Benz. The submachine gunner flinched as one of the American's 9 mm rounds ricocheted close to him, and James used that blink of an eye to seal the deal.

His handgun bucked hard. The slide recoiled backward, sending a single, smoking spent casing arcing into the air. The slide snapped forward, jacking another round. Beyond the end of James's muzzle the French operative staggered backward, surprise painted on his face, his mouth making a funny *O* shape. The man's throat was a torn and bloody mess.

The submachine gun tumbled from his grip as both his hands flew to his neck. Blood spilled out over his clutching fingers in a fountain. James took a step forward, his arm out, pistol leveled. He triggered his weapon a second deliberate time. The French assassin dropped to the ground.

The now-familiar wailing of a French police siren suddenly screamed to life on the far side of the parking garage where James had seen the patrol cars parked earlier. Moving without hesitation, he jogged forward and darted around the open door of the Mercedes. He stepped over the crumpled corpse of the driver, ignoring the wide, staring and empty eyes of the man he'd killed.

He slid into the driver's seat and kicked the corpse's tangled leg out of the corner of the car door. The engine was still running, and he pulled the door closed behind him, smoothly shifted into Reverse, cranked the wheel around and shifted the vehicle into Drive.

The lights of the spinning police light bar bounced out into the street in revolving yellow flashes. James stepped on the accelerator and the Mercedes leaped forward with enough momentum to snap the rear passenger door closed with a solid bang.

James cut down a side street, took a random left then another right and came back out on the main thoroughfare. He lowered his speed, signaled a right-hand turn and drove calmly out in the opposite direction from the crime scene.

He drove into the night at a sedate pace as more police vehicles raced past and converged on the scene in his rearview mirror. The black Mercedes was a pure pleasure to drive.

GARY MANNING REACHED UP with one long arm and unscrewed the lightbulb directly above the back door to the last structure. From the other side of the buildings the team could hear the rumbling exhaust of a diesel engine as someone in the compound started up a truck.

Manning turned and threw the bulb into the choke of weeds against the chain-link fence and Hermann Schwarz knelt in front of the paint-chipped door while Encizo and Lyons pulled security on the flanks. From inside his black khaki uniform shirt, Schwarz pulled a lock-pick gun and carefully inserted the metal prongs into the door's lock housing after checking to make sure it was, in fact, secured.

He made a fist and squeezed the trigger lever against the handle. There was a muted, metallic snap as the lock mechanism was manipulated, then the bolt clicked over and he turned the doorknob sharply to the right as far as it would rotate. He removed the lock-pick gun and secured it before looking up at Manning and nodding once.

The big Canadian let the M-4 dangle muzzle down, cross body from the rifle's shoulder strap. He drew his silenced 9 mm pistol and stepped away from the building's back wall. Schwarz lifted his knee off the ground, resting in a crouch on the soles of both feet. Encizo and Lyons gathered themselves.

"Do it," Manning said.

Schwarz rose like a dancer and stepped to the side, pulling the door open and pushing himself against the wall out of the way. Manning moved forward in a quick heel-toe shuffle. He darted into the building and immediately stepped to his left.

He was inside a warehouse with an exposed skeleton of metal alloy girders. Long, skinny fluorescent lights in banks of three burned overhead and spilled harsh illumination in oblong pools. Wooden crates and 55-gallon industrial drums on shipping pallets were lined against the north and south walls and down the middle run of the building. A small electric forklift sat in a corner at the front, plugged into a wall outlet by a long orange extension cord. The front door of the storage building was a single framework wide enough for a truck to back through, and set into a track of overhead rollers. It was closed.

Manning put his back against the inside wall and scanned his vectors with the silenced handgun. Right behind him Encizo entered the room, his own weapon up. The Phoenix Force commando mirrored Manning's choreography, stepping inside and to the right. He had barely set himself into position when Lyons entered.

The Able Team leader rushed forward, snapping his weapon back and forth across a precise ellipse as he pushed forward deeper into the building. He cleared out to the middle of the room and then went to one knee. Schwarz folded himself around the doorjamb and pulled the door closed behind him. He dropped to one knee beside the egress point and monitored the outside through a crack, his M-4 ready.

"In," he said.

"Clear," Lyons said from the middle of the building.

"Clear," Encizo echoed.

"Clear here," Manning said. "Let's do this, Rafe."

Immediately the Cuban holstered his silenced pistol and pulled his knife from its belt sheath. The claustrophobic structure smelled of sawdust and oil and body odor.

Encizo eyeballed the crates and boxes of various sizes, looking for the ones he'd seen off-loaded at the docks. He moved forward to a 5-foot-high stack set directly in front of Lyons's security position toward the front of the warehouse.

He slid the tip of his blade into the jamb of a crate and prized the lid off. The metal spikes released from the soft pinewood with a dull screech. Encizo quickly circumnavigated the box, popping it open with efficient thrusts and pushes of his blade. When he was finished he put the Gerber fighting knife away and pulled the lid free of the crate. He looked down and whistled softly.

"What about you, bro?" he asked Lyons. "You ever see a storage setup like this?"

Curious, Lyons rose up, pistol still held ready, and walked over to look into the box. His brow furrowed in consternation. He slowly shook his head. "No," he replied. "Mortar round. Obviously, but only five to a crate? And what's up with the warhead? And that plastic casing?"

Manning moved forward to look. He saw an 80 mm mortar round in a plastic sheath set in gray, cut-sponge packing material next to four identical munitions. The rounds were dark gray with a single black stripe just below the warhead. Below the stripe each was stamped with an identical serial number: BZ-EA-2277. The more traditional cone-shaped warhead found on mortar rounds had been replaced by a mushroom form, giving the munitions a bulging, slightly phallic appearance.

"Chemical or biological rounds?" he muttered. "Put one in your rucksack," he told Encizo. "We'll need Kissinger at Stony Man to tell us what we've got."

"We've got a fucking mess," Lyons almost snarled. "What the hell are drug runners, working for the Mexican intelligence service, doing with NBC-capable mortar rounds? They had a forward operating base in New Orleans for Christ's sake."

Manning nodded. He turned toward the rear of the building where Schwarz had taken up a security position by the exit. "Gadgets," he said softly. "What's your call on this? Can we blow them in place without spreading the shit in a cloud all up and down the east Mexican coast?"

"High explosives will do just that. What we need is a thermobaric charge. We get a quick hot ignition, preferably shaped for an implosion, then the stuff will instantly cook to an inert format."

Manning nodded. "We pack our Semtex in an earmuff configuration and call on the *Sea Witch?*"

"It would work on this bunker," Schwarz said. "But without the earmuff configuration the crap could spread on rocket impact."

"What if there were no real explosion?" Manning countered. "Just heat."

"It'd cook up into tar and we'd be good," Schwarz answered.

"Time we need for that, I wouldn't try it surreptitiously," Lyons said. "We get our cover blown with even one warehouse bunker left unchecked and we'd be screwed."

Encizo nodded. "Ironman's right," he said. "We didn't roll planning for this contingency."

"Adapt, improvise, overcome," Manning replied.

"Take down the compound then burn the lot?" Encizo asked.

Manning nodded. "Seems the only way."

"Oh, *now* we're talking." Lyons grinned.

ENCIZO AND SCHWARZ WORKED in tandem to place the Semtex shaped charges while Lyons covered the front of the bunker and Manning secured the rear entrance. Outside, a westerly breeze breathed in, stirring the weeds and trash and bringing the smell of the ocean to Manning through the crack in the door.

His earjack quietly purred. He lifted a thick finger and

settled the device. His other hand kept his trigger finger in place. "This is Field Element, go ahead," he murmured.

"There's been a problem," Barbara Price said.

"Copy, problem," Manning replied.

"We just got word that command elements of your target could be alerted to action against them."

"In the specific?" Manning demanded. Reflexively his finger tightened around the trigger of his M-4.

"We don't think so. We only know that a warning was passed that their operations are under scrutiny and to tighten security," she said, referring to the call Hal Brognola had received from the French agent, Henri. "We got the warning order on this just minutes ago, so if you witness a change in posture it is possible an alert went out."

"Copy," Manning said.

"Stony out." Price clicked off.

Manning turned and looked back into the warehouse, making sure each man had understood the transmission. Schwarz slid a pencil-shaped timing rod into his carefully crafted shaped charge. He looked over and gave Manning a thumbs-up and nodded. Encizo shifted down the line of biohazard mortars and nodded once, as well.

Lyons flashed him an okay sign from the front of the warehouse. Everything was rolling forward on a smooth track. No problem yet, Manning decided.

Then he heard the approaching helicopter through the opening in the door.

# CHAPTER SIXTEEN

Mack Bolan's cell phone rang.

He frowned and looked at the caller ID. He didn't immediately recognize the number. His eyes went to the motel-room bed where he'd laid out his sniper rifle on a cloth, then his gaze flicked to the room door and the window with the heavy curtains pulled across tight. He wondered if he'd been compromised.

He clicked the release button on the side of the little black cell phone and it unfolded like a spring-loaded stiletto.

"Who's this?" he demanded.

"It's Cal."

Bolan grunted in surprise. "How are things going?"

"Not well," James admitted. "It's why I'm calling."

Bolan looked down at the 4x power sniper scope he was adjusting after travel and frowned. "I'm kind of in the middle of something—how can I help?"

"I need you to intervene with the head shed," James said.

Surprised, Bolan leaned forward in his chair and set

the sniper scope down. He was concerned and curious why a member of Phoenix Force would be calling him to ask for help with Barbara Price and Hal Brognola. It wasn't as if David McCarter had ever had any reticence about speaking his mind to Stony Man control elements.

"Cal, what's going on?"

Quickly, James filled him in. He told him about the Marseilles operation going bad and the crash of the stretch Hummer. How he'd stayed behind with Hawkins while the others had extracted. How Stony Man had managed to extract him through open channels using Manning's company as a stalking horse to purchase a French lawyer. How the French government had figured out that it had been a U.S. black-ops unit responsible for the kidnapping and how they'd decided to deal with the perceived umbrage. He explained how the President had decided that for the sake of normalized relations Hawkins would have to be expendable and how both Brognola and Price had been powerless in the face of a direct presidential mandate to mobilize Stony Man resources—especially since the Stony units were undermanned and unraveling a plot to strike the U.S. homeland.

He also explained that he wasn't leaving Hawkins behind. No matter what.

"I need a lead," James finished. "Hal gave me the runaround. French security moved T.J. and we're no longer trying to figure out where he is. The hit team that came after me was stripped clean. I've got no clues, no bread crumbs to follow."

Bolan sighed. Every man who had signed up for the Stony Man project, including himself, had understood that it could come to this. Everyone had gone into the offered deal with their eyes wide-open. Every man on Phoenix Force and Able Team had agreed, and now that the deal had gone down, that the worst-case scenario had finally occurred, after too many operations to count, James didn't want to play by the rules anymore.

Bolan frowned. He wasn't much on rules himself.

"You'll be at this number?" he asked.

"Yeah. I'm holed up for now. I've got transportation, some light armament, some ID packages and a bundle of cash." There was a pause. Then, "And cable. I've got cable TV."

Bolan smiled. "I'll see what I can do. I'll try some pillow talk, but I don't know where that will get me. After I try the lady I'll call the Man from Justice. I'll call you in an hour."

"Great!" The relief was as obvious as a sunrise in James's voice. He paused and when he spoke again his voice was under control. "I'd appreciate anything you can do," he finished.

"I'll do what I can," Bolan said. "One hour."

The line went dead.

HAL BROGNOLA WALKED into the kitchen of Stony Man Farm. He saw Barbara Price standing next to a pot of coffee, a steaming mug held in her hand. She lifted her eyebrows in surprise at his presence there at such a late hour.

"Aaron make that coffee?" he asked, his voice wary.

Price shook her head. "No, I did, just about fifteen minutes ago. You want a cup?"

"I'll get it," he said. He went to the cupboard and pulled out a big mug. It read Happiness Is A Loaded Gun. He held it up and frowned. "McCarter's?"

"Carl's," Price answered.

"Should have guessed." Brognola poured himself some coffee.

"What's going on?" Price asked. "I just came over from the Annex for a few minutes to grab something to eat. The team is on-site in Mexico right now. We gave them the heads-up about possible compromise, but everything was unfolding smoothly so I decided not to suffer Aaron's coffee anymore. I'm about to head back to continue monitoring the mission. You here for that?"

"Yeah, let's go downstairs to the War Room instead." Brognola nodded. "I also just got word about our debriefing of al-Shalaan."

"He crack?"

"Wasn't hard at all. They kept him up for twenty-four hours in a chilly room, then offered him a way out of his mess and into a Witness Protection Program. He gave up what he knew."

Price set her coffee cup down. "That's great news. What's the story?"

"He only knew enough to give us a piece of the puzzle," Brognola responded. "He passed two polygraphs, so we think this is as good as it gets. The Saudi contact is named Mohammed al-Rhabin and he is, as we suspected, one of the eight hundred or so members of the royal family. The real shocker, though it's neither here nor there in terms of the plot, is that al-Shalaan is one of his sixteen sons. Al-Rhabin came under the influence of a known Wahhabite cleric while studying in Yemen two decades ago. He's used his money and influence to make contact with a corrupt Mexican intelligence official assigned to the consulate in Riyadh."

"He didn't give us a name?"

"He passed the poly saying it was all done through blind drops in Mexico City and in Dubai. He also believes there is somehow a French connection in this—but he didn't give us anything specific."

"Maybe the boys will pull a specific link out of the mess in Puerto Lobos," Price offered.

"They've done more with less before," Brognola admitted.

They started out of the kitchen, headed downstairs to the War Room. Both of them studiously avoided mentioning the situation in France. They had talked and argued and brainstormed until that horse had been beaten to death.

Price flipped open her cell phone. "Any updates?" she asked after contacting Hunt Wethers.

"Negative, Barb," Wethers said from the Computer Room. "We're keeping chatter down with the ground element until they finish prepping their charges. So far the *Sea Witch* hasn't picked up anything from Aslargo's cellular network."

"Understood. Hal and I'll be in the War Room, so go ahead and send our feed over there."

Wethers paused. "Couldn't stand Aaron's coffee anymore?"

"It's that sharply analytical mind that keeps you in work around here, Hunt," Price answered.

Wethers laughed. "I'm patching the feed through now."

"Price out."

The elevator doors slid open on the basement and Price and Brognola strolled down the hallway toward the War Room. Just as they reached the security door, Brognola's cell phone vibrated on his belt.

The Man from Justice looked down and then pulled the phone free. He read the number on the caller ID and frowned. He looked up at Price and gave a slight shrug. "I have to take this," he said.

She nodded, keyed in the code and entered the room, leaving him alone. He turned his back to the door and began walking back up the way he had come. A few paces down, he opened the phone and answered the call.

"What can I do for you, Striker?" he asked.

*France*

James tried to keep himself busy.

He used his nervous energy to prep himself for his next action. He showered, changed clothes and cleaned his pistol. He counted his stash of euros and prepped his identification paperwork. When that was done, he worked out.

First he warmed up by doing fifteen pull-ups using the doorjamb as a chinning bar. Then he alternated fifty rep sets of push-ups with fifty rep sets of sit-ups until he'd done two hundred each. Finally he did five hundred straight Hindu-style bodyweight squats over the course of fifteen minutes. To strengthen his grip, he took a copy of the metropolitan newspaper and crumpled a sheet up in his fist, then he added a second sheet to the ball and squeezed that into a compact ball. He continued doing that until he'd formed a wad of newspaper into a softball-size lump. The veins of his hands were pumped and full and his fingers ached slightly from exertion. Then he repeated the process using the second half of the paper with his other hand.

He forced himself not to look at the clock. Finally, almost in desperation, he turned on the television set and watched reruns of American prime-time shows dubbed into French.

When his phone finally rang, he shot a glance at the clock, noted the time then picked up the cell phone and answered it.

"I'm here," he said.

When he heard Mack Bolan on the other end of the line his heart leaped in hope for the missing Hawkins. As Bolan gave him the rundown, he felt a big smile begin to slide in place.

GARY MANNING WATCHED the helicopter coming in from the west, a searchlight slung under its belly like a cyclopean eye. The searchlight spun and rotated as the helicopter approached, the light playing across the desert floor like the gaze of a hungry predator. His mind went instantly to their vehicle parked at the bottom of the cliff. The camouflage netting was only a superficial precaution, and he didn't think it would hold up to scrutiny.

"Heads up, boys," he said. "Barb warned we could be compromised, and we got a chopper running down our alley from the west right now. Let's get this show started."

The men, grim-faced, continued their work. Manning turned his face back to the crack in the door and kept a watchful eye on the approaching helicopter. He keyed his earjack and spoke softly into the microphone.

"Ground Element to *Sea Witch*."

"*Sea Witch,* go ahead," Carmen Delahunt answered.

"You got no chatter of a compromise, correct?" Manning asked.

"Roger. Nothing on my end," Delahunt confirmed.

"I've got an inbound helicopter at the moment. I'm requesting you have the blacksuits ready the multiple launch rocket system in case this goes south."

There was a pause while Delahunt took this information in. "This was our Zulu option, Ground Element," she finally said, concern evident in her voice. "Are we at Zulu?"

"Negative," Manning said. "But with this shift in the wind I want to be ready to roll."

"Copy, Ground Element," Delahunt said. "We'll get it up."

"Ground out." Manning signed off.

He turned and noted the progress the unit was making then put his focus back on the approaching helicopter. He saw it start to fan out away from its linear approach and begin to track back and forth across the desert in a zigzag pattern. He didn't like what he was seeing at all.

OUT ON THE OCEAN in the *Sea Witch,* Carmen Delahunt put her blacksuit security team into motion. The four men, all of them special-operations veterans, sprang into action. Three of them moved forward and removed the front cargo hatch cover while the fourth directed the hydraulics control from the flying deck of the yacht.

An M-270 Multiple Launch Rocket System lifted smoothly from the hold and rose up to lock into position. The system was capable of launching twelve munition rockets in less than sixty seconds. The MLRS unit had been removed from its vehicle mount and placed on the cargo elevator at a secure naval docking location on the island of Puerto Rico as part of the U.S. navy's "gray fleet" command designed to support clandestine and covert maritime operations in the international war on terror.

The rocket system itself had ceased production in 2003, but luckily an astute and "outside-the-box" thinker in the Naval Special Warfare Command had realized the potential of the surplus systems and written a brief suggesting alternative uses for the systems.

The blacksuit fire team finished prepping the system for launch, then gave the high sign to the officer in charge on the bridge who, in turn, notified Delahunt that they were ready for action on her command.

Delahunt acknowledged the information and went back to monitoring her electronic and digital surveillance systems. Neither Aslargo nor his lieutenants had used their cell phones to contact the helicopter Manning had reported over his area of operations, which troubled the former FBI agent.

She reached over and pushed the arrow on the faceplate deck of an abstract tree—AST—multichannel digital receiving system, generating a sweep of independent digital receivers capable of switching between various cell-phone modes as required. To avoid silhouetting the yacht on the ocean, she had the window shutters drawn tight in the main cabin. Her face glowed an eerie green in the reflected light of her sensor arrays.

Immediately the mode-switching option paid dividends. A brusque male voice was speaking in rapid-fire

Spanish, interrupted occasionally by a feminine reply. Though she did not speak Spanish, Delahunt recognized the voices of one of Aslargo's lieutenants and that of his mistress, a Puerto Lobos woman named Bonita.

Instantly the language was passed in text format to the CPU next to the AST. The translation software began to burn through its binary options and an English transcription of the conversation began to scroll down the computer screen in front of Delahunt.

     Transmission Begins
Male Voice: He wants us ready. Mexico City called. I have to be quick.
Female Voice: Will I see you tonight?
Male Voice: Yes, at the casino, but later. After we check the mesa site. I'm not supposed to be using the cell phone so I have to go.
Female Voice: I understand. Hurry, I'll keep it warm for you.
Male Voice: I'll be there. If the helicopter reports nothing, it could be sooner. Goodbye.
Female Voice: Goodbye, Paco.
     Transmission Ends

Delahunt looked away from the screen and keyed her com link. Ground Element was going to need confirmation of their suspicions. Above her on the deck she could hear the Stony Man blacksuits moving around, maintaining the sentry watch and ship operations.

"Ground Element." Manning's voice was terse.

Delahunt swiveled in her chair. "I've had a confirmation," she said. "They're looking for interlopers."

"Copy," Manning said. "We are taking that under advisement."

"*Sea Witch* out."

Delahunt switched her channel selector. "You pick that last transmission up?" she asked Stony Man Base.

"We've got everything on-screen here," Price answered.

"You want to change anything now?"

Price didn't hesitate, and it was obvious to Delahunt that the Stony Man mission controller had come to her decision as soon as the translation had flashed across her screen in the Computer Room, where she was currently monitoring the situation.

"Copy that, *Sea Witch*," Price said. "Go ahead and get under way. Cruise into coastal waters and launch the Raven."

"*Sea Witch*, copy."

"Stony Base out."

Delahunt reached over and hit the intercom button next to her seat. Instantly the yacht captain, a twenty-year veteran of the U.S. Marine Corps Force Recon and small boat units, answered. "Go ahead for the bridge," he growled.

"Okay, you old jarhead," Delahunt said. "You've got your wish for some action. Take the boat in closer and have the boys launch the Raven."

The ex-FBI agent could hear the smile in the combat veteran's voice as he answered.

"Well, yes, ma'am."

# CHAPTER SEVENTEEN

"Pick it up, guys," Manning said. "*Sea Witch* just confirmed the helicopter I've got out here is part of a security response."

"I've got movement on the outside to the front!" Lyons hissed.

In the next moment the rest of the team could hear the rumble of a big diesel engine coming from outside the front of the bunker unit. Manning let the back door close and slid behind the concealment of a row of pallets. Lyons backed up to the cover of a long line of 55-gallon drums, his silenced pistol never wavering from the door. Encizo finished priming a timing pencil, then retreated, as well.

Schwarz coolly continued to prepare the last shaped charge. There was the sound of vehicle doors slamming and men calling out in Spanish. There was the loud hiss of an air brake and then of an idling engine from the other side of the bunker's front door.

Schwarz carefully placed the earmuff-configured

Semtex charge. The lock on the sliding door was popped open and the metallic snap of the release echoed through the inside of the bunker. Schwarz primed the timing pencil. The door began to rumble as it slid along its track runner, and the sound of the idling truck engine grew louder as the entrance opened.

The shadowed form of a stocky man in a cowboy hat with the familiar Remington 870 shotgun over one shoulder was silhouetted in the opening. The guard began to push the heavy metal door to one side. The parking brakes on the passenger side of the vehicle appeared, glowing red.

Schwarz somersaulted backward over his shoulder behind a stack of crates and froze in the shadow. His eyes darted around, seeking the other members of his team. He couldn't find Encizo or Manning from his location, but he could see Lyons behind an oil drum. The big ex-cop's silenced 9 mm pistol was up and ready as the Mexican drug soldier finished pushing the door open.

"Hurry up," the man snapped in Spanish.

Schwarz heard the truck driver respond and then the grinding of gears. The old U.S. army two-and-a-half truck began to back into the storage building, its rear gate already down and its cargo area covered by an olive-drab canvas tarp. The cowboy with the pump shotgun walked backward, guiding the driver who watched his hand-and-arm signals in the big sideview mirror on his door.

Three feet from the boxes of mortar rounds the Stony Man unit had just finished priming for detonation, the cowboy halted the truck by closing his fist. The air brakes on the truck hissed again. The driver swung open his door and dropped down inside the Quonset hut bunker. He wore a checkered flannel shirt like the first man and dirty blue jeans tucked into brown Cochran leatherwork boots. He wore a pro-backed Texas Longhorns college baseball hat, and his square face was framed by a close-trimmed beard. A S&W Model 696 .44-caliber 5-shot revolver rode in a black nylon holster on his hip.

From the passenger seat of the truck cab a third man opened the door and hopped out. A cigarette was tucked haphazardly into the corner of his mouth, the end gleaming red, the gray smoke almost invisible in the dim light.

He wore a blue chambray work shirt and had pulled his long black hair back in a tight ponytail. In the low light Schwarz could see the gleam of his gold teeth. The outline of a hard pack of cigarettes was readily evident in the chest pocket of his shirt, and the butt of a pistol was tucked into the front of his jeans. A large clasp knife rode in a leather sheath on his belt.

Schwarz blinked, and when he opened his eyes again, Rafael Encizo had appeared like a ghost over the man's shoulder. Schwarz narrowed his eyes, tense as Encizo's hand suddenly appeared from behind Gold Teeth's back and covered his mouth, smothering any cry and knocking the cigarette loose. Schwarz saw the man's eyes suddenly grow wide in surprise, then his features twisted into pain as Encizo drove home the point of his fighting knife into the man's kidney. Suddenly the bloody blade appeared and carved a second smile in the taut muscles of the man's neck.

Blood gushed from the long, clean laceration and spilled down the front of the Zetas drug runner's shirt.

It stained the shirt dark as the man's knees buckled and he fell forward. The spilling blood splashed down and extinguished the smoldering cigarette with an almost audible hiss. Encizo carefully eased the man to the concrete floor, and the body hung as limp as a rag doll in the man's grip.

The truck driver began to walk the length of his vehicle. Behind him the muzzle of Lyons's pistol tracked his every step. At the rear of the truck Schwarz caught a flash of motion out of the corner of his eye. He saw Encizo silently stalking toward the cowboy next to the demo-packed crates.

The cowboy walked up to the first crate and looked down. Schwarz kept his finger on the M-4's trigger. The Mexican drug soldier frowned and Schwarz knew he'd seen the earmuff charges. Suddenly the man's eyes went wide with understanding, and he turned to call out to the driver coming down the side of the truck.

He found Encizo standing in front of him. The cowboy opened his mouth, and his hand clawed for his shoulder-holstered weapon. Encizo pounced. His right hand sprang out, recoiled and sprang out again. He struck throat, heart and diaphragm in three quick heartbeats. He slashed first the man's upraised wrist, then stabbed his bicep on the opposite arm, smoothly crippling his ability to defend himself. Blood geysered under the flurry of his rapid multiple attacks. The man tried to call out but found his larynx savagely ruined. He gagged and sagged to his knees, and with two quick thrusts Encizo laid the Zetas's neck open on either side.

The man's eyes rolled up in his head and he fell over.

The truck driver saw the cowboy's outflung arm as he approached the end of the truck.

"What are you doing?" the man called out in Spanish. His hand went reflexively to the butt of the S&W Model 696 on his hip. He saw blood spilling in a dark rush across the dusty concrete floor.

Lyons quickly triggered three rounds. Two red gouges appeared in the truck driver's back just below his shoulder blades. The man gasped in shock and went to his knees. The third Parabellum round caught him in the top of the head and lifted a broken chunk of skull clear off the scalp. The man fell forward and hit the concrete with a wet, muffled slap.

Manning rushed forward, his M-4 up on his shoulder to cover the opening at the front of the bunker. Outside, the helicopter was directly overhead. A beam of sharp white light caught the hood of the truck and illuminated it before sliding off and skipping across the compound.

"We've got to take the towers out," Manning said. "Once those are down we can shoot and scoot around, mopping up."

"We could blow these charges," Lyons offered. "Then call in the rockets. As far as we know that batch of mortars was the only shipment of NBC weapons this crew has. Risky, but I think the odds bear me out."

"Let's save the call-for-fire as an ace in the hole," Manning countered. "This particular Zetas crew might have been hard-core commandos at one time but they've been living easy for too long now. If we can do this with small arms, I'd rather."

"Nothing to it, but to do it," Lyons agreed.

"Okay, then," Encizo said. "Let's roll."

*France*

JAMES LOOKED OUT THROUGH the windshield of his car at the unassuming brownstone building. Set on a tree-lined avenue in the suburbs to the east of Marseilles, the building's predominant feature was that it was unassuming. A lone light burned in a window on the fourth and top floors of the flat-roofed building.

According to the information Mack Bolan had passed on, the entire structure was a single residence owned by a man named Henri Galli. Mr. Galli was an intricate cog in the machinery of France's black-operations activities. Bolan had gone on to say that Galli was, in his own bureaucratic way, Hal Brognola's counterpart.

Fifty-three years old, a confirmed bachelor and experienced counterintelligence case officer with the National Police, Galli had used family and political connections dating back to postwar Vietnam to carve out a niche of influence in the shadier aspects of French internal and foreign affairs of state. He was most often used as a political cutout between men of power and those they could not afford to be seen communicating with.

In true French fashion he was having an affair with his twenty-four-year-old executive assistant, and James waited patiently until almost fifteen minutes to midnight for the young woman, a pretty brunette, to leave the man's building.

James watched Galli walk her out and see her safely into a taxicab, which he paid for. The French counterspy looked up and down his street before waving goodbye to his paramour and mounting the steps to his building. He closed the door, and a few minutes later the last light inside the building was turned off. The street became very quiet and James got out of his car. He slung the strap of a black nylon gym bag over his shoulder and crossed the street. He walked around to the building next to Galli's house, a two-story Queen Anne villa with a six-foot stone wall and black wrought-iron gate in front.

From his surveillance James had determined that an elderly spinster owned the house with only a single live-in maid for help. If the Aston Martin parked in the drive she used for excursions was any indication, the octogenarian came from old money and her address certainly bore out that supposition. More importantly for James, the woman owned no guard dogs and her wall butted up against Galli's property. A narrow strip of immaculate grass separated the brick wall from the rising side of Galli's four-story building, which was separated, front and back, from the street by tall, spiked iron gates.

By using the neighboring property as a staging area, he hoped to position himself inside the French spymaster's defenses for his final run at catching the man by surprise. He hoped he wouldn't have cause to give the old woman a heart attack in the process.

He was nervous about police presence in the area. This was a quiet, upscale neighborhood, and it was now well past the local residents' bedtime. He would be unable to explain his presence, and the naked truth was that his black face would not be an asset in this situation. There was no way he could afford to be hauled in by Marseilles police for a second time. He doubted even a lawyer as abrasively competent as Lejeune could get him out of that deep a hole.

He crossed the street, stepped through the line of old

oaks and onto the cobblestone sidewalk. He walked the half block to the corner of the woman's large house and turned down the side street. He hurried to the edge of her property to where a wide, clean alley designed to access the parking garages of the expensive properties along its length as well as the big vehicles used by the city sanitation department intersected the side street.

James turned down the alley, took a quick look around and then exploded into fluid action. He tossed his black gym bag over the wall and leaped after it. His hands found the lip and he hauled himself up and over, keeping low as he slid across the top of the wall and then dropped down to the other side.

He landed in a crouch on his feet on the inside of the wall, retrieved his bag and then set off, cutting across the back of the property, heading toward the border wall with Galli's building.

He reached the property line and looked up. The building rose up for three stories above the top of the wall. A fire escape began on the second story.

James, standing on the opposite side of the wall from Galli's property, reached into his bag and removed a two-pronged titanium alloy grapnel. The grappling hook was covered with hard black rubber and a knotted black hemp rope was tied with a Shepard's hitch to the eye.

James let the climbing rope play out around his feet and then ducked under the bag's strap so that it dangled from him across his torso. He played out a foot or so of line and then began quickly twirling the grappling hook. On the fourth revolution he released the sturdy tool and watched it arch up over the wall and cross the space between it and the building.

The clatter as it landed was muffled by the rubber sheath and he pulled back on the rope, seating the prongs tightly between two struts on the fire escape. Once that was in place he tied off his end of the rope to an elm tree in the lawn until he had formed a diagonal bridge leading across the wall and up to Galli's house.

He leaped up and caught the knotted hemp fiber rope with both hands. It sagged under his weight, but his knots held and he lifted his feet up and hooked them around the line. Quickly he began his angled ascent, scrambling hand over hand up the rope.

In a minute he had reached the lowest platform of the fire escape and he scrambled over the edge of the safety railing, landing lightly. A second-story double window faced out onto the fire escape. Heavy folds of curtain obscured his view of the building's interior. He turned and unhooked his grapnel before tossing it back across the wall into the neighboring property.

He turned around and reached for the sharply angled stairs leading upward. He sensed more than saw movement out of the corner of his eye and instinctively turned around once more, looking toward the source of the stimulus. The curtains covering the second-story window rustled as someone parted them.

Henri Galli's face appeared in the window.

ON THE *SEA WITCH* the blacksuits scurried in a well-practiced drill to complete their operational task. Once the boat was within range of the coast, the three crew members opened the rear cargo hatch and quickly began to assemble the Raven.

The RQ-11B Raven was an MUAV, or remote-controlled miniature unmanned aerial vehicle used by the U.S. military. The craft was launched by hand and powered by a small electric motor. The Raven was a compact unit with a wing span of fifty-one inches on a body frame eight inches shorter, at a weight of only a fraction over four pounds. The UAV had a flight range of roughly six-and-a-half miles, while ranging up to altitudes of one thousand feet at flying speeds between 28 to 60 miles per hour.

The Raven could be either remotely controlled from the ground station or flown on completely autonomous missions using GPS "waypoint" navigation. The Raven outfitted for the Water Witch Six ground support mission had a standard mission payload, including image sensor color video feed and an infrared night-vision camera. Images from the drone would be relayed back in real time to the communications transmitter onboard the yacht and then bounced via satellite to the Farm.

The yacht's coxswain hit the intercom button. "You've got a bird in the air."

"Copy, thanks," Delahunt said. She touched her earjack. "We're up and running."

"Copy," Price answered. "We've got images feeding in now."

"Copy," Manning whispered. "We'll be sure to put on a good show for you."

GARY MANNING LOOKED OUT the open door to the storage unit from behind the cover of the truck. He tried to ascertain the positions of the rest of the compound personnel, but his angle restricted his view.

Overhead the helicopter had begun moving out from

the center of the compound in growing circles, its searchlight sweeping across the ground. Through the open door the team could hear rough male voices talking back and forth to each other and they knew they could not hope to delay for very long.

"There's no way around it," Manning said. "We're too close to complete compromise. But we can't roll out of here without securing the NBC threat. Not with the Zetas having tried to set up a forward operating base in New Orleans. We've got to check each one of these warehouses for duplicates of those mortars before we can risk calling in the rockets."

"Plan?" Lyons asked.

"You and Rafe enter the warehouses. He knows the most about the packaging. Gadgets and I provide overwatch on the compound for your entries. We'll try to take out the towers and hold off the guards." He frowned and looked up, clearly troubled. "And the helicopter. Once we've secured the storage units, we can detonate the thermobaric charges and call in Carmen's rocket barrage."

"What if there's a whole bunch more of them?" Encizo asked.

Manning pointed out the open door. "Fuel depot. We cover 'em with gas and diesel so that when the HE rounds hit we get a burn factor."

Schwarz nodded vigorously, his face deadpan. "Good. I like it. Completely ad hoc and seat-of-the-pants. This is most definitely how we roll."

Manning smiled and held up one massive fist. Schwarz returned the grin and reached out to tap knuckles with the big Canadian.

"If you two are through flirting," Lyons interrupted, "I think we've got some people to kill."

Moving quickly, the team prepped for their departure. They knew the lack of activity on the part of the now-dead truck crew would attract attention, and someone would come to investigate. Working together while Manning used his M-4 carbine to provide overwatch, the other three muscled the bodies of the dead Zetas drug soldiers into the back of their truck. Then they rigged the front doors of the vehicles with antipersonnel grenades.

Once that was finished the team quickly cut back through the storage bunker toward the back door where they had made their entrance. Manning checked out through the crack in the door, saw no one and pushed through. He flipped around the door and dropped to one knee, weapon up and pointed down the narrow, weed-choked run formed by the back of the storage units and chain-link fence.

Behind him the Stony Man fire team surged out the doorway in linear procession and squatted next to the building while the back door swung closed.

Manning frowned; the helicopter was growing louder but the building shielded it from his view. If the pilot lifted the chopper straight up for elevation, the entire compound would be spread out below him like a chessboard and the infiltrators would have no place to hide.

Manning risked a look around the corner of the building and down the alley toward the center of the compound. He saw several men armed with Remington 870 shotguns rushing past the opening on the far end. Light stabbed at his eye and he looked above them to see the helicopter sweep in from the west and start a run directly toward his position.

Manning spun and caught Schwarz's attention.

"We're done for. Blow it!" he snarled.

# CHAPTER EIGHTEEN

*France*

James did not hesitate.

He rushed forward like a fullback off the line and struck the window. There was a crash and shards of broken glass scattered like razor-sharp raindrops. His dense, muscular frame exploded through the barrier and smashed into Galli.

The man squawked in fear and surprise and fell back. The two men struck the ground with James on top like a rodeo rider. He felt the smaller man's breath rush from him as they landed. There was the sharp crack of a pistol shot and a flash of light burst through the gloom in an accidental discharge. Still on top of him, James spun in his dominant position to address the primary threat of the man's handgun.

He saw the compact 9 mm Glock 17 in the Frenchman's right hand and he lunged. His hand closed around Galli's wrist and squeezed tightly, grinding the bones painfully. He drove a knee into the Frenchman's side to disorientate him, then smashed the hand holding the gun hard against the glass-covered floorboards.

The gun skidded across the ground like a flat stone on a smooth lake and clunked against a wall. James distracted the writhing Galli with another sharp knee to the side, then released his grip on the man's wrist with his own right hand and drove his elbow into the counterspy's temple.

The Frenchman shuddered under the impact and went limp. Instantly James spun into the mounted position high on his chest, pinning him to the floor. He fisted his own pistol and placed the muzzle against the side of Galli's head.

The man's eyes fluttered, opened then began to focus. There was a flash of fear as the man became aware of the vulnerability of his position. Then the counterspy's inner resolve forced the terror down and he blinked up at the gun-wielding James. A loose splinter of glass had opened a cut in his cheek the shape of a half-moon and blood trickled black down the side of his face.

"You are the American arrested at al-Shalaan's kidnapping," he said in English.

"That's some other black guy," James answered in French. "We all look alike."

"You have a gun pointed at my head," Galli said. He spoke French now as well.

"I wanted to talk to you."

"So talk."

"Get up."

James used his left hand to twist up the front of the

Frenchman's silk pajama shirt and hauled him to his feet. Galli came willingly enough and broken glass crackled under the soles of James's boots as the men stood.

"My window is alarmed," Galli said. "I imagine a response patrol is en route."

"No, it's not," James replied.

"I assure you I have an alarm system and that it is, indeed, turned on."

"I know you do." James shoved him forward down the hall toward a French Renaissance formal chair set underneath a gold-gilded mirror of the same period. "But your exterior breach monitors are contact switches. That's the most frequently used piece of alarm detection equipment and, interestingly, it's the easiest to circumvent. I, frankly, expected better. They're typically applied to moveable doors and windows in both homes and businesses. The contact switch consists of a switch and a magnet. You guessed it—when properly aligned, the magnet holds the switch closed. Does any of this sound familiar to you? Maybe the salesman explained it when he put them in? Maybe you skipped this lesson on Tradecraft 101?"

Galli moved to the chair and sat. His face had taken on a grayish pallor as James rattled off the technical specifications to his home alarm system. Once the Frenchman was seated, the American commando stepped back, leveling his pistol at the man's face, and continued talking.

"You'll note that window opens upward from the bottom. While the glass is shattered and a gaping hole into your house is readily apparent, Galli, the latch is still in contact with the jamb. The magnet is still connected to the current. You should have gotten pressure pads on the windowpane."

"One hardly expects a burglar to attempt to smash through the window in such a fashion," Galli replied, his voice droll. "But from an American…"

"Yep, I'm a real knuckle dragger," James said. "Plus the fire escape. I mean, I realize it's part of the original structure and everything is all 'retro-vogue' in Marseilles these days but, *please,* for a man in the intelligence game it seems a little haphazard."

"Please, I'm a bureaucrat in the Foreign Office, nothing so glamorous as all that." Galli turned his head to the side, offering a patrician profile. "Besides, building codes and architectural permits don't always take security into account."

"Pity."

"Yes."

James used his free hand to remove the black bag from around his shoulder. He set it down and dropped to one knee, pistol unwavering. He unzipped the bag and reached inside. When his gloved hand reappeared, it held a hypodermic needle.

"Time," James said, and his voice was cold, "is of the essence. I'm sure you're well-versed in counterinterrogation methods. Because of that I have no intention of being subtle. Inside this syringe is pure grain alcohol. Injected intravenously it will produce profound inebriation in under a minute. Your body will not be able to throw this up because it will have bypassed the digestive system."

"The KGB method," Galli acknowledged.

"Just so, Henri," James admitted. "It's a blunt instrument to be sure, but effective. Now, shall I sit on your lap, jam my pistol into your mouth and inject your carotid artery in the neck, or will you be so kind as to inject this yourself?"

Galli was silent for a long minute. Finally he said, "As you wish."

James reached out to hand him the needle. "I will shoot you to get what I want. I'll start with the kneecaps, so don't play coy with me."

"This is insane!" Galli suddenly yelled. "How does your government think it can get away with this?"

James looked him squarely in the eyes. "It doesn't, friend. I'm so far off the reservation I can't even see home from where I'm standing. That makes me a terrifying prospect for you, understand?"

"What is it you want to know?" Galli snapped. His eyes were glued to the big hypodermic in James's left hand. "Just ask me."

"The injured man, from the al-Shalaan incident. I want to know where he is."

"If I tell you, then you'll have to kill me," Galli reasoned. "You couldn't get to him before I alerted the authorities, so you'd have to kill me. If I'm going to die, I see no reason to help you."

The Frenchman set his jaw.

James stepped forward.

MANNING THREW HIMSELF back around the corner of the building as the helicopter raced toward the fire team's position. Behind him Lyons had stepped away from the shelter of the building wall and threw the butt of his M-4 carbine to his shoulder. The sound of the helicopter rushing down on them was deafening and the craft was barely thirty feet off the deck as it approached. A detached part of Manning's mind identified the hovering platform as a OH-58D Kiowa Warrior light Reconnaissance/Attack helicopter.

Manning saw the bright, hard beam of the searchlight flicker upward from the belly and move directly toward him. He triggered a 3-round burst from his carbine and blew the light out. A hail of bullets rushed out in answer from the copilot seat, and they buzzed around the big Canadian like angry hornets.

Behind him Schwarz pulled out the digital signal detonator and bypassed the timing pencils on his shaped charges. The explosion was immediate and overwhelming. The building's back door was blown off its frame and thrown into the fence, followed instantly by a jet of flame like dragon's breath. There was a near instantaneous whump as the fuel cells on the old truck inside caught and went up. The building shuttered, and the roof ripped free of its seams.

Shock waves rolled into the men of the Stony Man fire team and staggered them. For a second the concussive force made it seem as if cotton balls had been stuffed into their ears. Screaming shrapnel from the curved roof burst forth as ammunition stores began to explode inside.

The Kiowa shuddered under the impact, then canted hard to the side as the pilot fought the sudden, stunning shock. The engine screamed in protest but it was futile. The spinning rotors of the low-flying aircraft tipped and caught the top of the building next to the Stony Man warriors' position. The ripple of the impact shivered back up through the blades and vibrated into the aircraft's body. The chopper lurched again, then listed nose-first into the storage unit.

A ball of fire lit up the dark Mexican night and burning fuel fell in a jellied, flaming rain. Manning was thrown to the ground, then picked himself up. He tucked his carbine in close and prepared to move.

"Get the towers!" he shouted over his shoulder.

"I'm on it!" Lyons shouted back, then folded around the corner of the burning building and sprinted down the narrow run between the two buildings.

A Zetas soldier came around the corner, weapon up, and Lyons shot him in the head from twenty-five yards. The man stumbled backward from the impact of the high-velocity rounds and went down, his Remington 870 shotgun tumbling out of his hands. Lyons continued on.

Behind him Encizo reached down and put a hand under Schwarz's shoulder to help the other man rise to his feet. When both of them were standing, they stumbled, found their footing and began to race forward. The pair moved past the blazing wreckage of the helicopter and Schwarz saw one of the pilots writhing in his seat restraints as he was burned alive.

The sickly sweet smell of burning flesh mixed with the toxic stench of aviation fuel and the man's piercing screams rent the air. Schwarz granted him mercy with a double tap of 5.56 mm bullets from his M-4 carbine.

At the far end of the back run, near the north fence line, two drug soldiers appeared. One wielded what seemed to be the standard-issue Remington 870 shotgun and the other, perhaps a supervisor or sergeant of some sort, carried a mini-Uzi submachine pistol.

"Sons of bitches!" the Uzi-gunner shouted in Spanish. Both groups fired their weapons.

Encizo and Schwarz went low, sweeping their rifle muzzles up and triggering bursts with simultaneous timing. The shotgun jumped and boomed in the shotgunner's hands and the mini-Uzi chattered its own response. Schwarz felt buckshot pellets rip at his clothes and heard Encizo cry out in surprised pain as some of the shotgun spread caught him, as well.

Schwarz's M-4 burst struck the Zetas gunner center mass, one of his rounds burning into the breech of the Remington and snatching it from the man's hands as four more 5.56 mm rounds burrowed into his chest and shredded his lungs.

The man with the mini-Uzi shifted his fire, but his excitement had caused him to let the recoil lift the muzzle of his weapon. Encizo hissed against the wound in his side and gunned the man down. The mini-Uzi dropped as the dead man spun and landed face-first on the still-leaking body of his partner.

Schwarz turned toward Encizo. Behind them they could hear both Manning and Lyons firing their weapons toward the center of the compound. Schwarz looked down at the growing stain of red seeping across the side of the other man's fatigue shirt.

"How bad?" Schwarz demanded.

Encizo shook his head. "I'm fine. Ironman was hurt worse by that damn jellyfish! Let's roll," he said, pushing himself up.

With weapons up they proceeded toward the fire storage unit beyond the burning wreckage of the helicopter. The flames cast behind them threw distorted shadows on the wall. Encizo went to one knee again and picked the lock on the back door while Schwarz stood guard.

Encizo finished and rose, pulling the door open. Schwarz charged through, weapon up, and peeled off to the left, followed almost immediately by Encizo. Inside the building, they began to rapidly check packing material. Outside they could hear the tower gunner's Squad Automatic Weapon open up.

MANNING DUCKED BACK around behind the corner of the building as the west and north towers pinned him under a brutal cross fire. Red tracer rounds knifed through the air in brilliant tracks of rigid illumination. Zetas drug soldiers began advancing on Manning's position under the cover fire, adding the staccato booming of their Remington 870 shotguns to the raucous din.

As intense as the situation was, the gunfire was Manning's secondary consideration. Out in the desert west of the compound, along the narrow dirt track of the access road, a convoy of headlights was rushing toward the battlefield the narco-supply depot had become.

"Cover me while I move!" Lyons roared.

Manning shifted automatically and began raking the muzzle of his M-4 back and forth in a Z-pattern, triggering 3-round bursts. Lyons fired two shots at the north tower and saw sparks arc off the metal safety rail in front of the SAW gunner. Surprised, the man stopped firing and jumped back.

Lyons charged forward, firing from the hip. As the Able Team leader sprinted toward a forklift, a gunner appeared from behind the rear of the utility vehicle, a mini-Uzi machine pistol chattering and bucking in his hands.

The Able Team leader caught the man first with his fire and drove him back into the knobby rubber tires of the industrial forklift. The man staggered, patches of pink and red blossoming like flowers on his chest.

Lyons reached the dying man and drove the butt of his weapon into the side of the gunner's head and knocked him down.

Manning put his hard sights on the north tower gunner who had recovered from his close call and was now spraying the forklift with a vengeance. Manning pulled his first shot left, but his next burst caught the man in the chest and drove him back against the sliding door of the tower housing.

The SAW gunner tumbled backward and dropped his weapon to the grating before sliding down slowly, leaving blood smeared behind him on the metal door. Manning turned and fired at a Zetas hardman who had gotten too close, driving the man back behind the cover of a random line of 55-gallon drums.

Manning did a snap check on Lyons just as the Able Team warrior popped up out of a crouch and stepped from behind the cover of the forklift. He saw the egg-shaped sphere leave the ex-LAPD detective's hand like a shot put, visually tracing its arc as it covered thirty yards and bounced off a concrete apron around a set of three fuel pumps and rolled under a black Lexus SUV parked there.

"Jesus!" Manning swore.

The big Canadian twisted away and threw himself backward from the hellfire he knew was coming. There was the hard, sharp boom of the grenade going off followed by the whump of the luxury SUV's fuel tanks erupting. The night was illuminated by a glare every bit as bright as when the helicopter had exploded.

Manning felt a wave of heat wash into him like the Santa Ana winds and in a sudden, second-long vacuum of sound he heard a man screaming in agony. Stony Man's warriors had brought flaming justice to the Mexican desert.

All of this paled with what came hard on the heels of the first explosion a heartbeat later. The high-explosive grenade shredded the hose lines to the free-standing fuel pumps and mangled the pump housing. Fuel spilled out like a river rushing over a waterfall and the torrent was instantly ignited. The flames spread quickly, and the massive reservoirs under the fueling station were ignited. The explosion ripped the ground like a bunker buster bomb falling from the belly of a B-52.

Inside the storage bunker, the explosion deafened Encizo and Schwarz. Stunned by the intensity of the blast, the two men looked at each other.

"Ironman," Schwarz said.

# CHAPTER NINETEEN

Calvin James admired the French counterspy's courage. If the life and freedom of a teammate had not been on the line and the circumstances different, the ex-Navy SEAL knew he could have found a valuable ally in the man.

None of James's conflicted feelings mattered to T. J. Hawkins, who was lying in a prison hospital bed somewhere with only one slim chance of freedom. That chance was James.

"I'm sorry," James said. "This will hurt."

Galli spit. "I don't need your apologies!"

James placed the hypodermic between his teeth. He shifted his pistol to his left hand and Galli's eyes followed the movement. "Kill me and you'll never find your friend, bastard."

"I know," James replied.

His hand reappeared from the inner pocket of his coat and Galli's eyes widened in recognition. The man struggled to rise from his seat, but James was faster. Twin braces of stun-gun darts shot out and spiked into the man through his silk pajama shirt. Blue veins of electricity arced and danced as James juiced him.

The French spymaster locked up and bucked hard against the voltage, the muscles of his jaw knotting and his teeth grinding together. James hit the trigger again and sent another brutal current through the wires.

When that finished washing into the Frenchman, completely disabling him, the Phoenix Force operative threw down the stun gun and leaped forward. The muzzle of his pistol struck Galli, driving hard into the soft flesh under the man's jaw and forcing his head back cruelly, exposing the neck.

Galli made a mewling sound as he struggled to bring his muscular-skeletal system back under his own control, but James was too big, too strong, too fast. He removed the hypodermic from between his teeth and stabbed the long needle into the bulging target of Galli's pulsing carotid artery.

He pressed hard with the gun muzzle, pinning the disorientated man's head back against the seat. His thumb was on the hard white plastic of the plunger and he pushed the pure alcohol into the man's system.

When the dose had been administered, James jumped back off the man and threw the needle down the hall. He found the drained stun gun and kicked it after the hypodermic, ripping the darts and attached wires from Galli's chest.

James looked down at his watch, marked the time, then began to watch the French counterspy for signs the inebriant was taking effect. He knew from past experience that he would not have to wait for very long.

"You son of a bitch," Galli murmured. His voice was

thick and his head lolled on his neck. When he lifted his face to stare at James, his eyes were startlingly blood-shot. Cotton-white spiderwebs of spittle gathered in the corners of the man's mouth.

James looked at Galli with distaste. He was a medic and he much preferred to use his skills after that fashion. But he was also a pragmatist, and the bald, baseline truth was still the bald baseline truth: he could either do everything in his power to save Hawkins, or he could leave him to his fate. Sometimes the choice was that simple—do what it took or capitulate.

He sighed, feeling tired. If his plan unfolded according to design, Galli would have nothing but a bad hang-over and a couple of missing days to show for his endeavor. So far, about absolutely zero had gone according to plan.

James reached out and caught Galli's slack jaw between his fingers. He squeezed and snapped the man's face toward his own. He leaned in close. The effect of the pure alcohol on the Frenchman was severe, and by bypassing the liver and digestive system James had manipulated the man's insulin levels in a crude but powerful fashion. The man's breath stank of rotten fruit as his shocked system switched over to burning ketones with incredible speed.

The confusion of the insulin shock was biologically greater than the straight "drunk" of the injected alcohol, which was a powerful and brute instrument all on its own. The confusion was so profound and based on inde-fatigable biological factors, not on personal willpower. Resistance training was of little help, though strong-willed individuals usually held out longer than those more submissive by nature.

James sighed and moved forward. It was time to start asking questions.

"GOOD GOD!" Barbara Price yelled.

On the oversize wall monitor the Mexican night lit up like an erupting volcano as the fuel cells under the gas pumps exploded. The images from the Raven were digital clear and digital sharp. The rolling column of bright orange flame and thick black smoke filled the screen's parameters completely.

"That Ironman," Kurtzman said dryly. "He makes a big splash."

"All right," Price said. "First the helicopter, then the fuel depot. There's about zero chance Aslargo doesn't know his days at Puerto Lobos are finished."

Kurtzman looked up from his keyboard. "You think he's going to rabbit?"

"He's going to rabbit or he's going to man a second wave of response." She pressed the tip of a slender finger against the swell of her lip and looked toward the ceiling. "What he won't do is sit in his hacienda twiddling his thumbs. I think we have to prep for secondary operational contingents now."

On the screen they saw Gary Manning and Carl Lyons cross streams of automatic fire to scythe a gun tower sentry out of his post. Price nodded once, then spoke into her mike.

"*Sea Witch,* orientate west please."

"Copy," Carmen Delahunt said.

On the screen the Raven's camera shifted off the battle and pulled the desert west of the main gate into focus. A line of headlights snaked up the road toward the burning compound.

"*Sea Witch,* pull the Raven and get it over the GPS setting for our primary target's main residence."

"Copy that, rolling out now," Delahunt answered.

Price switched over to the open operational channel. "Ground Element," she said. "Confirm you are aware of eastbound reinforcements."

"Copy, a whole line of them burning up the road," Manning answered immediately. The sound of weapons' fire was clearly audible in the background.

"I'm pulling my bird's eye onto Lobos Primary," she said. "I'm thinking you may want to let the *Sea Witch* roll on this engagement."

There was a pause, and Price knew Manning hated the idea of taking a shortcut on checking the storage buildings. There was nothing to be done about it, she knew. Stony Man wasn't a combined arms infantry division or even a Ranger Battalion. The four operatives and limited support system was all they could field. The reality on the ground dictated tactics and things were always the way they were, never the way they should be.

"Copy," Manning answered. "I'm falling back. *Sea Witch,* wait for my call. I'll tell you when the wolf is at the door, over."

"*Sea Witch,* copy," Delahunt answered.

MANNING SWITCHED OVER to his tactical channel and his voice filled the earjacks of the Stony Man fire team. "Fall back to exfiltration point," he said. "We've got too many cowboys rolling on our site to complete this as planned."

"Copy," Lyons answered.

"Copy," Encizo and Schwarz echoed.

Manning began to fall back. He triggered four 3-round bursts at a group of hardmen advancing on his position, forcing them to scatter for cover. Bullets whizzed through the air around his head and dimpled the siding of the buildings next to him, kicking up gouts of dirt around where he crouched.

He cut loose with more covering fire as Lyons fell back from his own forward position. Across the compound and outside the fence on the road a Hummer rolled up to the gate, floodlights blazing. A camouflage-uniformed soldier sat in the open gun turret of the vehicle behind a M-60 E 7.62 mm machine gun.

The man swiveled the general-purpose machine gun to provide cover as a soldier hopped out of the back and sprinted toward the gate to open it. Behind them several more Hummers rolled ahead of two troop transport trucks. Men began jumping out of the vehicles, all of them armed with M-16 assault rifles.

The cavalry has arrived, Manning thought wryly.

He put the iron sites of his M-4 on the head of the M-60 gunner and shot him from 150 yards out. The man was knocked backward against the turret lip, then bounced forward to sag against the butt of his weapon. Blood gushed from the head wound.

The soldier struggling to unlock the gate snapped his head back to look at his teammate, and when he turned back toward the lock, Manning shot him, too. The man dropped to the dirt road and flopped like a fish in the bottom of a boat.

Manning burned a pair of 3-round bursts into the

windshield of the lead vehicle. The first 5.56 mm rounds pebbled the safety glass and the second grouping punched through to hammer the driver in his exposed face and throat. Off to Manning's left he heard an explosion, then, just as quickly, a domino pattern of secondary explosions. A ball of fire rose into the sky from his right-hand side.

"I'm at the grapnel site," Lyons said over the tactical channel.

"Rafe and I have eyes on you," Schwarz said over the com link as he ran. "If we're going to go, let's go."

"Copy," Manning answered. "I'm falling back now." He used his thumb to dial up the fire selector on his weapon one notch. "You copy that chatter, *Sea Witch?*" he asked.

"I did. You ready for Danger Close?" Delahunt asked.

"Bring it," Manning said.

Then he turned and ran.

LYONS SENSED MOVEMENT and twisted, bringing up the muzzle of his M-4. He saw Manning come out of an alley between two storage units and his finger went lax on the trigger. Red tracers burned through the air and split the space where the big Canadian had been as he rounded the corner.

Behind him Encizo had already reached the ground and was stripping the camo netting off the Excursion as Schwarz came down the rope. Manning hooked through the fence and sprinted toward Lyons.

A clean-shaved Mexican in OD fatigues appeared on the rear run, the M-16 in his hands up and ready. Lyons triggered a burst that burned inches to the left of the running Manning and hammered into the confused soldier. The man was knocked backward and his assault rifle fell away.

A second soldier appeared in the opening between the buildings, saw his brother go down and threw himself behind cover as Lyons triggered a burst at him, as well. Manning threw himself down on the ground next to Lyons and fired toward the north in the opposite direction covered by the Able Team leader.

Men armed with assault rifles and dressed in OD uniforms began to swarm out from between the burning storage vehicles, and both Stony Man operatives found themselves forced down on their bellies by the withering automatic fire.

"Get down the rope!" Manning yelled as he shot two men.

"Go ahead!" Lyons said. "I got it!" He put a 3-round burst into the belly of a gunner wielding an Ingram M-11 machine pistol.

Manning made as if to argue, saw an opening, shot a soldier, then closed his mouth. Arguing with Lyons was useless. "The rockets are inbound!" he yelled.

"I'm coming!" Lyons yelled over the sound of his firing weapon. "Just go!"

Manning spun on his belly and began crawling on his elbows to the spot where the rope went over the edge of the bluff. He ducked his head under the sling of his rifle and grabbed the rope with both hands. Lyons triggered burst after burst to cover him while edging backward in an awkward shuffle under the intensity of the returning fire.

A deadly sphere the size of a baseball suddenly arced

out of the night, backlit by the burning fires. It landed and bounced wide, out of Lyons's reach, and there was nothing for him to do but to duck his head.

The explosion was so loud Lyons felt a scream ripped from his lips in the instant before his right ear went deaf. He felt shrapnel rip into the length of his body along the right side, and he felt the concussion try to pull his carbine from his hands but he stubbornly held on.

He felt slow and stupid, almost drunk from the shock. He forced himself to turn, to bring his weapon up and around, but it felt as if he were swimming through mud. He couldn't hear very well, then suddenly his ear popped and the sound of the battle came rushing back into his consciousness.

He saw the crater formed by the exploding hand grenade and frowned. Something was wrong. He shot someone with a blazing M-16, then twisted and fired at someone else. He saw the aluminum-alloy grapnel hook lying loose on the ground, its prongs twisted like Italian noodles.

He rolled over onto his stomach and fired wildly. The climbing rope attached to the grappling hook was nowhere to be seen—it had been blown apart by the grenade blast. His first thought was to wonder if Manning had gotten off the line in time.

His second thought was the realization that he was trapped on the bluff.

Another black sphere arced toward him out of the night.

# CHAPTER TWENTY

*France*

James backed his car into the garage attached to his suburban safe house. He hit the remote button and lowered the door. Once it was closed, he got out of his car and unlocked the side entrance to the house. He removed his pistol and carefully explored the building, making sure everything was the same as when he'd left it.

When he was sure he was secure, he returned to his car in the garage and pulled out the sleeping Henri Galli. He hoisted the unconscious counterspy over his shoulder and walked him into the safe house. He had the Frenchman's hands cuffed behind his back with plastic ties as a precaution, but he was more concerned about the man's respirations being compromised by the high blood alcohol content, rather than the man coming to and trying some desperate gambit for escape.

He put Galli down on the bed in the small, secondary bedroom and attached a pair of handcuffs to his right ankle and the bedpost at the bottom of the bed frame. He checked his respirations, twelve, and then felt his pulse, fifty-five. Galli's breaths were deep and regular, his heartbeat was sluggish, which was to be expected, but steady and strong. He propped one of the pillows under the Frenchman's back to keep him propped in the unlikely event he vomited, then left the bedroom.

What James had been able to get out of him had been troubling. Getting Hawkins was going to be incredibly difficult. He was still in Marseilles, but the clinic was a small, private facility reserved for political and extremely dangerous convicts with medical problems deemed too serious for regular prison medical centers. It had been designed with security in mind, and an elite counterterror unit of the National Police had been called in to supplement the regular security personnel.

Added to that was the fact that according to Galli, Hawkins had not regained consciousness yet. This meant he would not be assisting in any escape plans and that moving him could be dangerous. James would need to locate, extract, stabilize and transport an unconscious and critically injured man without backup or any resources from Stony Man Farm.

In many ways the extraction was harder because lethal force wasn't a true option. If he pulled Hawkins out but caused an international incident by killing French forces, he doubted if Hal Brognola could clean up the mess. The extraction would have to be casualty free if he were going to pull it off—or he'd have to give up completely.

He thought briefly of attempting a prisoner exchange, a simple straight trade of Hawkins for Galli. He considered the problem. Much like the Italians the French did not have the same iron-clad institutionalized refusal to trade prisoners that America or Britain did.

Without backup or governmental resources, though, there would be no way to ensure that a special unit wouldn't simply stage a takedown on him if he made open contact. He rejected that plan out of hand.

James went to the refrigerator and pulled out a brown bottle of domestic beer. He opened it, took a drink then carefully checked his alarm setting and every window and door in the safe house. He made a mental note of the vehicles he could see from his windows and if any of his neighbors in the upscale neighborhood seemed to have taken an unusual interest in him.

He finished the beer and set it on the table, then went to check on Galli. The man's pulse and breathing had risen slightly, indicating that some of the effects of the inebriant were wearing off. He prepped a bio-inculcator with Versed and gave the counterspy another shot.

James sat and watched the comatose man's breathing. He realized what he would have to do. If he wanted Hawkins, he would have to go in and get him. It was that simple.

THE GRENADE LANDED and rolled to a stop in front of Carl Lyons.

Ignoring the machine-gun fire hammering his position, he surged up and forward, grabbed the hand grenade and whipped it out from in front of him. The deadly egg sailed back toward the fence and landed hard to bounce once before exploding. Geysers of dirt jumped into the air. Shrapnel ripped out in an umbrella pattern.

Then the missiles landed.

The warheads struck in a wave of overwhelming explosive destruction. Fireballs streaked out of the sky and rammed into the compound. The earth shuddered under the impacts, and Lyons felt the vibration come up through the ground and shake his body hard enough to rattle his teeth.

Clods of dirt fell around him like rain and washes of heat rolled into him in waves. The sound was deafening and brutal. He tried to lift his head and another shock wave slammed into him. In between the hammer falls of the explosions he could hear secondary detonations as the fuel tanks on vehicles were ignited.

Burning fireballs turned the night as bright as day, and Lyons felt naked and exposed in the brilliant illumination. He lifted his head, and dirt hammered into him. He spit and blinked and saw figures spinning and rolling as building after building inside the compound was hammered to pieces.

Lyons jumped up and looked around quickly. Nothing moved on the rubble-strewn and burning landscape. He spun and jogged over to the edge of the bluff and looked down, afraid of what he would find. He saw Encizo crouched by the front bumper of the Excursion with his weapon trained on the cliff top. Schwarz knelt beside the prostrate form of Gary Manning. The big Canadian's left leg was bent out at an unnatural angle. It was obvious the man had fallen when his climbing line had been severed during the initial hand grenade attack.

"Throw the grapnel down!" Encizo shouted up at him.

Lyons turned and scanned the fence line, searching for the grappling hook. After a tense moment he found it stuck in the ground where it had been blown clear by one of the explosions. He ran over and picked it up before returning to the edge of the bluff. He saw Encizo moving forward with an end of the rope in his hand as Schwarz finished putting a battlefield splint on Manning's broken leg.

Lyons tossed the grappling hook down, and Encizo sprang forward and retied the end of the knotted rope through the eye-loop. Behind him Schwarz helped Manning to his feet and started for the SUV.

"Here it comes!" Encizo yelled.

He spun the rope around on a tight axis and then released it. The grappling hook arced up and shot forward to land at the top of the cliff. Working quickly, Lyons snatched it up and then secured it to a sturdy desert scrub that had somehow survived the bombing attack. He took one quick look around and then shouldered his weapon and went over the side of the bluff.

Dropping hand over hand, he quickly made his way to the bottom of the rope and dropped the last few feet to the ground. He turned and ran for the SUV.

He slid into the shotgun seat as Encizo fired up the engine and threw the Excursion into Reverse. Manning gritted his teeth in the backseat and cursed explosively. Schwarz was retrying the splints that had come loose in the shuffle to get into the SUV. He pulled a morphine lollipop from his field kit and passed it to the man.

"How you doing?" Lyons asked the Canadian.

"I'll be fine," Manning replied from around his lollipop. "How did the damage assessment look up top?"

"Like we turned a drug compound into a burning crater," Lyons answered.

"Good."

Encizo took the Excursion into a tightly controlled spin, got the nose pointed in the proper direction and floored it. Rooster tails of dirt spit up behind the spinning tires and the SUV surged forward.

Lyons hit his earjack. "Stony Ground, Element Six is injured but good. The MLRS strike was five-by-five. We are extracting at the moment. Can we get a situation update?"

"Copy," Delahunt replied. "I've got a bird's-eye on the primary now. He took the news poorly. I have a four-vehicle convoy pulling out as we speak. He appears headed for the coastal road and running south."

"Understood," Lyons replied. "We're rolling intercept now."

FIVE MINUTES LATER Encizo fishtailed the Excursion off the dirt road and onto the north-south Mexican national highway. On firmer traction he quickly picked up momentum and soon had the speed gauge needled at just past 90 mph. The big Ford shook on its suspension as they barreled down the road and up ahead red taillights appeared in the night.

The Raven had trailed the convoy until they had passed out of its maximum flight range, then returned to the *Sea Witch*. The yacht itself had begun to conduct a parallel course with the racing drug runners but had been quickly outpaced.

"We've confirmed only hostiles in this convoy?" Lyons asked.

"Affirmative," Delahunt replied. "Aslargo and two of his lieutenants got into the gray H3 Hummer and his men piled into the black Escalades running in front and behind him. Everyone was male and everyone armed."

"Copy. Out," Lyons said.

Through the windshield the shape of the convoy rear vehicle came sharply into view. The Escalade looked heavy, riding low on its suspension from what Lyons suspected was obviously body armor.

"Let's try a 'pick' maneuver to get past them," he said to Encizo. "We need to peel off as many extra guns as we can before we tackle the H3."

"Watch and see." Encizo nodded.

He raced up behind the heavier vehicle, which was straddling the centerline and taking up the whole road. He tried to pace on the left and the driver swung over to cut him off. Encizo snapped his steering wheel back the other way and shot forward on the right.

Still doing more than 80 miles per hour, he ran the front of the Excursion parallel with the speeding Escalade then whipped it over, striking the vehicle's tire with his heavy, reinforced bumper. There was a loud sound of tires squealing as the other SUV jerked to the side and its spinning tires caught the soft gravel on the shoulder of the road.

The vehicle went spinning off into the desert and struck a boulder hard. A star-pattern burst blazed from the back window, but the rounds flew wide and the Excursion was past the wreck and running hard up on the rear of another Escalade SUV.

Three Stony Man commandos rolled down their windows and prepped their weapons for a firefight. In the Excursion's high beams they saw a dark-skinned man lean out of the rear window holding a H&K MP-5 in his burly, tattooed arms. The bodyguard triggered a long, ragged burst at the pursuing vehicle.

Lyons fired his weapon, answering back blast for blast. He saw his rounds spark off the top of the Escalade and dimple the reinforced glass of the rear windows. He edged his chattering carbine over to the left and managed to catch the drug runner in the face.

Encizo put the pedal to the metal and surged forward to ram the other SUV. Inside the cab, everyone was thrown against their seat restraint harnesses and Schwarz began to fire out his window, as well.

In front of them the rear doors of the bodyguard's SUV flew open and the muzzles of two automatic weapons appeared over the seat rests. Encizo cut the wheel to the left again as bullets punched softball-size holes in the Excursion's windshield, spraying glass like snowflakes. Lyons fired his M-4 one-handed out the window and put a wild blast directly through the Escalade's open rear doors.

One of the firing submachine guns suddenly swung up and burned off its magazine into the dark Mexican sky. A body tumbled over the backseat and bounced off the Escalade's rear bumper. Encizo jerked the wheel left to avoid the falling body and his right front tire caught the corpse, sending that side of the Excursion up into the air like a bucking horse.

Manning leaned out his open window and fired his weapon above Lyons's head. Red tracer fire burned over the front of the vehicle as it swung back in line and hammered inside the enemy SUV. Suddenly the second Escalade lurched off to the left-hand side of the road and sped into the desert, apparently out of control. As they shot past the vehicle, both Lyons and Manning raked the car with fire from their M-4 carbines, shredding tires and blasting out the safety glass.

"Here we go!" Encizo shouted.

Just ahead, the H3 containing Aslargo and his lieutenants came into view.

## CHAPTER TWENTY-ONE

The rear doors of the H3 swung open as the Excursion raced forward and two hand grenades tumbled into the roadway. The deadly little bombs struck the pavement and bounced down the center lane toward the onrushing Stony Man commandos.

"Grenades!" Lyons shouted.

Encizo didn't bother to reply. He twisted hard on the steering wheel, trying to pull onto the shoulder, but the grenade closer to him took a bad hop and he was forced to gun the vehicle in the other direction. He pushed the vehicle between the two bouncing grenades like a man threading a needle, and stomped on the accelerator.

The twin explosions came hard as he cleared the grenades and bits of shrapnel blew out the rear window of the team's SUV. Lyons poured fire through the opening in the back of the H3, and it was returned from at least three separate sources. Bullets whined off the hood of the Excursion and skipped away while several bounced up and knocked more glass out of the broken windshield.

Encizo narrowed his eyes against the shards and slivers of broken glass the wind stream carried with it. Manning continued to fire out of his window, but Lyons had shifted the muzzle of his carbine inside and was returning fire straight out the broken hole of the front windshield.

The Hummer suddenly pulled into the left-hand lane and the lead vehicle, another big black Escalade identical to the other two, fell back. The Hummer cut in front of the larger SUV, and Encizo found his path blocked by the final bodyguard vehicle.

"Bastard," the Cuban hissed, and once again attempted to raise his speed.

Up ahead he could see the highway take a gentle downhill curve to hug the shoreline. He was forced to brake to take the curve on the blocky suspension of his vehicle. His tires screamed in protest as he took the turn and he fought against the inertia of his maneuver, steering wheel rattling hard in protest. Suddenly, Lyons was thrown hard against his seat as Encizo gunned the SUV hard against the angle of the turn.

The Excursion ran up to the bodyguard vehicle as it hugged the outside corner of the turn. The rear window was down and a hardman leaned out his window and fired one of the crew's ubiquitous Remington 870 pump shotguns with its shoulder stock folded down. They were close enough that the man's every feature was clearly distinguishable in the Excursion's high beams. The man squinted against the bright lights and triggered a blast.

The right headlight on the Excursion exploded, showering sparks and going black. The man racked the slide on his assault shotgun and leveled it again. The Stony

Man team's vehicle cut the inner corner of the roadway on the turn and crossed the center. The front end of the Escalade tore into the rear of the SUV, and Lyons fired on the shotgunner from less than ten feet away.

The man's face exploded into gory mush and red spray. The Remington 870 tumbled from his hands and bounced off the hood of the Excursion. The impact popped the engine hood into a warped comma shape as the front bumper plowed into the bodyguard's vehicle.

The angle of Encizo's maneuver was dead-on, and the Escalade slid wildly out of control. Again Lyons and Manning sprayed the tumbling vehicle with their weapons as their now-battered SUV shot past the wreckage.

Encizo drove with his head hanging out the window. Schwarz had climbed up onto the edge of his door to fire at the H3 running hard in front of them. Lyons reversed his M-4 and began striking the crumpled engine hood of their vehicle with his rifle's buttstock to flatten it out.

With a screech of ripping metal he was able to knock it loose, and Encizo pulled his head back inside the Excursion's cabin. The Hummer was running flat-out about a hundred yards ahead of them, and the three Stony Man commandos began to pour a savage fusillade of fire at the rear of the vehicle and its back tires. Rounds sparked off the road, scratched the rear doors of the vehicle and began to spiderweb the safety glass.

Finally the repeated assault yielded a successful strike and a 3-round burst by Schwarz blew the rear passenger tire off the rim. The heavy frame of the Hummer sagged as the tire blew out, and the spinning metal wheel touched off an avalanche of sparks as it bounced onto the pavement.

The Hummer began to skid out of control and the driver overcorrected before jamming on his brakes. The big luxury SUV locked up and turned parallel to the roadway. The rear end swung around 180 degrees until the engine block was pointed toward the Stony Man crew.

The ruined rear tire caught on the shoulder of the road and it was over. The Hummer tumbled like rolling dice on a craps table, and bits of the vehicle began to fly apart as it smashed through the desert landscape of cactus and boulders.

Schwarz burned off the rest of his clip into the crumpled vehicle as Encizo brought the team's Excursion to a stop. Lyons and Schwarz leaped from the vehicle and began approaching the smoldering wreckage of the H3 while Encizo and Manning kept their own weapons trained on the vehicle in a protective overwatch.

Lyons and Schwarz drifted left on their approach to avoid crossing up the other two men's angles of fire. They moved forward cautiously with their weapons at their shoulders, muzzles trained on the ruined H3. A man armed with an H&K MP-5 popped up from the rear passenger side like a demented jack-in-the-box.

He held his submachine gun out and began to spray a wild figure eight, his face a mask of blood from a gushing head wound. His angry screams were cut short by simultaneous short, accurate bursts by Schwarz and Lyons. The man pitched forward and hung limply against the door, his arms dangling loosely.

Lyons moved forward, letting his M-4 drop loose on its sling as he pulled his pistol clear for the close in work. He hurried up to the smoldering vehicle just as yellow flames began to flutter and catch in the sand below the engine where oil had leaked onto the ground.

Raising the pistol, Lyons peered quickly into the vehicle, sweeping the weapon back and forth. He reached in with a free hand and moved something, then straightened and turned to face the team's Excursion. He threw Encizo and Manning a thumbs-up.

"Let's roll out of here before somebody comes looking for that asshole," Encizo said.

IN A MANSION ON THE ESTATE outside Caracas, Venezuela, Marcos Sincanaros gripped the cut crystal of his tumbler in an iron fist. He sipped the fiery, expensive rum and contemplated the painting in front of him. It was an oil-and-canvas rendering of a subject that had kept him enthralled since he was a young boy: Tarot cards.

In the frame a magnificent black stallion reared up, positioned before a wall of orange flame. On his back the charger carried the Knight of Wands. The armored knight's cape formed the blood-orange-colored flame, flowing down his shoulder and swirling dramatically around his warrior steed. The knight wielded a flaming wand clutched in a gauntlet-covered hand. A winged horse reared on the crest of his dark helmet.

Sincanaros shivered with delight and turned to face the painting's mate. The Knight of Swords was rendered in an aerial scene on the east wall of the ostentatious room. The perspective gave the admirer a point of view from above the knight as he streaked across a blue-and-white sky on a blond horse thrusting two swords out beyond the nose of his flying mount. Three swallows darted below them. The knight was dressed in yellow-green armor and his great helm was adorned with four long, gossamer blades like the rotor of a helicopter.

Sincanaros looked to the painting that completed the set. It made him feel in control to have completed collections. It thrilled him in some indefinable way that power and woman and drugs could not touch. Only murder came close.

On the west wall hung his commissioned painting of the Tarot card the Knight of Cups. A knight in dark emerald armor rode away from the viewer while the horse looked back, watching with one eye. They rode amid an iridescent turquoise background. The knight had wings of blue-white colors and before him he held a reddish-gold cup aloft from which a crab crawled. At the lower right corner of the painting a peacock faced outward, its tail raised.

Sincanaros felt his breathing slow, his heart stop racing. He took a drink and looked over at the woman he'd thrown to the floor. He felt good as he watched her cower. For a brief period of time he had felt out of control. Phone calls had come, from Galli in Marseilles and Reyes, the intelligence agent in Mexico City.

That Arab bastard al-Shalaan had talked. The prince was angry. Galli had been assaulted. Reyes's Zetas cutouts had been assaulted and their terror weapons seized. Bellicose Dawn was over. Over before it had even started. He felt fear in his belly and he clutched his glass.

The woman before him was the young daughter of a business rival. He would use her up and throw her away as a message to those who thought they could cross him in anything. Hurting the young woman would take his mind off his recent failures.

He smiled and the young woman began to cry.

BARBARA PRICE SPUN in her chair, surveying the men the War Room. It was a depleted cast of the usual characters. Hal Brognola sat beside her and on his right Aaron Kurtzman had rolled his wheelchair tight in next to the conference table. Of her operational forces only Carl Lyons, Gadgets Schwarz and Rafael Encizo were present.

"Gary's fine. He has a compound fracture of the tib-fib. I had to order him to take some time off once the cast was on, but we'll probably be able to use him in some support or overwatch capacity as he's ambulatory. Running, jumping, kicking...not so much."

"It's like Agatha Christie's *And Then There Were None* around here lately," Schwarz said. "The teams have taken some dings before, it's the nature of the beast, but this has been insane recently."

"Law of averages, I guess." Price sighed. "We run a tight margin, and as a whole we've usually always beat Murphy's Law. But the odds have always been stacked against us."

"True enough," Encizo agreed.

The door to the room opened and Carmen Delahunt entered carrying a stack of files and a cup of coffee. She nodded toward Price and took a seat.

"Nice shooting in Mexico, *mamasita*." Encizo laughed.

Delahunt smiled. "Some of it might have been the GPS systems, but I did type them in..."

"Is that the printout from the analysis done on the mortar round Rafe brought back?" Brognola asked.

Delahunt nodded, and pulled a small stack of papers out of her folder and slid the sheets across the table. "It sure is," she said. "It had a chemical container warhead just like they suspected."

"What was in it?" Price asked. She picked up the lab result breakdown and frowned.

"No way!" Schwarz shouted. He looked up and caught Delahunt's eyes. "Are they sure?" He sounded incredulous.

"BZ-EA-2277," she answered. "They're sure."

"A hallucinogen? Like what?" Brognola demanded. "Like LSD?"

"Yes and no," Delahunt said. "While this report is a chemical breakdown and spectro-analysis, the weapon compound itself is biological."

"Who makes it?" Lyons asked. The red mark from the jellyfish sting had already begun to fade but was still readily apparent on his face.

"That's the problem," Delahunt said. "Nobody. And when it *was* made, it was made by us."

"Us?" Price asked, looking up.

"Us as in U.S.," Schwarz said.

"Start at the beginning," Brognola said with a sigh.

"And keep it pithy. Chemistry wasn't my favorite subject in school," Lyons said.

Delahunt opened her mouth but Schwarz cut in quickly. "Do *not* ask what his favorite subject was. You'll be sorry," he warned.

"It's like having children," Price said, shaking her head.

Lyons nodded, his expression earnest. "Yes, exactly. Murderous trigger-happy children, but, yeah, children."

"Go ahead, Carmen," Brognola prompted.

"Wait," Schwarz said. "I know I said 'us' as in U.S.,

but I just remembered. Wasn't Iraq's Agent 15 project supposed to be basically the same thing?"

Delahunt nodded. "I'm aware of that connection. Both BZ and 15 are the chemical 3-quinuclidinyl benzilate, or QNB. However the stamp said 'BZ' and BZ is, or was, the NATO code name."

Schwarz nodded and frowned, obviously troubled. He leaned back in his chair and began to fidget with a black pen. Encizo looked at him, then Carmen Delahunt.

"Start from the top, Carmen," he said. "What's QNB?"

"In a nutshell? BZ is a compound related to atropine, scopolamine and other deliriants. Dispersal is aerosolized solid configured primarily for inhalation, or possibly as an agent dissolved in one or more solvents for ingestion or even percutaneous absorption.

"It acts as a competitive inhibitor of acetylcholine at postsynaptic and postjunctional muscarinic receptor sites in smooth muscle, exocrine glands, autonomic ganglia and the brain. BZ decreases the effective concentration of acetylcholine seen by receptors at these sites. Because of this, BZ causes peripheral nervous system effects that in general are the opposite of those seen in nerve agent poisoning." Delahunt paused and gave a small smile. "In a nutshell."

"Where's Cal when you need him," Encizo moaned. "I thought dive tables were complicated!"

"Actually 'in a nutshell' would be more like 'drug makes people go crazy,' the end," Lyons pointed out.

"Here's what's important, though," Delahunt said. "BZ produces effects not just in individuals, but also in groups. Sharing of illusions and hallucinations or 'mass hysteria' is not just common, it is the *exact* effect. I read a report summary where two gassed BZ-intoxicated individuals took turns smoking an imaginary cigarette clearly visible to both of them but not to anyone else." Delahunt looked down and read directly from the page. "'When one observed subject mumbled, "Gotta cigarette?" his delirious companion held out an invisible pack. He followed with, "S'okay, don't wanna take your last one." In another test it was reported two victims of BZ played tennis with imaginary rackets.' Imagine a mortar attack of that stuff on a military barracks or a shopping mall."

"I thought our stores and NATO stores were destroyed?" Schwarz asked.

"I thought Stony Man didn't exist," Delahunt replied.

"Sweet," Lyons murmured. "I like you, Carmen. I really do."

"Okay," Price cut in. "Let's start adding up what we know. Phoenix goes to Marseilles to pull a hostile extraction on a Saudi terror middleman. Able is deployed to New Orleans to rescue a government confidential informant."

"Both missions unfold less than perfectly," Brognola inserted.

"Both missions unfold less than perfectly," Price repeated. "And two seemingly unrelated bad-guy organizations are using an identical code phrase, 'Bellicose Dawn.' The Saudi middleman is linked to Mohammed al-Rhabin, a prince and mover in the Saudi intelligence service. He's also linked to a Mexican intelligence agent named Reyes. The same Mexican intelligence agent running covert ops using supposedly traitorous Zetas. Zetas who have bioweapons supposedly destroyed by the U.S.

in 1988." She paused. "We can connect the dots. But just because we have a linear progression doesn't mean we understand everything."

"Not just the U.S., but NATO," Schwarz clarified.

"What?" Price turned toward him.

"BZ wasn't just U.S. juice. It was NATO, it was EU," Schwarz said by way of clarifying.

"What about Gabriel Gonzales's contention that his boy Lagos was taking orders from a Frenchman?" Lyons pointed out. "What did he tell the interrogators? It was a *totally* sissy French name. Henri. Yeah, he said in the last month this Henri had been giving orders, sometimes cutting Reyes out."

"Was there a last name on that?" Brognola sat up and leaned forward. His consternation was as plain as a neon sign across his face.

"I'll double-check the transcripts," Delahunt said. "But I'm pretty sure all he said was the first name." She shuffled some of the paperwork in front of her and frowned. "Wait. I recall something else…" The room remained quiet while the ex-FBI agent cross-checked her reports and intelligence summaries. "Here it is," she said finally. "I have a second hit."

"Give it to me," Kurtzman spoke up. His fingers flew across the keyboard built into the conference table. "I'll run a global search through all files and uplinks."

"It was the Marseilles police report. The name of the hooker the police found in the room after Phoenix did their takedown. That name was annotated as having a flag from some of our Interpol reports. The woman is a suspected freelancer for French intelligence, procurement and courier work mostly, but also linked to some more dubious ops involving her skills as a…ah…" Delahunt stammered.

"Whore?" Lyons offered politely.

Delahunt cocked an eyebrow at him but nodded. "Well yeah, basically."

"So Phoenix goes to take down a terror network node, and the guy just happens to be in the company of a call girl used by French intelligence?" Price asked.

"Yes. And here's why it stuck in my mind," Delahunt continued. "Her handler and recruiter is suspected to be a counterintelligence agent named Henri Galli."

"Hold on." It was Kurtzman's turn to request patience. The big man's fingers hammered into the keys as he jumped screens. "Here's something curious. I cross-indexed BZ with NATO and with our Monsieur Galli's name. I have a match."

"What is it?" Brognola demanded, his voice tense.

"He was the coordination and communications officer for French military intelligence in 1988 on Project Tabula Rasa." Kurtzman looked up and grinned. "That would be the liaison mission set up by non-NATO parties to ensure that stockpiles of BZ were destroyed in accordance with all agreements."

"Can I go to France?" Lyons asked. "I'd like to go to France. I'd be very polite, I promise."

Schwarz kept his face angelic. "I believe him. You can trust him. I'll vouch for him."

"Not so fast, Carl," Brognola said. "I have a piece of this puzzle, too. Well, I might. It looks that way, but I need to make some calls and double-check." He turned to Price.

"Look, Gary's out, and we're down shooters big-time. Why don't we send the boys to Mexico City to pull a little recon on this Mexican intelligence connection Reyes, get the lay of the land?"

"If you think that's the way to proceed, then okay, Hal," Price answered. She frowned. "Is everything okay?"

"I don't know enough to even put this on the table yet." He was hedging, and Price knew him well enough to see it. He knew her well enough to know she could tell.

"Let me make some calls," he repeated. "I'll get back to you shortly on this. Let's see what the Mexico City connection gives us."

"All right," Price said, and watched him hurry out of the room.

OUTSIDE THE DOOR Hal Brognola immediately pulled out his cell phone. He dialed a number by memory and listened impatiently to the digital buzz. It continued. A computer modulated and automated female voice informed him his party was not available and requested he please leave a message.

Brognola swore. The recording prompted him with a sharp beep.

"Damn it, Striker, where are you?" he demanded. "Never mind. Call me back as soon as you get this. We may have a major complication with the extracurricular activity going on in Marseilles."

He snapped his phone shut and began walking for the exit. He was halfway down the hall before it occurred to him where Gary Manning had probably gone once he'd been pulled from the active duty roster of Phoenix Force.

"Goddamn it!" he bellowed, and pulled his phone back out.

# CHAPTER TWENTY-TWO

*France*

"It's called Nubain," James explained. "There is a side effect of slight euphoria but the painkiller is localized. I'll give you this shot right below the knee. It'll numb the area well, but shouldn't have a large systemic effect."

"All right," Manning agreed. He watched while James gave him the shot with a hypodermic needle from the glove-box medic kit.

James gave the injection at the point where Manning had bloused his pants above the top edge of his sports cast. "Anyway, it was hallucinogenic? Instead of shrapnel or, say, radioactive compounds, they were going to disperse hallucinogens?" James asked.

"Yup," Manning answered. The two men got out of the vehicle and looked up and down the deserted stretch of coast before beginning to unload their equipment.

James put his back to the lights of Marseilles and looked out across the gulf waters. His broken leg wrapped in a sports cast with a hard rubber-soled traction on the bottom, Manning unloaded the kayak from the storage rack on the Highlander SUV.

"Isn't that a little Dr. Evil and inefficient?"

James looked at his watch and used the compass to shoot a casual azimuth in the general direction he had pinpointed on the map. In a south-by-southeast direction he saw the lights of the island complex. He turned and watched the broken-legged Manning carefully double-checking their gear. The big Canadian used black rubber bungee cords to attach a ballistic shield to the middle section of the kayak.

Manning shook his head no to James's question. "I don't know. It was a terror op. Any attack on the populous would generate horror. But the camera images of men and women and children driven into violent insanity? Pretty gripping. Then the chemical rounds are linked to U.S. government programs? Just a couple of attacks like that on big sports venues or malls would have people living in perpetual fear of terrorist boogeymen. If anything the air time would be larger—especially if the drugged people hurt each other instead of casualties being caused by foreign operators. Mothers hurting their children, husbands hurting their wives, teachers attacking students or vice versa. It would generate horror in a way a straight attack couldn't."

James nodded his agreement, then bent and picked up the front end of the kayak. "You got that cast sealed up watertight?"

"We're about to find out," Manning said with a laugh. "I think so."

James stepped into the warm Mediterranean and felt

the seawater close in around his boots and pant legs. He walked out until the water was up to his knees, then set down the kayak.

He and Manning climbed into the sleek, low-profile craft and picked up their double-bladed paddles. Manning dug the end of his into the water and pushed off hard against the bottom. The watercraft shot forward.

James leaned forward and dug his oars into the waves and began to pull. "I'm still amazed how quickly you were able to gather and deploy this much off-the-books logistical support. I know we've used your corporation for cover before, like when we went into Iraq, but are Hal and Barb aware of just how much capability your company has?"

"They're not stupid people," Manning pointed out. "But they've never really utilized my corporate connections." Manning paused and continued rowing. "Maybe they don't like the idea of using civilian enterprise to augment what Stony Man is doing. It's a gray area."

"Stony Man is a gray area." James laughed. The shore was disappearing behind them.

"Yeah but it's *their* gray area."

"True enough."

They were out in the Gulf of Lion now, knifing through the light chop on the indigo-colored water. The rocky atoll they were headed toward was coming into clearer view with each paddle stroke. The kayak's low profile kept them from becoming silhouetted against the night sky. The government complex on the islet was a clandestine facility run under the cover of a French oceanic and maritime research facility studying industrial pollution in the gulf. In reality it was a black site detention-interrogation center.

As such the defensives were kept inconspicuous and the only patrols in the harbor area of the gulf were gendarme maritime units and the regular force coastal defense agencies. Twice James and Manning stopped paddling and leaned forward as police cruisers motored slowly by. Both times the low-slung kayak went unnoticed.

When the mile-and-a-half trip was over, they slipped out of the warm Mediterranean and up onto the sandy beach that covered the southern edge of the islet. The atoll was approximately a half mile square with a sandy beach taking up about two-thirds of the lower shoreline. Scrubby vegetation was predominant on the lower areas of the atoll while thicker growth was concentrated farther up the hillside. Most of the atoll's northern coast consisted of a sheer rock cliff running between ten to fifteen yards high near the building's location. Two hundred yards west of their position an empty steel-and-concrete pier sat at the end of a single-lane macadam access road that led up the little island toward the complex. Streetlights with low-wattage lamps dotted the lane, forming interconnected pools of soft illumination.

*T.J., here we come,* James thought. He helped Manning submerge the kayak into the waist-high surf and the two men began their approach, Manning packing the rectangular-shaped ballistic shield. Neither man carried a firearm but instead was heavily loaded down with stun, smoke and gas grenades as well as police tactical stun guns. For emergencies each man carried an XM-26

LSS bolt action 12-gauge shotgun with 5-round box magazine.

The weapon had a collapsible stock of the same design used on the M-4 carbine and a foreshortened barrel, making it highly adaptable in close-quarter combat situations. Manning and James carried nonlethal rubber and beanbag antipersonnel rounds.

Above them the dual lamp of a tower-mounted searchlight circumnavigated the island on a predictable path, as much lighthouse warning for ships in the Gulf of Lion as security illumination on the islet. Moving at quick time, Manning and James jogged up the beach, left the sand and began to climb the hill. Each time the searchlight rotated to their vector they knelt and froze, turning their approach into a choreographed ballet of infiltration like a childhood game of Freeze Tag.

Within ten minutes of landing, the two Phoenix Force operatives approached the final line of brush and vegetation before a denuded area stretching for ten yards around the periphery of the complex. James and Manning came to rest beside a thick stand of azaleas, the lavender and white blossoms giving off a heavy perfume. He set his shield facedown on the loose soil.

James scanned the ground looking for electronic sensors or trip wires but could discern none. His information from Henri Galli had been spotty due to the nature of his method of interrogation. The blunt facts had come readily enough, but details were hard to extract in the time constraints he was given to. Basically the complex relied more on low-profile subterfuge for security rather than intensive, aggressive defense measures.

Beside him, Manning sized up the building. A 6-foot-high chain-link fence topped with three lines of out-ward-leaning barbed wire encased the main building on all four sides. The fence was set out from the building approximately 150 yards across a concrete apron.

Facing the southern exposure was the fence's only gate, which sat across the beginning of the macadam access road leading down to the pier. Parked behind the gate was an empty Toyota Land Cruiser. Just beyond that, Manning saw, was a helipad.

The helicopter was a La France Tours Model 7, the French version of the Bell JetRanger. Behind the helicopter the front of the building was broken by a set of metal double doors on the side nearest them and a freight elevator in a small concrete block annex twenty yards west of the entrance.

Ten windows ran along the eastern exposure of the building, though James and Manning both noticed that all the openings were dark, with drawn blinds. On the roof of the building a guard post was erected to a height of thirteen feet above the top of the structure. The dual lamps of the motorized searchlight were fixed to the top of the post, sitting just above a small radar dish and satellite relay.

Manning reached over and nudged James, calling his attention to the sentry tower. He leaned over and asked in low tones, "You see any direct roof access to that tower?"

James narrowed his gaze and frowned in concentration. Large bay windows made of heavy safety glass had been set with a 360-degree view in the tower. They were close enough now that they could see the guard post's single occupant. A pair of large binoculars sat at the man's elbow. There was no catwalk or access ladder that the ex-SEAL could see from his angle.

"Negative," he replied. "I'm guessing that means the tower is connected directly into the building."

"Probably the security office, right?"

"Well, probably not a surgical room or the staff lounge," James agreed. "I see your point, but I think the approach is too exposed for us to assault the tower before he raises an alarm. Not if we have to go through those windows."

"That leaves out the front doors and that freight elevator," Manning added, thinking out loud.

"We didn't have time to prepare," James said. "We're just going to have to improvise. No plan is going to be perfect. Just less obvious."

"Window through the side, then," Manning answered. "We'll be under the searchlight once we get close. We'll pop the window off the frame or smash it and go in. If T.J. is confined to a bed, we can't use the roof for pickup anyway—it'd have to be open areas."

James frowned. "Alarms?"

"Have to risk it." Manning shrugged.

"Well, luckily, you do have a broken leg. So that helps."

Manning smiled. "Which is why I'd rather cut through the fence than climb over it."

James nodded, then shook his head. "Look, I think we should just use the climbing pole."

"Hey-diddle-diddle right up the middle?"

"Hey, I'm a SEAL not a Marine," James said, grinning. "But I think the KISS principle might be our wisest choice. Over the fence to the building, then up the side to the tower, use the spring-loaded center punch to enter and take him out. We can't have them in control of that high ground when we go for extraction anyway."

"Nothing's ever easy." Manning sighed. "I'll time how long it takes for the searchlight to travel around in a full circle, then we'll roll."

Shrugging off his gear bag, James pulled a sectional ladder clear. Manning watched and timed the circling light as James put together the pieces of the aluminum-alloy collapsible ladder. Of the three separate pieces he carried, he linked only two for the fence crossing.

The light swept past them as they crouched behind the azalea bushes. The two men turned their faces away from the brilliance to avoid too much denigration of their natural night vision.

"What was the time?" James asked.

"Sixteen, almost seventeen seconds," Manning answered.

"Oh, that's plenty of time for a healthy kid like you."

"Next pass," Manning agreed.

They waited, poised for the light to come back around. Again they turned their faces away from the shining light and when it had passed, they sprang into action.

Picking up the sectional ladder, James sprinted forward and hooked it on the topmost strand of the triple row of barbed wire that topped the chain-link fence. He anchored it tight against the wire and sank to one knee beside the base of the ladder, holding it fast.

Manning snatched up the ballistic shield and raced forward to scramble up the ladder one-handed. The only indication he gave of his broken leg was the slightly sharper tone his exhalations took. He went up and over the top of the fence, threw the shield down and, bending double at the waist, reached down to grab hold of the fence with his lead hand.

He locked first one hand, then the other into the fence and somersaulted himself over the top, flipping 180 degrees to land on his feet. He hissed as the nerves of his broken leg sent pain signals coursing up from his shin. He ignored them and sprinted for the building wall after snatching up the ballistic shield. The light was making its approach on their position as he slid into place in the protective lee of the building between two curtained windows.

Working smoothly, James unhooked the ladder, laid it flat on the ground next to the fence line, then somersaulted over one shoulder and into the protective cover of the wild azalea bushes. He remained motionless as the dual lamps of the searchlight passed with mechanical smoothness over his position. He sprang up, retrieved the collapsible ladder and hooked it on the fence again. This time it was his turn to scramble up its length.

At the top he spread his body across the strands of barbed wire and flipped the ladder over the fence to the other side. He leaned against the inside of the fence and stuck a booted toe into one of the diamond-shaped wire links for purchase before pushing off and dropping to the ground.

The searchlight started around toward the eastern exposure of the atoll. James reached over with both hands and picked up the ladder. The top had tangled up with the razor wire. He stepped back and twisted the ladder in his hands, jerking it free. The searchlight started to slide down the fence line, still motoring smoothly toward his position in its uninterrupted pattern. James snapped his head to the side, saw the fast-approaching light and cursed.

The Phoenix Force commando pulled the ladder to him and began to run. The column of light swept toward him. He saw Manning crouched against the building's wall, watching him intently as the searchlight came toward him. He felt his right eye, the one closer to the beam, go blind from the glare of the light for a moment, then he was under the shaft of light and into the safety of the dead spot close to the building.

He went to one knee beside Manning, breathing heavily. Without saying anything, Manning quickly unhooked the third and final section of his collapsible ladder from James's rucksack. He bent and began to attach the third part while James held the ladder steady against the ground and watched the blacked-out windows for any signs of movement.

Once the ladder had been finished, they waited for the light to pass over their heads, then started the second phase of their assault. James stood and gently lowered the now 10-foot ladder into position against the edge of the building to avoid any banging noise.

When it was braced securely into place, he nodded at Manning, who picked up the ballistic shield and repeated his scramble up its length. Manning reached the edge of the flat roof and rolled across the lip. This time James immediately followed behind him. Once on the roof he sprawled flat and waited for the searchlight to traverse his position while Manning maneuvered across the roof to the base of the sentry tower.

The light passed by and James sat up. He hauled the

ladder up and ran around the raised rectangles of the solar panels, skipping over the exposed conduits and heating vents dotting the roof. He frowned as he approached where Manning crouched by the tower.

The easy part was over. One false move now spelled the end to any hopes Hawkins had of seeing safety. James ignored the greasy cold splashes of adrenaline as they churned in his stomach, his fear not for himself but for what failure would mean for his friend.

"Go," Manning whispered.

James put the ladder into position.

Manning raced up the ladder toward the east window of the guard tower. Without hesitation his teammate took his turn carrying the ballistic shield and ascended the ladder directly after him. The big Canadian had a spring-loaded center punch used by fire rescue crews to shatter car windshields.

The ladder bounced against the tower as the Stony Man warriors charged up its length. Manning arrived at the top of the ladder and reached up like a pro basketball player about to slam home a dunk. The tempered, tapered point of the center punch met the glass. Below him James could clearly hear the thunk as the handheld device's spring popped.

The metal probe snapped out and there was the almost musical sound of glass shattering. Manning leaped up off the end of the ladder and rolled over one shoulder and into the room, James close behind him.

His head cleared the top of the window and he saw a cramped room filled with a bank of metrological instruments, a desktop PC and an intercom. A pair of large binoculars had been knocked to the floor next to a Gail assault rifle and overturned chair. Glass was scattered around the room like litter in an abandoned field. James tossed the ballistic shield onto the desktop directly below the shattered window. Manning was on top of a uniformed guard, his bio-inoculator in his fist while his other covered the man's mouth as he wrestled against the guard's frantic punches from the submissive position.

James rushed forward to offer support just as Manning snorted in frustration and clipped the guy a short, inside roundhouse blow to the point of his chin. The big Canadian's punch snapped the man's head to the side and stunned him long enough for him to pump a dose of anesthetic into his bloodstream.

James looked around the room, looking for camera monitors or alarm controls. He saw a steep, narrow staircase leading down from the northwest corner to the building below them. Manning got to his feet and began using his plastic ties to bind the sentry's hands and feet.

A doorknob rattled at the bottom of the staircase. James moved out of view of the stairway. Manning looked up at him and his teammate put a long finger to his lips. A male voice called out a question up the stairs. The Phoenix Force commandos waited silently, hearing a curse.

Then the sound of someone climbing the stairs.

## CHAPTER TWENTY-THREE

"I tried," Hal Brognola said into the phone. "If they've still got Henri, I don't know about it. If you can get through to them, it would help—but I'm not having any luck, which leads me to believe they're rolling hot."

"I'll try, Hal. It'd be pretty damn ironic," Mack Bolan said, "if Henri is our cell leader and they let him go. At this point I think just getting T.J. home is their top priority."

Brognola paused for a moment. "It'd put him pretty much off his guard if they took Hawkins and let him go. He'd feel pretty secure in the knowledge that we didn't know a damn thing."

"So watch him and see if he's at the top of the food chain."

"He'll be cagey, but it's a plan we've used before."

"He's experienced and he's got governmental resources behind him," Bolan pointed out.

When he spoke Brognola could hear the sound of a plane passing overhead in the background and from the noise level he realized Bolan had to be close to an airport. "But if we can make a case stick instead of wiping him out, it might go a long way toward smoothing ruffled French feathers," Brognola said.

"True. Difficult to pull off, but Cal and Gary can work miracles."

"We'll see what happens when they call back." Brognola sighed.

"I'm out."

"Talk to you later."

Brognola hung up and looked over at the clock on his desk. It was down to the waiting. From outside his office window the sounds of D.C. were muted and distant. He leaned back in his chair and closed his eyes. He thought about calling Barbara Price and putting her in the loop. He decided to let sleeping dogs lie, at least for the moment. She had enough to worry about getting a depleted Stony Man force into position in Mexico City.

The big Fed chewed remorselessly on his unlit stogie, while looking out the window. He felt old.

*France*

THE VOICE CALLED OUT AGAIN as it headed up the stairs to the security tower.

James ducked behind the waist-high wall that secured the staircase opening from the office area in the tower. Manning knelt and pinned the unconscious guard to the ground with a knee across his neck.

Feet pounded in the narrow stairwell as the man jogged up onto the observation floor. Outside, the searchlight continued its endless pattern. The man's head cleared the top of the wall and Manning could see the shock register on his face as he saw the broken window.

The man wore a tan-and-khaki uniform from which a neck like a stone pillar emerged. His hair was obviously his pride, and it grew thick and was combed back over his ears at the very limit of what military regulations would allow in a rakish pompadour. James popped up from behind the retaining wall and snatched him up by that thick neck and full hair.

Twisting hard at the waist, the Phoenix Force commando yanked him over the wall and slammed him onto the linoleum floor. The man croaked in outrage, but James already had one strong hand around his neck like a vise, choking off any outcry. The man was no stranger to the gym and had a weightlifter's build. He latched on to James's wrist and began to pry his fingers off his throat.

Manning hopped forward and drove his knee into the top of the man's head, stunning him momentarily. He was ready with the bio-injector and shoved into the French officer's exposed carotid artery. The man bucked frantically, but the drug coursed through his system with each wild pounding of his heart and saturated his brain in seconds. James rose and brought his shotgun around to cover the stairs while Manning used plastic riot cuffs to bind the man, then finished up by gagging him.

"That was close," he said.

"This whole thing is going to be close," James answered. "I wish it was Jack or Charlie Mott with us."

"My guy's a good man. He's been flying helicopters

as an independent contractor for the Department of State in Baghdad. He won't fold."

"Let's do it, then," James said, then nodded.

The two men rose and began to descend the stairs down into the complex.

JAMES PUSHED OPEN THE DOOR and stepped into the room. He quickly moved to the left side of the door to give Manning space to follow him. They were in a large, open area with tile floor and several electronic consoles. Tables ran along the walls holding closed-circuit television monitors, intercom stations, alarm centers and video-camera feeds. A locked case was set against the wall that held two Gail assault rifles and two Heckler & Koch MP-5 submachine guns. There were two doors, one set in the north wall and an identical one on the west wall.

James moved forward, scanning the room for movement or clues. An office chair on wheels was sitting in the middle of the room a few feet out from a desk holding a switchboard-style office phone, a laptop and a mug.

Manning moved past him and began to read a fire evacuation map posted on the wall underneath a hard plastic screen. James looked at monitors to try to find a clue as to where Hawkins was being held.

He saw several people in white lab coats walking down long interior corridors with linoleum floors and fluorescent lights as they passed identical single doors of nondescript brown wood. Clear plastic file holders were set into the wall next to each of the doors he could see. Some held paperwork while others were empty. In addition to what he assumed were medical personnel in the lab coats, he saw an occasional security officer in the same tan uniforms the men in the tower wore. Each one wore a pistol holstered on his belt.

Manning tapped the plastic cover over the building blueprint. "Okay, I know where we are. You have any clue where T.J. might be?"

"Shit!" James snarled.

Manning turned to see the north door to the room swing open. A tall, lean man in a tailored uniform walked through the door, a cup of coffee in his right hand. There was a pistol on his right hip. He stopped short as he looked into the cavernous muzzle of James's shotgun.

Manning stepped forward and delivered an uppercut elbow strike that caught the man on the point of his chin. The guard's head flew up, then his knees crumpled and he dropped to the floor. His coffee mug fell from his fingers and shattered on the floor, spraying hot liquid everywhere.

The big Canadian reached down and grabbed the unconscious man by his lapels and pulled him farther into the room. He shoved him under a desk and James gave him a shot to put him to sleep. Manning stared at the room's two doors, half expecting a platoon of reinforcements to come charging in.

When none did, he turned back to James. "You think we should try to put on a couple of uniforms? It's a stretch, but it might slow reaction time."

"I've pointed this out before but it bears repeating. I'm black. You're a giant lumberjack. This facility is just too small. They'll pick us out immediately."

Manning nodded at the obvious logic. "I guess we'll

do it the hard way. Do you have any clue about where our boy is?"

James tapped a screen. "All the official-looking egg-heads seem to be going in and out of the rooms in this hall. I, of course, don't know which hall it is or how to get there from here."

"Deduction, my dear Watson," Manning said. "Count the rooms, tell me which side the doors are facing in relation to the screen."

"Six rooms. Facing in from the left side of the screen."

"Only one hallway with six doors along the same side of the hall. Simple," Manning replied.

"Something has to go right once in a while."

"Of course it's on the side of the building the exact farthest from our current position in the security office."

James gestured lazily with his hand. "And there you go."

"We'll take the west door."

THE TWO COMMANDOS CAME OUT of the west door of the security office and immediately found themselves in what was obviously a reception area. They could see the metal double doors of the complex entrance they had identified from the outside of the building. The open area contained a desk, standing empty, under a single overhead light. Opposite the desk, against the same wall that housed the door they had emerged from, were three comfortable chairs.

A hallway led into the complex from their right and one on the far side of the desk directly opposite them. They took a quick survey of the area, saw the security camera in a corner above a potted plant and began to sprint for the hall running westward from the reception desk. A line of pictures on the wall showed photographs of the current French prime minister, followed by the Defense and Interior ministers.

Moving fast, they entered a long narrow hallway broken only twice by doors on their right.

Their plan was simple. Find the hall they had located on the security camera, then grab someone and make him or her talk. As long as speed and surprise remained on their side, the simplicity of their strategy would serve them.

They turned the corner at the end of the hallway and almost immediately found themselves face-to-face with an attractive middle-aged woman in a lab coat, her brunette hair pulled back in an austere bun.

Manning struck without hesitation. He scooped her up in his arms so that her back was against the inside of the ballistic shield he carried. He propelled her backward into the first door they came to. James pushed into the room immediately after him. A figure lay prone on a hospital bed under an oxygen tent. The sound of the artificial-respiration machine was a loud and persistent mechanical rhythm in the room.

"Shh," Manning whispered. He felt slightly ill by what circumstances were forcing him to do.

James pushed up close to the woman and questioned her in rapid French. "Where is the American? He came in yesterday. Where is he? Answer me! Answer me!"

The woman stuttered, "W-oh-nine, up the hall."

James looked at Manning and nodded once. The auto-injector made its pneumatic cough and the woman's eyes rolled up in her head. Manning lowered the drowsy woman onto the floor. His hand went to his belt and he pulled his cell phone clear.

Using the walkie-talkie function, he broke radio silence for the first time since driving up to the Gulf of Lion with James.

"Make approach and hold pattern," he said.

"Copy," the pilot responded.

Manning put his phone away and looked at James. "I don't see how this is possibly going to work."

James smiled. "That's the spirit, baby."

They opened the door and left the room behind them.

Ten steps down the hallway it began to fall apart.

The guard rounded the corner ahead of them, walking beside a bald and bespectacled man in a lab coat. The two Phoenix Force commandos continued their forward charge, both realizing they would never make it across the distance to close with the men.

The guard reacted like a pro. Shoving the man in the lab coat to one side, he groped for the butt of his pistol where it rode on his hip. The man in the lab coat stumbled back around the corner with a loud squawk of protest as the military officer pulled his Glock 17 from its holster.

The XM-26 LSS bolt action 12-gauge shotgun in James's hand roared, the sound of the weapon firing deafening in the narrow hallway.

The riot load of beanbags burped from the barrel and slammed into the military sentry with sledgehammer force. James reached up with one hand and snatched the bolt action back as Manning charged past him, the shield up in front of him like a force field. The French security officer staggered and spun under the impact of the beanbags. His feet tangled up in themselves and he went down hard.

Manning brought the shield up over his head, then drove the bottom edge into the stunned man's unprotected stomach. The guard folded up around the blow like a book snapping shut and made a harsh retching sound.

The big Canadian skipped past him and turned the corner to put the ballistic shield into position. James was three steps behind him, letting the shotgun fall to the end of its sling as he pulled the auto-injector free. He descended on the guard like an avalanche, burying an overhand haymaker into the side of the soldier's neck and following up with a precisely placed shot of Versed from the bio-inoculator.

James felt his heart hammering in his chest as he spun and put the auto-injector back behind his belt buckle. He tossed the Glock 17 away, sending it skidding down the hall. He looked past the broad stretch of Manning's shoulders where the man crouched behind the ballistic shield. He saw the civilian in the lab coat who had been walking with the security officer now standing at what looked like a nurses' station frantically speaking into a phone.

"W-0-9!" Manning pointed to a room halfway down the hall toward where the man was calling for rescue.

"Let's go! Let's go!" James said.

Manning surged up and hurried down the hallway while James unslung his cut-down shotgun and followed closely behind. It seemed almost suicidal to leave doors at their rear that they hadn't properly cleared, but time was collapsing around them like a house of cards.

Manning reached the door to W-0-9 and took up a position near it with the shield. Without hesitation James raced past him and struck the door with his shoulder. The door pushed open easily and he entered the room.

On the bed was T. J. Hawkins.

Next to his bed stood a guard with a drawn Glock 17. The Frenchman spun as James barreled into the room and triggered two quick shots from the 9 mm pistol.

# CHAPTER TWENTY-FOUR

The sharp flat, twin bangs of the handgun cracked hard in James's ear a heartbeat after he felt the searing sting of a slug rip across his shoulder near his neck. He felt the hot splash of his own blood soak the collar of his shirt, and he sprang forward in a desperate attempt to get to the weapon.

He saw the flash and heard the report of the pistol even as he lunged. *This is it,* he thought. But the shot was wild and the sentry cursed in anger. Hawkins surged up out of the bed, his eyes dull and bloodshot, and cracked the cast on his left arm across the guard's wrist.

The man's arm was knocked wild as the bones of his wrist were bruised by the hard plaster of Hawkins's cast. The Glock went spinning and the man howled as Hawkins moaned from the pain caused by his sudden exertion and sank back into the bed, retching at the effort. In an almost frenzied state the wounded James struck the man.

He used the arm on his wounded shoulder to grasp

the stumbling guard in a half-grip, Muay Thai clench hold. With his good arm he began to hammer punches into the man. Confused and overwhelmed, the French sentry attempted to jerk his head free to avoid the hammer blows. Suddenly switching tactics, James released his hold and the man windmilled, wildly off balance and falling backward.

James did not hesitate. He put the heel of his combat boot squarely on the man's chin in a picture-perfect front snap kick and dropped him. The man crumpled into an unconscious heap directly beneath the pulled blinds of the room's reinforced window. Panting hard and soaked in his own blood, James looked over at the ashen-faced Hawkins.

"Son of a bitch shot me," James said.

Hawkins smiled weakly. "What the fuck took you so long?" he whispered, then passed out.

Pistol shots rang out in the hallway and angry, shouting voices preceded Manning backing into the room. Rounds ricocheted off the ballistic shield he held and whined away before lodging into the building's drywall, leaving craterlike wounds at their impacts.

"Jesus!" Manning shouted, sounding like a tourist on a roller-coaster ride. "Are we good? Are we good? Please tell me we're good!"

James pulled his left hand away from his shoulder and frowned at the blood he saw there. "We're as good as we're going to get—lock the goddamn door."

Manning put the ballistic shield between himself and the solid wood of the room door before throwing the dead bolt. Behind him James began a rapid trauma assessment of the unconscious Hawkins to determine his travel requirements. He had discussed the situation with

Manning beforehand and both men had agreed that if the former Delta Force commando was on a respirator, then they would leave him. Moving him would kill him.

What James saw now was bad enough, and he was thankful his friend was unconscious. The youngest Phoenix Force member was covered in bandages and casts. He was hooked to an IV tree of saline solution attached to a bolus of antibiotics. James could see the tubing was connected by a surgically implanted PIC line in the man's chest, and there wasn't an inch of skin that remained exposed that wasn't mottled yellow and purple. A feeding tube had been inserted via nasal canula.

Manning pulled the heavy racks of sensory equipment that monitored Hawkins's condition in front of the door, forming a makeshift barricade. Bullets punched through the wood of the door, splintering it. The Canadian turned toward James as the ex-Navy SEAL began prepping the gravely injured man for movement.

"Get the bed against the wall," he said.

James nodded and kicked the wheel lock loose on the hospital bed. As he pushed the bed over, Manning undid the buckle holding a bandolier across his chest. He dropped to one knee and threw the bandolier on the floor where he began peeling his Semtex shaped charges loose.

"Get the shield and lie on top of him," Manning instructed. "The back blast will be trapezoidal in shape. If we're in the left corner of the room on the door-side wall, I can focus the blast away from us. It'll knock the window and back wall out, but that side of the room in the geometrical angle is going to get fried, as well."

"We're good," James said, taking up the ballistic shield. "Better warn the pilot."

Manning shook his head. "The blast *is* the signal. He should be overhead right now."

"Let's do it," James said.

Manning scooted across the room in a half crouch, keeping below the height of the sensory equipment that formed the bulwark of his defenses against the pistol shots raining into the room from the outside. He began to expertly place the preconstructed charges. He prepped them for ignition and scrambled back across the room to where James stood waiting with the ballistic shield.

"You ready?" he demanded.

"Let's do it."

Manning scrambled onto the hospital bed, covering the unconscious Hawkins with his own body. James slid into place next to him and locked the bottom edge of the shield against the side rails to more securely weather the blast.

"I'm good!" he shouted.

"Fire in the hole!" Manning answered.

There was a flash of light.

The oxygen was gone from the room. James could hear nothing.

The concussive force rolled into the ballistic shield, carrying a rush of noise with it. There was the rattle of loose building textiles against the composite material of the shield, then a rolling cloud of billowing black smoke obscured the room from sight.

James forced himself up. He could see the sky like a backlit canopy through the swirling smoke, and he threw the shield away from him. Behind him Manning was pushing himself up off the bed and scrambling into position.

A triangle-shaped hole had been punched through the north wall of the room where the window had sat. James moved and snatched the bed by the forward edge of a side rail. He jerked it after him, and the wheels protested as they began to strike debris.

Manning grunted with the effort and lifted his end of the bed. James tightened his own grip and heaved it off the floor, leading the way through the ruin across the spilled detritus. A fire was burning against the east wall and deep craters had been punched into it as if by sledgehammer blows.

James looked back and saw how relatively unscathed his own corner of the room had been by the residual blast damage. The contrast was stark. Manning had done a consummate job with his controlled demolition. He tried to grab the bed with his other arm, but his wound seemed to scream in protest and he felt the hot wet flow of more of his blood. He gritted his teeth and forced his body to perform.

Then he was outside the choking confines of the hospital room, and he sucked in air like a drowning man. He cast about him widely but couldn't see the helicopter. He felt Manning driving the bed forward and allowed himself to be directed farther away from the blast hole.

The smoke thinned and his ears popped, and suddenly he could hear the drumming of the helicopter overhead. He looked up as rotor wash began to beat down on his face and drive the circling smoke away. He saw a civilian Sikorsky with the massive engine turbines of a construction workhorse. The pilot looked at him through a dark visor out the side window and bounced the helicopter off the tarmac as he brought the bird down. The side door to the cargo bay was already open, and it yawned like the mouth of a cavern.

James put his head down and dug in with his legs. The two Phoenix Force commandos raced across the short space, heads bent against the driving, relentless force of the rotor wash, and reached the cargo bay of the Sikorsky.

James used his forward momentum to throw himself over the lip of the bay floor and carry the top of Hawkins's bed up onto the helicopter. He went up on one knee and gasped out loud at the pain from his shoulder. He yanked the hospital bed toward him, the metal scissor-legs collapsing flat the way they were designed to do, and saw Manning shoving hard with both hands on the rear of the bed, forcing it into the nominal protection of the helicopter bay.

Behind Manning, James saw a French security officer emerge from the swirling smoke, a pistol in his hand. He tried to shout a warning, but it was carried away by the driving white noise of the Sikorsky engines. He scrambled to try to alert Manning as the Frenchman raised the Glock.

He tore a flash-bang grenade from his harness as he lunged forward, and he saw Manning look at his sudden movements with quick comprehension. The Canadian looked behind him and saw the security guard taking aim in a hasty two-handed Weaver stance. He set his jaw and ignored the threat, pushing the gravely injured Hawkins farther into the helicopter and safety.

James pulled the pin on his stun grenade and saw the muzzle-flash from the barrel of the guard's pistol. Manning stiffened as the 9 mm round struck him high on the left shoulder and his blood spit up and splashed across the white sheets of Hawkins's hospital bed. The big Canadian sagged under the impact and threw himself forward to cover his wounded teammate's body with his own. James released the flash-bang and saw it arch outward, its cylinder body spinning end over end.

He was thrown backward as the helicopter pilot gunned the engines for a takeoff. The guard raced forward, firing his pistol, anger and determination stamped in harsh lines on his face. Bullets rattled off the inside of the helicopter. As the grenade bounced and rolled toward the Frenchman, he saw the movement and instinctively threw himself away from it.

The sharp flash of brilliant light was blinding, and the hard flat bang was audible even over the Sikorsky's engines as the stun grenade detonated. The guard was thrown to the ground by the concussive blast of the nonlethal device and the Sikorsky shot out over the dark indigo waves of the Mediterranean, heading south and running hard for open water.

James forced himself up off the floor and grabbed the handle to the bay door. He snarled with the effort and slammed the heavy portal shut along its runners. He turned and looked at Manning, who remained hunched over the bottom half of Hawkins's bed.

Worried, James made his way over to the man, but the Canadian lifted himself up before the ex-Navy SEAL made it to him. Manning grimaced in pain and clutched his wounded shoulder. He saw the expression on James's face and gave the worried team medic a reassuring thumbs-up.

"We made it!" he shouted at James. His voice sounded incredulous. "Remind me to give our pilot a bonus."

*Stony Man Farm, Virginia*

"DID YOU KNOW ABOUT THIS?" Barbara Price asked.

"No," Hal Brognola answered. He looked uncomfortable, then admitted, "Not in any formal sense. I had my suspicions." He paused. "So did you. We knew they were going to get T.J."

"What about Henri?"

"I couldn't alert James in time. Henri was left in the trunk of a car outside the government offices in Marseilles. He's already been found and released."

"So he must not think we know he's the primary facilitator behind the disparate Bellicose Dawn elements."

"That thought had crossed my mind," Brognola admitted. He was just glad the conversation had progressed past what he might or might not have known about the extracurricular actions of James and Manning. Or how Mack Bolan might or might not have fit into them.

"He's a little too slick of an operator to try to pull a 'follow the leader' operation on," Price pointed out.

"I know, but what if he was just the field officer? What if he's got somebody behind him? I mean, his putting this thing into motion I get. He did it for the money. But who pulled the trigger? Who wrote the check?"

"The Saudi, al-Shalaan for one, at least in part. But that was secondary. The main perpetrator has to be someone who would profit, in some way, from a terror attack inside the U.S. It's that simple."

"And that's wide-open," Brognola replied. "Unless

we can figure out how Henri would profit by instigating this Bellicose Dawn, we have to assume he's just hired help."

"The prince and the Mexican connection?"

"We have to take them down, but right now they look like spokes in the wheel. Major players, but not the kingpin."

"What if we have a cabal, a joint operation?"

"That's not what the interrogators are getting from al-Shalaan. Henri knew al-Shalaan could get to the prince and to the Mexican connection, for that matter. He put al-Shalaan into the prince's path, probably picked the prince out as a likely moneyman from French intelligence files."

"There is the possibility that this is somehow a sanctioned operation."

"I guess. I mean, we have to keep an open mind, but I sure hope to hell not. If so, the buck stops with Henri."

"If we find out elements of the French government have basically declared an act of war on the U.S. and the Man doesn't want the public fallout—and I can't see him doing so—then we could never get to the bottom of this."

"We'll have stopped the attack and dismantled the network."

"It's going to hurt letting the kingpin at the top of the pyramid go. Our boys have eaten some real casualties on this one."

"Barb, I'm not sure we'll be able to move on the Saudi. He's a freaking prince in the family of one of our strongest allies in the Middle East. The Man has given his nod to the takedown of the Mexican connection, Reyes, but he's still sitting on the fence about the Saudi.

Political blowback could hurt us too much to make a kill cost-effective."

"This stinks." Her voice held an undertone of anger, and bright points of color showed on her cheekbones.

Brognola put his unlit cigar in his mouth and clamped down hard. "We don't have to like it. Shadow wars are never pretty. There's always a bigger picture to think about."

"It's times like this I get real jealous of Mack."

Brognola looked away and sighed. "I know exactly what you mean."

"THE AZTECS USED TO sacrifice about two hundred and fifty thousand of their own people every year," Schwarz said. "They would cut out their hearts while they were still alive."

"Okay, that provides us with a template on how to deal with this guy," Lyons pointed out.

Encizo nodded from behind the wheel of the black Dodge SUV. Around them a rambling shantytown sprawled from the edges of Mexico City. The Stony Man crew kept the blacked-out windows on their SUV rolled up tight against the smell.

The road they traveled was made of dirt and heavily rutted, dotted with puddles of dubious origins. Bored, apathetic faces stared out at the expensive vehicle from the safety of clapboard and aluminum-siding shacks. The poverty was appalling and left Carl Lyons uneasy. He was no stranger to Central and South American privation. Able Team had made the lower half of the Western Hemisphere a primary area of operations since the unit's inception.

Encizo guided the big vehicle through narrow alleys while hungry dogs barked and chased them. Up ahead a line of railroad tracks broke the sprawling shantytown and massive warehouses began to line its length. Beyond these the silent mausoleum of factories built by American companies that had exported jobs to exploit cheap labor reared up like austere, prefabricated mountains.

Encizo cut the SUV onto a single-lane dirt road that paralleled the train track. The vehicle's suspension rattled and hummed but inside the climate-controlled cab the ride was smooth and virtually silent. Up ahead a chipped and cracked asphalt lot opened up just past a broken gate in a dilapidated chain-link fence. A battered and rusted sign warning away trespassers in Spanish hung off to one side like a forgotten letter.

The building across the old parking lot was abandoned, dotted with broken windows and gaping emptiness where doors had stood. A line of crows had taken roost across the top, and Encizo slowed the vehicle as he pulled into the old parking lot.

"How are we sitting for time?" he asked.

Lyons looked at his watch. "We're a good hour before the meet, according to the CIA stringer," he said. "We couldn't have got here any sooner with flight time anyway."

"Not with the Saudi warning the Mexican," Schwarz added.

"Do not get me started on the Saudi," Lyons snapped, his voice bitter. "I'm going to be a very unhappy boy if the President decides to go easy on the prince."

"Big picture, big picture." Encizo shrugged.

He guided the SUV around the side of the building.

A pair of filthy alley cats hissed in surprise at the sudden appearance of the monstrous vehicle and scrambled for the safety of some overflowing garbage containers. Lyons eyed the building warily as Encizo drove around it. He reached under the seat and pulled an Ingram MAC-10 clear.

"Politics give me a rash," Lyons muttered. He snapped the bolt back on the compact submachine gun and seated a .45 ACP round.

"I just wish we had more time to check out this setup," Schwarz said from the backseat. He removed an identical MAC-10 from a briefcase on the seat next to him and chambered a round. "We don't know this guy from Adam."

"Barbara had it right," Encizo answered. He pulled the SUV into a parking spot just behind an empty freestanding garage inside the fence, putting the vehicle out of view of the main building. "Now that Reyes knows we're onto him, his only option is to play ball. He was taking money from the Saudi, the CIA got a hold on him when they found him taking money from Chavez in Venezuela and kickbacks from the Zetas. The guy's dirty, but he's a gold mine of information."

Encizo reached over and pulled his own prepped and ready Ingram from the inside compartment of his door. Each man on the team wore a windbreaker over a backup shoulder-holstered pistol. They had no intention of hiding their firepower when they went into the meet.

As the team stepped out of the vehicle there was a thunderous roaring as a freight train began its approach of the rail yard off to the side of the building. Lyons looked around. This was the location of the meet with the man who was supposed to take them to where Reyes was hiding.

"This strike you as overly isolated for a simple meet-and-greet?" Schwarz asked.

"Why, whatever do you mean, Grandma?" Lyons asked, then added, "Fucking CIA man. I hate crossing ops with them. Our styles are just *way* too different."

The freight train began to slow even further. The engineer popped its brakes with a deafening hissing noise accompanied by the screaming of steel on steel as wheels locked up on rails. Encizo eyeballed the upper reaches of the building as they approached the back. The windows looked back at him, silent and dark.

Closer to the ground the building was taken up by a concrete loading dock and roll-up bay doors for almost two-thirds of its length. The other section was broken by a single metal door set at the top of a short flight of concrete steps. Spiky lines of graffiti covered the wall and doors. Displaced air from the sliding train pushed scraps of paper across the broken asphalt like stringless kites.

Mexico City was one of the worst polluted cities on the face of the earth and here, in its underbelly, the stench was sharp and chemical.

The train pulled up next to the yard, clattering in a deafening din as boxcar after boxcar slowly rumbled by. Though they stood close together, the men couldn't hear each other speak. Lyons frowned and made a gesture with his hand.

The other two immediately spread out, forming into a loose triangle as they finished their approach to the front of the building. Schwarz looked to one side and saw line gouts suddenly erupt in the earth. He reached over and shoved Lyons to one side, then flung himself in the other direction. The line of bullets stitched up the middle of them while off to the side Encizo had lifted his MAC-10 and began to spray it at the top line of windows on the building. For the Stony Man crew it was SNAFU as usual.

Situation Normal: All Fouled Up.

# CHAPTER TWENTY-FIVE

The Ingram MAC-10 compact submachine gun was designed for close, almost point-blank range and ease of concealment, but the heavy .45 ACP rounds were more than powerful enough to cross the space between ambush sniper and the men caught in the path of his murderous fire. Encizo's burst had no trouble slamming into the building.

Lyons rolled with the hard shove his teammate had given him and somersaulted over one shoulder. He came up and quickly scanned the building for the attackers. He saw nothing other than the single sniper trading shots with Encizo and quickly crossed his stream of .45 ACP rounds with the Phoenix Force commando's.

Bullets rebounded off the wall and shattered what slivers of glass still remained in their frames. He saw brilliant bursts of muzzle-flashes and tried to bring his own fire to bear accurately as he continued to race toward the building. The freight train had formed a blanket of painful white noise on the entire area and Lyons felt acutely strange, able to register the feel of his recoil and the heat of escaping gases but still almost entirely unable to hear the report of his own weapon in his hands.

Off to one side Schwarz bounced up off the parking lot and raced for the single pedestrian door set to one side of the building. Behind him Encizo continued firing burst after burst into the area of the sniper in an attempt to suppress his gunfire. The freight train continued to roll on past their position in an endless line of flatbed trailers and boxcars.

Grunting with the effort, Schwarz raced toward the building, his Ingram submachine gun up and ready. Closing with the short staircase, he let go of the subgun with his left hand and leaped into the air like a sprinter running hurdles. He caught hold of a metal safety rail running the length of the stairs and vaulted over to the top of the steps.

He tucked his elbow in tight against his ribs and drew the Ingram close to his body. With his free hand he grabbed the doorknob and twisted, jerking the heavy door open on protesting hinges. The sound of the train rolled into the building and echoed off the walls so that the din and racket was actually worse the closer the Stony Man crew got to the massive warehouse structure.

Schwarz darted inside, immediately finding himself in a cavernous, open space some three stories high. He scanned the gloomy interior and let the door swing closed behind him. He had expected the structure to contain floors, but he quickly shifted his tactics to compensate for the open space.

He pivoted and dropped into a crouch toward a formation of ladders and scaffolding set against one wall.

Through a forest of metal bars and steel mesh he caught an impression of movement, triggering a burst and hearing the sniper do the same. Lead slugs ricocheted wildly inside the building and muzzle-blasts flared, casting crazy shadows.

Realizing he had to cut an angle on the sniper, Schwarz dived forward across oil-stained concrete and came up before triggering a second burst with his Ingram. He saw a black-clad figure lean over a railing with a scope-mounted M-16, its black buttstock jammed tight into his shoulder.

The man fired down at Schwarz, and the Able Team electronics whiz threw himself toward the uncertain cover of a line of 55-gallon barrels. One of the roll-up bay doors directly beneath the sniper suddenly slid open to a height of about three feet, and Schwarz had a brief glimpse of Rafael Encizo lying flat on his stomach, Ingram held out in front of him.

Realizing Lyons was about to make entry into the abandoned factory, Schwarz raked the scaffolding with automatic fire, still desperately seeking an angle to catch the sniper. He couldn't force a clear trajectory out of the mess, and his rounds scattered in a wild pattern around the hunched and ducking man.

The sniper rose, straightened his weapon and returned fire, his assault rifle set to 3-round bursts. Volleys of 5.56 mm rounds began to hammer into the barrels Schwarz crouched behind. Below the man, Lyons pinpointed his position and turned his own Ingram MAC-10 skyward. The chatterbox rattled in his hands, and a stream of dull gold casings arched out like water from a hose and bounced and rolled across the concrete floor.

The .45-caliber slugs began slamming into the mesh and metal framework at the sniper's feet, and the man suddenly began sprinting toward one side of the platform above them, while still trying to turn and return Lyons's fire. Schwarz used the opportunity to merge his own stream of gunfire with Lyons's, only to have his magazine run dry.

He dropped the magazine from the well in the pistol butt and curling gray smoke followed the empty box. He pulled a secondary magazine from his coat pocket and slid it home before chambering a round. In the brief time it took for the Able Team commando to switch out magazines, the faceless sniper had managed to reach the temporary safety of a double girder, overhead-bridge crane control panel and engine housing.

Schwarz cursed. The control area was like a fortress of metal squares and thick welded beams. He tried an exploratory burst, but the Ingram was less than precise. He would have to settle for burst cover fire unless he could work his way in closer for a more accurate shot.

The situation was fast approaching a stalemate, Schwarz realized. Without drawing closer, the Ingrams were too inaccurate to pose a threat at the current range, but to get closer the Stony Man operatives would have to cross open space easily within the range of the man's assault rifle.

Lyons sprinted across the space between his position and the barrels Schwarz was using for cover. He rolled over and came up next to his teammate as Encizo continued to fire from the edge of one of the bay doors.

"This is insane!" Lyons yelled. "The asshole can't

possibly think the CIA will let him get away with setting up a meet and then ambushing American agents!"

Schwarz lifted his Ingram and sprayed another quick burst. "Maybe he thinks he can run, maybe he did it for money from Reyes."

The sniper poked the barrel of his M-16 around the edge of the panel and squeezed off an answering burst; Encizo returned fire.

"The only way to find out is to take him alive," Schwarz said.

"You want to cross that open space and charge up a vertical ladder?" Lyons demanded.

"No, but I was hoping you would." Schwarz laughed. "You are known for your temper."

"Kiss my ass, Gadgets!" Lyons muttered, the MAC-10 bucking in his hands.

Schwarz scanned the wide-open floor space of the factory. He realized that with his elevated position and superior range, the sniper still had every advantage— even though he'd blown his initial attack.

"Let's just go," Schwarz said.

"What!" Lyons shouted, his voice incredulous.

"Let's just boogey out of here. I mean it. Let him think we ran."

"We need to know what that guy knows!" Lyons argued. "Reyes is a ghost. He's our only lead."

"To find out," Schwarz pointed out, "we need him to come down."

Lyons opened his mouth to reply. He paused, then closed his mouth and cocked an eyebrow. He turned toward Schwarz and nodded once. "Okay, let's do it," he said.

"Rafe!" Schwarz shouted.

"Yeah?" Encizo shouted back.

"Get the car!" Schwarz yelled. "Trust me!"

Encizo looked at him, then nodded. In a second he was out the door. Lyons dropped a magazine from the pistol grip of his Ingram and inserted a fresh one while Schwarz provided covering fire.

JAMES WATCHED THE Farm come into view and despite himself, he felt like he was coming home. He was angry and depressed to have discovered that he'd held a key player and then just let the man go. He was more troubled by the fact that Brognola seemed convinced that the White House may have deemed the man off-limits in keeping with the needs of the "big picture."

After cleaning several security checkpoints, he pulled the red Pacifica to a stop in front of the main farmhouse and shut off the engine. He climbed out of the roomy vehicle and threw his overnight bag onto his good shoulder. The other one was covered in bandages under his clothes. He walked into the house and was immediately greeted by Buck Greene, the head of Stony Man security.

"Good to see you, Cal," the chief said. He held out his hand, then nodded toward the bandage peeking out of his shirt next to James's neck. "How's the wound?"

"I'll live," James replied. "It's not that bad really. It wasn't deep into the muscle, just an ugly scratch."

"Good. Hal and Barb are waiting for you down in the War Room. If you want, I can take your bag to your room upstairs."

James handed the man his bag and nodded. "Thanks, Buck. No rest for the wicked."

"Good seeing you," Greene said, and took the overnight satchel as the Phoenix Force commando headed for the elevator to the basement.

On the lower level he quickly found his way to the War Room and entered. Both Price and Brognola rose to meet him, and he accepted their greetings warmly. Quickly, though, he got to the point.

"I should have put a bullet into Henri Galli when I had the chance."

Price looked at Brognola, who frowned. "I understand how you feel, Cal," the big Fed said. "But there's a lot going on."

"Like what?" James demanded.

"Like who Henri called when he was released from that car trunk you stuffed him into," Price said.

James turned to look at the woman. "Say what?" His voice was incredulous. "He made such a rookie mistake?"

"I think he did it on purpose," Brognola said.

James raised an eyebrow. "Really?"

"I received a very cryptic e-mail written in obtuse language from an anonymous public server in a Paris Internet café."

"Your office e-mail floating around the university district of Paris?"

Brognola shook his head. "Nope. To get that e-mail in the Justice Department you have to be inside the system, or have access to someone who does."

"What did it say?" James asked.

"It simply said, and I quote, 'Things have gone too far. Repercussions for both parties too damaging if situation made public. Maintain big picture. Monitor source for compromise,'" Brognola said.

"Then?"

"Then," Price broke in, "Akira's electronic monitoring of Henri Galli all of a sudden managed to crack the encryption on his cell phone. Galli made a single call and then disconnected that phone."

"He gave us the tip of the pyramid?"

"He gave us the tip of the pyramid," Brognola echoed, nodding. "They fed us a pretty significant bone to protect French and U.S. relations. The man in the Oval Office is pretty much inclined to nix a hit on a member of the Saudi royal family. We get the kingpin and permission to send the prince a very pointed message."

"That doesn't feel like resolution," James said. "Galli was the one who directed T.J.'s interrogation. He was the planning and logistic mastermind behind an attempted terror plot on U.S. soil."

"Technically it was a nonlethal attempt," Price pointed out. She didn't sound convinced herself. "And you were able to thwart it before it happened."

"That BZ would have caused widespread pandemonium, undermined public security and most certainly would have resulted in deaths," James argued.

"And that's why we're sending you after the man that put this plot into motion," Brognola said.

"And that is?"

"The media darling Marcos Sincanaros."

REYES HIT THE GAS on his Katana street bike and raced out of the building. He was pretty close to panicked. The Saudi prince had been very clear in his warning; it was all coming down. Loose ends needed to be tied up, and he hadn't been left with a lot of time to assemble a cleaning crew off the books.

What had started out as easy money from connection-making and influence-peddling against the arrogant Yankees had quite suddenly backfired. The Zetas organization on the East Coast was wrecked. Their commandant butchered. It was time to take the money and run. He'd tried to shake the investigators off the prince's tail for him, but it hadn't worked out. Too bad, so sad. Now it was time to go.

He gunned the powerful motorcycle across the abandoned asphalt parking lot of the old factory and out the front gate. The American investigating team had made its escape and it was time for him to do the same. He used the toe of his boot to push the bike into a higher gear and he cranked with his wrist, holding the throttle wide-open.

He shot through the gate and out onto the access rode lined with shantytown shacks of aluminum siding and cardboard. Suddenly up ahead, next to the rusting derelict of a train engine parked and forgotten on the old tracks, Reyes saw one of the American agents, the big blond bastard, standing out in the open with his submachine gun. The man flipped him the middle finger and Reyes went to lock up his bike, send it into a slide and change direction before the fool opened fire.

His rear tire caught on the hard-packed earth, and he felt the motorcycle start to respond. Suddenly he sensed movement and looked up. Too late he saw the Americans' vehicle, a massive SUV, rush out of a narrow alley in the shanties to run into him. Behind the blacked-out visor of his helmet Reyes screamed.

Rafael Encizo's face was expressionless as he rammed the big vehicle into the man. The heavy bumper struck the Japanese bike and sent it skipping end over end down the road, tossing the rider like a rag doll in a spinning pinwheel of limbs.

The corrupt Mexican intelligence agent struck the ground and bounced, his limbs almost instantly folding into unnatural angles. Encizo hit the brakes on the SUV to allow the motorcycle to bounce away and avoid becoming entangled with it. He watched the body of the ambush assassin rebound off the ground like a rubber ball and sprawl in an ungainly slide onto the old, weed-choked railroad tracks.

"Oh, that's going to leave a mark," Schwarz muttered, and winced.

Encizo twisted the wheel and threw the SUV into a sideways slide as he brought the vehicle to a stop. He opened his door and bailed while across from him the Able Team electronics expert did the same, both men bringing their compact submachine guns up to provide cover.

From his decoy position Carl Lyons raced toward the fallen man, his own submachine gun covering the motionless figure. Encizo sized up the situation and immediately turned to provide cover as the two Able Team warriors converged on the broken body.

Lyons knelt and put two fingers against the motorcyclist's throat while Schwarz covered him. The Able Team warrior pulled some clothing to one side and felt again. He looked up at his teammate and shook his head.

"No pulse," he said.

"Yank the helmet," Schwarz demanded.

Setting down the Ingram, Lyons quickly undid the

chin strap and pulled the helmet free. The man's head bounced oddly and came to rest at an almost obscene angle. The neck of the assassin was clearly broken.

"That's Reyes," Schwarz stated.

"Well, I guess we're done in Mexico City," Lyons announced.

"Shake him down for a cell phone or something. It might pay off," Schwarz pointed out. "I'm sorry, guys. I know we needed him alive. I didn't realize he'd be riding a bike instead of driving a car when I set up the plan."

"Shit happens," Lyons said.

"Unless Hal and Barb have found out who set the Frenchman in motion, we've got no one left to run down other than the prince," Schwarz stated.

"Find anything?" Encizo called.

Lyons looked up. "No, he was running clean."

"Let's get out of here, then," Schwarz said, looking around. "The natives are starting to get curious."

Lyons stood and nodded.

"Let's roll."

# CHAPTER TWENTY-SIX

Barbara Price sat across the table from Hal Brognola in the War Room. Beside her, at the head of the table, Aaron Kurtzman was busily keying information into his computer. The green light from the screen flashed.

He used a blunt fingertip to tap a series of keys a final time. He grunted and frowned, then looked up at Brognola and Price. "No one can do it fast enough," he said. "Even the on-call units from the army and navy will take too long to mobilize."

"Damn it!" Brognola slapped a hand down on the table with enough force to slosh coffee around in its mug.

"Well, there we are," Price said, her voice tight. "Our choice has been made for us. We either postpone the strike or go as we are."

Brognola held up his hand and began ticking off fingers, one by one. "Rosario, David, T.J., now Gary. Hell, Calvin is far from one hundred percent. His shoulder is shot to hell. Carl looks like he got in a fight with an ugly stick and lost."

"He looks like that most of the time," Kurtzman broke in.

Brognola gave him a sour look. "Three guys. Three guys and an injured Calvin."

"We have basically Able Team plus one," Price pointed out. "We've sent Able into just as dangerous situations, just as outnumbered." She paused. "It doesn't take anything away from Rosario to say Rafael's a damn good man."

Brognola sighed heavily. "No, of course not. But we've been running them hot and heavy since this began."

"When don't we?" Price answered. She held up a hand to cut off the big Fed's protests. "Hal, I'm not arguing just to prove points. You know what the men are capable of, the same as I do. I'm saying that they'll *want* to put the nail in the coffin on Sincanaros, and send the Saudi prince a message he won't soon forget. With the rest of the government's covert action teams tied up there's no one left to exploit this opportunity. Of course it's risky. Risky is what we do."

Brognola puffed out his cheeks then slowly released his breath. He shrugged. "You're right, Barbara."

He turned to where Kurtzman was waiting and nodded. "Call them in, Aaron. If we're going to do this, then every minute counts."

CARL LYONS SCRATCHED the receding welt on his face. "Let me get this straight," he said. "Cal's pain-in-the-ass Frenchman warns the Saudi. So the prince knows he's under surveillance, and the first thing he does is set up a tour on a personal yacht the size of a cruise ship with a cabal of Islamic radicals and their bodyguards?"

"Arrogance is his sin," Kurtzman said. "It is that simple. It's what made him think he could get away with helping fund a terror op against the U.S. in the first place. He thinks he's untouchable."

"Apparently he is," Schwarz said. "The President said no dead Saudi princes, right?"

"Right," Brognola said. The Man from Justice leaned forward. "But he *only* said no dead Saudi princes. Everyone else on that ship is fair game, at least as it stands now. The Yemenis expatriate clerics, the Waziristan bodyguards, the Dubai financiers. It's a honeypot operation in spades, and the President feels just fine with you surrounding that prince with piles of smoking corpses. Hell, if the prince wasn't on that ship, the Man would probably authorize a Hellfire missile, Oman territorial waters or no Oman territorial waters."

"But if we want them, then we need to start loading up on the plane ten minutes ago," Price said.

Lyons's face split into a huge grin. "That's all I need to hear."

Encizo turned in his seat and looked at Schwarz. He jerked a thumb at Lyons. "You know, this guy kind of starts to grow on you."

"Sure." Schwarz nodded, face earnest. "Just like a fungus."

JAMES LOOKED AT Hal Brognola from his seat across the table from him in the War Room. "Why aren't I with the rest of the team?" he demanded. "My shoulder is fine."

Brognola looked at Price. The mission controller nodded and turned to face James. "You're not with the rest of the Stony Man unit because time is ticking and we need to be in two places at once."

"How so?"

"Marcos Sincanaros."

James leaned forward, his face registering his surprise. "You got him sanctioned?"

"Yes, we did," Brognola acknowledged.

"*Him* you can get a sanction for, but not the prince?"

"Let's just say the President doesn't feel it would be counterproductive to our efforts in the war on terror to piss off a certain South American leader," Kurtzman spoke up.

"Why do the strikes need to be simultaneous?" James asked. "I understand the rush to catch the prince and his cohorts on the yacht, but why can't Sincanaros wait till we've finished with that?"

"Because despite the help of your good friend Henri Galli," Price replied, "when the prince gets his 'come to Jesus moment' on that yacht, Sincanaros will know exactly what's happening. Reyes was an expendable middleman, but Sincanaros is the real deal, a big fish. He'll be plugged into the networks capable of giving him plenty of warning and if he goes to his sponsors for protection, we'll be fighting an army to get to him.

"If you hit him tonight, then things will be a hell of a lot simpler," Price added. "At this moment, after the kind of runs we've been having, Stony needs simple, and how. Jack Grimaldi will be your pilot and backup. You want some payback for what happened to T.J.? Forget Galli. He's just a well-paid errand boy, no matter what kind of an idiot he is. Sincanaros is the one who put this together from the beginning. He just used

Galli's connections and savvy to bring in al-Shalaan. We need to send the Saudi a pointed message—but the loose ends, as best they can be, are tied up when Sincanaros goes down."

"Let's do this, then," James said. "Where is he?"

"We traced his sat-phone signal to a resort villa in Venezuela," Kurtzman said. "I pulled up the National Intelligence Estimates for that area over the last week to see if we had any cross-pollination with other groups. Apparently the Agency has placed several traveling diplomats from Colombia's FARQ as moving through the airport nearest his villa two days ago."

"He can facilitate that kind of transnational movement?" James asked. "Even if only on a regional level?"

"Hell," Price broke in. "The FBI counterintelligence boys think he bought the good senator from Maryland, remember? Sincanaros is just the kind of none-state actor D.C. fears most in this current day and age. Überrich, über-connected and politically motivated. I read the supplemental report out of the General Accounting Office's audit and transcripts division. From his purchasing record it seems the BZ terror attacks were a way for Sincanaros to leverage the American dollar and *really* hurt us."

"You're kidding." James whistled. "One man can do that?"

"Jeez," Kurtzman said. "Look at how much damage George Sorros did to Britain's currency, and that was just plain greed."

"And French intelligence knew about this?" James demanded.

"It's not that simple. One agent acted rogue, as a

mercenary. We suspect that certain elements inside the French establishment suspected but couldn't prove the gist of what was going down. There's enough plausible deniability built into the project for the Oval Office to say it's too iffy to move on," Brognola said.

"Besides," Kurtzman added, "what are we going to do? Declare war on France? Even a secret war?" The man shrugged his massive shoulders. "What are you gonna do?"

James cocked an eyebrow. "What am I going to do?" He smiled. "Sounds like I'm going to kill Sincanaros."

JACK GRIMALDI KEPT the Q5 Lacrosse helicopter deep in the cloud cover and navigated by his instruments.

Beside him in the long-range helicopter, James methodically checked and rechecked his equipment. Occasionally he would doze off to catch a quick catnap and at other times he would systematically work the muscles of his body in isometric contractions to avoid stiffening up during the long flight.

Out over the southern Caribbean right before it became the Atlantic along the eastern coast of the South American continent, they conducted a refueling operation with an Air Force plane specially designated for the task by the Officer in Charge of the Southern Command at the personal request of Hal Brognola.

Once that was done, Grimaldi put the nose of the aircraft on a southwestern azimuth and ran it hard. He kept his speed at just under 280 mph and avoided designated air-traffic flight zones and military radar from half a dozen national agencies.

The night was cobalt-black as he made his final approach. He reached over and put a hand on James's shoulder to alert the man before keying his headset.

"We're on the approach," Grimaldi said. "Look out, and you'll see the regional highway. The island of lights in the hills south of that road is Sincanaros's mansion. Keep the road north and the property south, and you should land right on target."

James nodded. "At five hundred feet there's not a lot of time to screw it up."

"Not enough for you to recover if you did, anyway." Grimaldi grinned. "You tell me when you're ready, and I'll drop down."

James went through his prejump drill, securing his harness and double-checking his equipment and primary weapon. He was dressed, not for a full-scale assault, but for a quiet kill. He was going to sneak in, make a sharp, relevant point on behalf of the United States, and sneak out again, hopefully without anyone being the wiser.

He turned to Grimaldi and gave the man a thumbs-up before removing the flight helmet. The Stony Man pilot nodded his understanding and James felt the helicopter begin to change elevation. The aircraft floated downward, dropping out of the clouds, and the checkerboard landscape beneath began to grow and sharpen into focus.

James looked out of his window and quickly orientated himself using the landmarks delineated by Grimaldi. The highway was a curving black line through dark tree-covered hills, connected by bridges where it crossed fast-moving rivers and deep but narrow canyons choked by heavy, green brush. North and east of the drop zone the lights of a medium-size city were prominently displayed, but just to the south of the highway the Phoenix Force commando could easily pick out the set of buildings belonging to Sincanaros.

Grimaldi looked over at him and pointed at the altimeter before giving James another thumbs-up. James felt the helicopter slide into a gentle, precision hover as the Stony Man pilot settled in at five hundred feet above the ground. He looked out the window and saw the clearing in the terrain they had picked as a drop zone from the satellite imagery of the surrounding area.

James cracked the copilot door and felt the rush of wind enter the cockpit. He turned in his seat and backed out, stepping onto the helicopter's landing skid. He felt the pull of the rushing air tugging at his clothes and he felt the sensation of the earth falling away beneath his feet. He grabbed the handle and slammed the cockpit door shut.

James took a step backward into space and the hovering helicopter veered sharply away from him. Gravity snatched at him and he began to plummet, gaining speed rapidly. Immediately his hand went to the rip cord and he deployed his parachute. There was no backup. At five hundred feet he'd be on the ground too quickly to ever deploy one in the advent of a mishap with his primary canopy.

There was the rustle of silk in the wind. Already the air was warmer as he drew closer to the ground. The parachute, an old-style T-50 colored black and designed to get him to the ground as quickly as possible, fluttered up and out behind him as he fell. James had time to wonder if he was screwed, and then the chute flared and caught, jerking him hard in his heavy nylon body harness.

The fall immediately became controlled, but he was still dropping incredibly fast. He plunged, not floated, to the ground and he saw the black earth rising up to meet his boots. He put his feet together and kept a springy bend built into his legs. He hit the ground and went instantly with the force of his fall, rolling along his leg and the side of his body to absorb the shock.

He grunted with pain as a hidden rock slammed into his side. Then he was past it and coming up into a sitting position. His parachute descended around him and he quickly began gathering up the soft, billowing folds.

James was on the ground and the clock was running.

HALF A WORLD AWAY Carl Lyons and his team were racing toward the dawn.

The plane they were in, flown by Stony Man pilots Charlie Mott and Jock Reno, cruised at thirty-seven thousand feet. They conducted their own refueling operation with a U.S. naval plane over the Azores, then turned sharply south.

Hours later the cold, dark waters of the Gulf of Oman off the southwestern coast of Iran lay beneath their wings. Mott set the plane into a low, slow loop over that section of ocean while from low earth orbit a National Security Agency satellite tracked the massive luxury yacht on the sea below them and transmitted the GPS coordinates to the plane's sensory equipment.

In the back of the airplane Lyons looked at his wristwatch and frowned. The timetables for the operation were starting to accordion inward around him. It made him edgy and irritable. Unable to continue sitting still and waiting, he unhooked his seat belt and made his way up the center aisle to the front of the plane.

Mott turned toward him as he entered the cabin. The pilot's usually jovial exterior was missing, and Lyons's cop street sense clued him in that something was wrong. He frowned and closed the cockpit door behind him.

"I was just about to call you up here," Mott said.

"Why? What's wrong?" Lyons demanded.

He looked past Mott and out through the cockpit windshield. Morning was fast approaching, and the sun was a luminous star pattern of light emerging on the horizon. According to their briefing, Mott had intended to circle wide out over the drop zone and make the final approach onto the target with the rising sun at their back. Something was very wrong.

"I made contact with a situation report as agreed upon. Stony Man control told me to go into a holding pattern. I thought at first the NSA sat had lost our target but that's not the case," Mott said.

"What exactly is the case?" Lyons said.

"The White House has told Stony to put a hold on the assault."

"What! We're hanging our asses out over Iranian waters and they want a hold!" The ex-LAPD detective turned and slapped the aircraft bulkhead in frustration. "Why didn't you tell me this when it first came up?"

"Because Stony Base only just told me the reason. At first I thought we had a communications or meteorological problem that was going to complicate your drop," Mott fired back. "Barb's waiting to talk to you."

"Oh, this just gets better and better," Lyons muttered. He eased himself behind the copilot, Jock Reno, into the seat reserved for the communications officer on a larger crew. He slid an aviation headset on and jacked straight into the encryption broadcast transmitter built into the cockpit control panel.

"Stony Base, this is Able Actual," he barked into the headset.

"Able, this is Stony Base. Hold for Stony Six," Akira Tokaido's voice came back.

There was a long pause while an anxious Lyons swore he could see the sky growing lighter. Then Price was on the radio. "Able, this is Six."

"Six," Lyons said. "Tell me my party is fine."

"Able, the weathervane just swung 180 degrees down on the beltway. You are to maintain a hold to deploy pattern."

"Jesus Christ, Barb!" Lyons snarled into the microphone. "The sun's coming up over hostile waters here. The coast is lined with radar stations left over from the days of the Russian Bear, and our target is cruising toward sanctuary at a good head of speed."

"I have Hal working this," Price snapped back. "The advisers in the Oval Office aren't sure they want such a strong message sent."

"What!" Lyons exploded. "Those mortar rounds were coming straight for the U.S. and that son of a bitch below us helped pay for it."

"Stand down, Ironman!" Price snapped. "We're doing what we can."

"Stand down?" Lyons responded. "Stand down? I'm not a soldier. I've never *been* a soldier. I stopped being a cop so I wouldn't have to put up with this kind of bullshit, Barb! Stand down? I'm over the goddamn target right now. Delta Force has to stand down because of politics, the Marines have to stand down because of politics, Able Team doesn't damn well stand down because of politics. We drive right through politics!"

Price's voice was ice cold when she answered, her words terse and clipped as she spit them out. "You will stand down. End of story. Anytime you want to turn in your resignation you can, and I'll get you your old job back. But as of right now this mission is on hold. I'm the mission controller telling you that's the way it is." There was a hiss of static as she paused. "What's it going to be, Ironman?"

Lyons rose and snatched his headset clear. He threw it down with disgust on the chair. Mott studiously looked the other way. "You tell Ms. Mission Controller I'm ready and waiting to go." He paused, nearly choking as he added, "At her word."

He slammed the cabin door so hard Mott could swear it rocked the plane.

# CHAPTER TWENTY-SEVEN

Hal Brognola paced back and forth.

He walked from one end of his office in the Stony Man farmhouse to the other, turned on his heel and counted off the steps back to the opposite wall. His desk was covered with open files, tactical maps and satellite photos. He was holding his NSA diplomatic upgrade cell phone to one ear, and he kept bringing an unlit stogie to his mouth with his other hand. He crunched down on the unlit cigar then jerked it free.

"Am I still here?" he snapped into the phone. "Of course I'm still here. I'm waiting to talk to the President. What am I going to do? Get bored and wander off?" He paused and forced himself not to explode. The voice on the other end of the line spoke, and he felt all the air drain out of his body as if he'd been punched. "Fine. Yes. I'll be at this number."

He snapped the cell phone shut. It was always a very bad sign when he didn't get to talk to the President directly. When the man's security adviser intervened in the conversation, the big Fed almost never liked what was coming next.

Brognola crossed to his desk and stabbed the intercom button. "Barb?" he snapped.

"I don't need another bullheaded man taking his frustrations out on me!" Price fired right back.

Brognola stepped back from the intercom on his desk and looked at it. He frowned, then sighed and stepped back over to it. "Okay, okay," he said, voice softer. "I take it Carl took the news about as well as we thought he would."

"He doesn't need to worry about the Iranian navy," Price said darkly. "I'll shoot the plane down myself."

"Think of poor Charlie." Brognola chuckled. "Besides, I got the National Security Adviser on the line instead of the Man," he added.

There was a pause, then Price said, "That's never a good sign."

"No, it's not." Brognola sighed. "I'm beginning to think we're a victim of our own success," he said.

"How so?"

"By catching the attacks before they happened they became an abstract to the suits and ties doing the President's thinking for him. Let the French connection go. Let the Saudi connection go. Not worth the media headache, blah-blah-blah. Typical talking head's bullshit. I'm worried they may try to pull the plug on the Venezuelan connection, as well."

"What!" It was Price's turn to shout.

"Who's yelling at whom now?" Brognola said, his voice grim.

"Fine, fine." Price calmed herself. "Why would they do that?"

"They haven't," Brognola stated. "Not yet. I'm just feeling a lot of cold feet on this one. It's not like Sincanaros is a drug dealer. He's a legitimate businessman with plenty of international influence. Once the will to act starts to erode, it can avalanche pretty damn quickly. We've both seen it."

"It's not supposed to happen to Stony Man," Price said. She gave a short harsh laugh. "Now I sound as bad as Carl."

"Just be ready," Brognola warned. "Sincanaros is tied pretty tightly to al-Shalaan. I think that's sealed his fate but just be ready for the winds to change."

"Christ!" Price sputtered. "Cal's already on the ground."

"Well, it'd be a damn shame if we lost radio contact with him."

There was an answering silence on the end of the intercom. "I've got to go, Hal," Price said finally. "I've just been informed we're experiencing technical difficulty with our South American com-links."

The intercom clicked off and Brognola chuckled to himself. Then he went to the cabinet behind his desk and began to prepare a glass of antacid.

MOVING FAST, James cut through heavily wooded hills. He was well-prepared for a silent infiltration and kill. His combat harness contained garrotes and several slim-bladed stilettos. In addition to a silenced H&K MP-5 SD-3 submachine gun, he carried an unmuffled M-1911 A1 handgun with an extended magazine on his left hip and a silenced 9 mm Glock 19 pistol in a shoulder holster. His only acknowledgment to big bang firepower were several fragmentation grenades secured to his harness in case things went south in a bad way.

He maintained a tactical map in the cargo pocket of his black fatigue pants, but he had committed the layout of the mansion grounds to memory. Sincanaros had spent his money lavishly. Hunt Wethers had lived up to his academic reputation on the cybernetics team in the service of Aaron Kurtzman, managing to locate the architecture company out of Buenos Aires, Brazil, responsible for the construction contract and then hack their records to provide the raw statistical data necessary for an in-depth infiltration plan.

A dense wall of concrete block four meters high by one meter thick surrounded the entire estate, which covered an area the equivalent of fifty-three football fields. According to the architectural plans, and confirmed by spy satellite imagery, only two openings pierced the thick stone wall: the well-guarded gate on the main drive and an insignificant culvert that channeled a small, swift stream out of the estate and into the surrounding hills.

Sincanaros was a rich man, and he had built his estate and villa with an eye to security but it was neither a medieval fortress nor an armed camp. The Venezuelan entrepreneur had used his money to run in some very dangerous circles, but he had always left the dirty work to others, as such he'd always felt himself safe enough on his own property in his homeland.

James begged to disagree with the man's assessment.

The terrain of the South American country at this altitude reminded James more of Colorado, or northern

California than the jungles he had envisioned when first learning of the geographic location housing Sincanaros. A thick row of evergreens lined the concrete security wall on the inside, effectively obstructing the view of anyone beyond the boundary of the property.

James skidded down a slight, scree-littered slope heading toward the babbling stream at the bottom of the gully. He stopped and surveyed the wild brambles encroaching the Sincanaros's estate. The blueprints and plans had outlined the security systems in place, giving an overview of the multilayered defenses the South American businessman had put into place.

The villa security system consisted of three main elements: indicators, alarms and video cameras. The indicators registered an event with the computer software housed in the villa, such as the opening of a door, cutting of the wire running along the top of the block wall, or the breaking of a window. According to the commercially obtainable software templates available, Sincanaros's computer did not issue an alarm automatically but instead registered the potential breach to the centralized computer screen manned by an observer. The same center also housed the closed-circuit TV monitors for the several cameras positioned around the villa estate.

Piece of cake, James thought wryly.

Moving in close to the wall, the Stony Man commando quickly surveyed the stretch for cameras. The sensor wire was running along the top, but he could see no security camera pod and he broke from the cover of the bushes and headed for the depression in the block wall that housed the culvert grating.

James ducked under the lip of the culvert, shrugging off his pack as he did so. He crouched in the cool water of the stream, feeling it soak through the leather and canvas of his boots as took the Semtex from the pouches on his harness. Stripping off his tight leather driving gloves, he began to place precise amounts of the explosive compound along the wrought-iron structure at the points where it was secured through the aluminum body of the culvert and into the concrete block.

By applying the charges in an exact manner, he could reduce the sound of the explosions to very soft bangs, like muted pistol shots, too quiet to be heard across the distance to the main villa. The charges themselves had been expertly constructed by Stony Man weaponsmith John "Cowboy" Kissinger. The ex-DEA agent had calculated exact charges of the demolitions to loosen the reinforced rebar from its moorings to such a degree that James could remove it by hand, thus further reducing the noise signature.

Shaped charges in place, James scooted to the edge of the culvert and stepped around the edge. The initiator timing pencil popped and the detonation cord followed suit, igniting in a rapid series of firecracker pops. Brief match heads of yellow flame flared, followed by small plumes of gray smoke that rolled out of the tunnel formed by the culvert.

James swung back around and checked his work. He smiled grimly after inspecting the metal bars and seeing the erosion. He sucked in a lungful of air to gather his strength and shot both of his hands outward. The heels of his palms struck the grate in the center and easily snapped it clear of its moorings. The metal grid fell into the gurgling stream with a small splash, and James immediately hustled through.

He paused at the mouth of the culvert as it opened up onto the Sincanaros compound. Slowly he peeked his head around the corner and looked out. Immediately he saw the security camera mounted on a metal bracket to the concrete wall, its black lens pointed directly at the culvert mouth.

James ducked back around the corner and out of sight. If the personnel at the CCTV monitor were on top of their job, he had already been seen. Chances were, however, that only prolonged exposure to the camera would be noticed.

He gritted his teeth and burst out of the culvert. He took two hard steps and somersaulted over a shoulder and passed under the camera to come up on his feet outside the camera's range.

He paused and took a look around, orientating himself to the map he had memorized. He could see the lights of the main villa just about two hundred yards away. Beside the main house there was a four-door garage with a drive leading up from the main lane past the villa. The driveway continued past the garage and tied into an asphalt road that meandered through the property.

As James watched, one of the garage doors opened. A Toyota Land Cruiser pulled out of the garage, turned west on the property road and began approaching James's position, gaining speed as it came.

The Stony Man commando hugged the ground as the Land Cruiser slowly rolled past.

He kept his finger on the trigger of his H&K MP-5

and pressed hard into the grass, willing himself to be a shadow among shadows. The Land Cruiser crept down the road where it boarded the stream and moved past the culvert without slowing. Keeping one eye shut to spare his night vision, James watched the vehicle-based sentries cruise past his position.

Once the Toyota had traveled down the road, James was up and running. He crossed the drive and entered the bush on the other side. He tried to approach the house from cover, darting in and out from stands of trees and cultivated bushes, but the landscaping became sparse the closer he got to the house and very quickly he found himself with nothing but open lawn to cover.

Keeping one eye on the slowly patrolling Land Cruiser, he went for the garage next to the main house, running fast with weapon up. He made the corner of the building without an alarm being raised and scrambled onto the roof, breathing hard.

He hugged the top of the building and began to search the windows in the second story of the villa that faced him. The villa was a one-level ranch-style and rambling in design. A pool took up the area directly behind the house, and the whole area was landscaped with an elaborate flower garden. The front porch was a low brick platform covered by an extension of the roof supported by two brick pillars. A set of enormous Brazilian oak doors comprised the main entrance, each of the doors carved with a dramatic *S* monogram.

James stood and quickly took a second, more sustained survey. Seeing no one, he quickly sprinted across the roof and leaped into the air. He jumped the distance between the roof of the garage and the red clay shingles of the house, landing lightly. He scrambled across the incline toward an upstairs window and halted to see if any alarm was raised.

His internal countdown was greeted by silence. Carefully he approached the window, holding the H&K MP-5 SD-3 up and ready in one fist. Sincanaros's bodyguards were well-trained and well-armed professionals. As employees of the man, they were de facto conspirators in a terrorist cell bent on attacking the United States. Still, if at all possible, James would studiously avoid killing anyone except for the terror facilitator. Washington, D.C., had wanted its message to be pointed but clean, otherwise a Hellfire missile would have been fired through the middle of those intricately carved front doors.

He looked around the edge of the windowsill.

A single lamp burned a soft yellow, leaving the corners of the room draped in shadow. A king-size bed filled the northwest corner of the room, sitting kitty-corner from a desk and chair against the east wall. A wide dresser was positioned next to the window through which James peeked, next to a wardrobe. The bed itself was covered with a rich-looking gold quilt.

The room appeared empty, and James's eyes were drawn to a dramatic oil painting of what he instantly recognized as a Tarot card. A burning stream curved the length of the painting where a nude woman floated face-down, her left arm stretched out with the hand wrapped around a large wand. A tiger was curled beneath her, its tail lying lightly across her shoulders. A gold brazier with flames flaring was nestled in the curve of the stream.

From behind him James heard the unmistakable

racking sound of a pump action shotgun. The Stony Man warrior whirled and saw a man in khaki step out of the walkway between the garage and the main villa, the business end of the weapon pointed his way. James pivoted aside just as the 12-gauge shotgun boomed.

The window exploded, shattering as the shotgun pellets blew it to slivers. James didn't hesitate. He pivoted again and dived through the window, the rest of the glass in the window imploding.

For better or for worse, he was in the house.

HAL BROGNOLA HUNG UP the phone.

He turned and looked at the people in the Computer Room. Every face was turned toward him: Hunt Wethers and Akira Tokaido looked up from computer screens while Carmen Delahunt and Barbara Price stood on either side of Aaron Kurtzman's wheelchair.

He shook his head.

"Call Charlie and turn him around," he said. "The powers that be have convinced the President not to go ahead with action against the prince."

"Goddamn it!" Kurtzman shouted. He turned his head to the side and scowled. Then he held up a hand. "Sorry. Just frustrated."

Every face in the room was grim. This wasn't supposed to be the way Stony Man worked. Other covert units got called off, not them. But here it was.

Price stepped forward. "Where does that leave Cal?"

"Can we pull him?" Brognola asked.

"I told you—he's rolling hot right now," she said, her voice a harsh whisper.

Brognola smiled. "Then we're good on the South American front."

Price nodded and turned to Tokaido. "Okay. Call Charlie. Tell him to pull out and run for Baghdad International Airport—the clearance over the airspace has already been arranged."

Tokaido swallowed, hesitated. "What if Carl is on the line?"

Price gave him a hard grin. "Then it sucks to be you."

JAMES HIT THE FLOOR and got up to his feet. The H&K was in his hands and ready. He crossed the room and flung open the door. He had pored over the floor plan extensively on the flight down and felt confident of his ability to find the master bedroom from any point in the house.

He hit the hallway beyond the bedroom door at a dead run. He sprinted past two doors to a T intersection in the hallway and turned left. The short hallway ended in double interior doors. The entrance to Sincanaros's inner sanctum lay right before him. He crossed the distance and tried the heavy gilded door handle, found it locked and stepped back. He lowered the muzzle of the MP-5 and blew the handle apart. He lifted up a big boot and kicked the ruined door open.

So much for clean and quiet—but no matter what, he would put the end to any further threats to America from this quarter. The door burst open and he charged through it. This is what justice looked like out on the sharp end: violent, sometimes sloppy, but brutally efficient and deadly committed.

He saw the woman in the bed and heard her scream as she lifted the covers. He ignored her and turned in time to see his target, Sincanaros. The man was naked and scrambling for the door to the master suite's bathroom, a black pistol in his hands. He had abandoned the woman to try to save himself.

For James, at that moment, it was all instinct. He was like a computer-guided precision machine on an unstoppable path. Here was justice.

The H&K MP-5 stuttered in James's hand. Red gouts of blood opened up on the soft flesh of the fleeing man, and his pistol tumbled from lifeless fingers. Sincanaros fell to the ground and his blood pumped out onto his thick pile carpet. The woman was still screaming, and James knew the scene was horrific to her. He thought about what those BZ bombs could have done in a crowded shopping mall or sports venue and his finger worked his trigger again.

Smoking shell casings popped out of the ejection port on his submachine gun as the 9 mm slugs riddled the man. Sincanaros stayed down, his eyes wide-open and staring, the back of his head cracked open.

James saw the man's leaking brains and knew he was done. He turned toward the woman where she cowered in the bed and began running straight for her. She screamed again, and he leaped onto the bed as he lowered the muzzle of the smoking H&K submachine gun. The mattress sagged under his weight.

As his feet sank into the bed, the woman's shrieks became hysterical and sharp. His finger tightened on the trigger and the submachine gun bucked hard in his hand. Behind the woman and above her head, the 9 mm Parabellum rounds shattered the picture window overlooking the pool and expansive grounds.

He hurried past her cowering form and threw himself out through the shattered portal. He felt gauze curtains and heavy drapes drag at him as he plunged through. He floated for a moment in the air, then struck the concrete patio just outside the veranda-style windows. He landed in a crouch, saw motion and turned. A khaki-dressed figure rounded a corner by the garage, holding the familiar silhouette of a SPAS-12 shotgun.

The silenced H&K stuttered in his hands and the man fell away, leaving a red mist in the air as he dropped. James twisted and spun, saw the backlit water of the Olympic-size pool, and darted around the edge. On the road behind the pool area he saw a Toyota Land Cruiser racing toward him, and he knew he'd never make it to the fence.

He went down on one knee behind a concrete pillar next to a short flight of stairs only to see concrete chips fly as someone opened fire on him from the house. His hand went to his earjack and he jabbed the transmit button.

"Let's go! Let's go!"

But all he got in response was the shrill scream of static.

# CHAPTER TWENTY-EIGHT

Hal Brognola stormed forward. "What do you mean, we've lost radio contact!" he demanded.

Kurtzman furiously worked his keyboard. "I'm telling you—we should have it. The NSA connections are up and linked fine. I've just finished my second diagnostic. I just can't get Jack or Calvin up on the air."

Price turned to Brognola. "Are you sure we haven't been left out in the cold?"

"Son of a bitch!" Brognola snarled. "Not after everything we've done!"

"You think the NSA com-links were cut by Washington?" Carmen Delahunt asked.

"I've never lost commo like this before," Kurtzman said. "It's like it just went dead."

Brognola stood. "Screw them. I don't know what's going on—and I'll never be able to ask. But let's do an end run."

"An end run?" Tokaido asked, puzzled.

Walking briskly past him, Price already had her personal cell phone out and was working the buttons.

"Jack?" she said. "Good."

She began speaking fast.

OVERHEAD THE Q5 LACROSSE swept past the wall to the estate and hurtled across the lawn. Taking cover behind a cabana, James plucked an antipersonnel fragmentation grenade free and used his thumb to yank the pin. He triggered a burst at the window of the house where he was taking fire from and then let the spoon fly off the deadly egg he held in his hand.

The Land Cruiser locked its brakes and went into a power slide as it approached his position. A weapon fired from the passenger window. James threw his grenade at the vehicle, feeling a sudden, sharp pain in his shoulder, and then the flow of warm blood as his stitches gave way.

He dropped to one knee as the grenade flew across the width of the pool and bounced near the vehicle. Someone screamed, then came the deafening sound of the grenade detonation. He fired another burst at the house, then raked the side of the Toyota.

James turned and began to run. The H&K MP-5 ran dry, and the bolt locked open in the rear position. James threw it away and sprinted onto the wide expanse of lawn. Relief washed over him when he saw the helicopter.

The shotgun pellets ripped into the back of his leg and tore his hamstring. He screamed and went down, then felt the rush of rotor wash as it swept over him. Grass and dirt exploded out of the ground next to his head as another shotgun blast came close.

James pushed himself up and pulled the Glock 19 from his shoulder holster. He realized the range was too extreme and forced himself to roll over, leaving the weapon behind. Buckshot struck near the elbow and he was splashed with his own blood.

He yelled despite himself, and it was as if a hand came down from heaven to set him on his feet. His heart was pounding in his chest and his arm and leg felt as if they were on fire. He hobbled forward, felt his leg give way under his weight and went down on one knee.

He saw Grimaldi tumble out of the door of his helicopter.

"No!" James roared at the man.

Grimaldi shouted something back, but it was lost in the noise of the helicopter engines. James saw bullets spark off the airframe and saw several windows spiderweb under the impact. He forced himself forward.

The ace pilot caught him and James sagged into his arms. He saw more gouts of dirt erupt as rounds continued to fall around them. He forced himself forward, leaning against Grimaldi because he was sure the man would never leave him.

*We're not going to make it,* he thought, but he felt strangely elated. Sincanaros had paid the price for his attack, and the satisfaction he had felt gunning the terrorist down still fueled him. They reached the waiting helicopter, and Grimaldi roughly shoved him through the open door. Glass from the pilot window rained down around them.

James clawed his way across the seats and into the copilot station. Grimaldi scrambled in after him and began to work the controls, not bothering to shut his door. A stray bullet flew in, cracked the altimeter and then ricocheted into the bulkhead. James didn't flinch. He heard the screaming pitch of the helicopter's power plants change, then the strange feeling of his center of gravity being above him returned and he knew they had taken off.

He turned to Grimaldi and saw the man's face was a mask of blood. There were two fist-size holes in the Q5's windshield, but the veteran Stony Man pilot's hands were rock steady on the yoke.

Incredulously he saw the pilot working his cell phone, the screen lighting up as the call connected. The pilot turned toward him and smiled. A runnel had been carved out of his forehead by flying glass. "It's Barb," he yelled. "She wants to talk to you."

James eased himself down in his seat and began to laugh.

# The Don Pendleton's
# Executioner®
## HOSTILE ODDS

## A small town is caught between warring factions...

The illicit activities of an organized crime family take Mack Bolan to California, then to Oregon, where he uncovers a deadly power struggle. Profits from prostitution and drugs tied to local businesses are being funneled to a radical ecoterrorist group willing to strike out against anything—and anyone—in their way. A war is brewing and, faced with mounting casualties, Mack Bolan will have to use his own methods to clean up the environment.

*Available March 2009 wherever books are sold.*

# James Axler
# Outlanders®

## SHADOW BOX

A new and horrific face of the Annunaki legacy appears in the Arizona desert. A shambling humanoid monster preys on human victims, leaving empty, mindless shells in its wake. Trapped inside this creature, the souls of rogue Igigi seek hosts for their physical rebirth. And no human—perhaps not even the Cerberus rebels— can stop them from reclaiming the planet of their masters for themselves….

*Available May 2009 wherever books are sold.*

# TAKE 'EM FREE

## 2 action-packed novels plus a mystery bonus

## NO RISK

## NO OBLIGATION TO BUY